Key of Iron & Fate

Katherine A. Darling

This is a work of fiction. Names, characters, places, and incidents either are the product of the author's imagination or are used fictitiously. Any resemblance to actual persons, living or dead, events, or locales is entirely coincidental.

Editor: Adie Hart

Cover Artist: Etheric Designs

Internal Art: Etheric Designs

ASIN: B0CTTT9H4C

ISBN (Paperback): 978-1-961972-03-2

Author's Note

Your mental health is a priority, and I want to do my best to help protect it. Some of the topics in this book can be upsetting to certain people. While I cannot list every trigger, I want to warn you of those I can (if you have no triggers, please feel free to skip). This book contains discussions of parental death, scenes of gore, discussions of humans being eaten, explicit sexual content (all consensual), violence, and forced marriage. If any of these bother you as a reader, you might not want to continue.

Thank you for reading Key of Iron & Fate, and I hope you enjoy it!

Chapter 1

"A magical contract was struck. Was it wise? I fear not. But the deal was made and my blood shall pay the price for years to come." – Lord Rhett, First Lord of Sídhetír.

"Breathe," I said. "Just breathe."

Oren shook his head, making his pale, almost white hair brush his high cheekbones. "I cannot."

"You can," I said, slicking his hair back before straightening his tailored jacket. Today was Oren's twenty-first birthday. As the seventh son of Lord Jonathan Byrne, he would inherit his father's title and land. Part of that responsibility was being presented to the fae representatives of the Day and Night Courts.

His already fair skin lightened, taking on a green hue. "I cannot. I swear, Aidan, I cannot do this. Please don't make me."

"I'm not the one making you."

The burden of heir did not sit gracefully on Oren's slight shoulders, but he had no choice. Magic bound him to the land, and there was no freedom from those shackles.

The door swung open with a loud creak, making us start. Lady Hester Byrne, Oren's mother, strode in. Her white-blonde hair was drawn into an elegant chignon, contrasting against the green silk of her high-waisted evening gown. Hands folded over her narrow waist, she walked to her only child, every movement as liquid as water.

"My son," she said, voice soft and as delicate as she was. "Why are you still in your rooms?"

He shifted, putting me between him and his mother—Oren was small enough in stature for me to provide an adequate shield. Lady Byrne shook her head at his antics, though she refrained from commenting. I was often Oren's protector, even though he had six older brothers who all loved him.

"He's nervous, my lady," I supplied, smoothing my brown waistcoat.

She peeked around me, but Oren buried his face between my shoulder blades. "All you have to do is say hello and greet a few guests. Your father is not even going to make you speak."

"Can't I stay here and read?"

"No." While soft, her tone was forged of iron. "You must come down to *your* party. All of your brothers are here."

My own twenty-first birthday had come and gone seven days ago, but I felt like a river existed between Oren and I. He'd been cherished, sheltered, and loved, while I'd had to confront the realities of this world at a young age when Mother died thirteen years ago. I was blessed, though, because I'd become a ward of Byrne Manor and Oren's companion.

"May I have a moment with him, Lady Byrne?"

"One," she said. "Lord Byrne will come himself if Oren doesn't appear soon."

No one wanted a confrontation between Jonathan and Oren. Lord Byrne didn't possess much patience for his youngest son. If he had to retrieve Oren, he would turn brusque and Oren would burrow deep within himself.

Oren looked at the ground, his shoulders slumped, and his pale hair covering his delicate face. He was his mother's son in look and manner. Gentle. Delicate. Graceful. Those qualities didn't make for a good Heir of Sídhetír. As the lord, Oren would have to deal with the fae on a regular basis. If they smelled weakness, they would pounce like beasts and tear him to shreds.

Putting a hand under his chin, I lifted his face and slicked his hair back again. The silky strands didn't want to cooperate with the current fashion, preferring to hang around his face.

"You can do this," I said. "I believe in you. Go. Meet the fae representatives."

"I might be able to do this, but I don't want to. I don't want to be Lord of Sídhetír. I want to go to school."

My hand fell to my side. "You have no choice."

Magic didn't allow substitutes, whether the heir wanted the burden of lordship or not. The contract had been made long ago, and it couldn't be altered—only broken. And if it was broken, fae would pour from their realm and wreak havoc on the mortal plane. Like before.

Oren's sky-blue eyes were stark as he stared at me like I could perform a miracle. I couldn't. I was no one, and there were no miracles. Only the price to be paid for a choice made long ago by a man who was long dead.

With a deep breath, he straightened his gray waistcoat, which was embroidered with green vines and golden flowers. Oren buttoned his deep blue jacket, put on his crisp gloves, and smoothed his hair back; it didn't stay, instead flopping around his forehead. I rearranged his cravat until it rested perfectly. He was the portrait of a perfect lord.

Almost, I thought, smiling at his troublesome hair.

He left the room and greeted Lady Byrne, who waited in the hallway. She slipped her hand into the bend of his elbow, and they disappeared from view.

I waited in the center of Oren's room for several minutes, until I was positive they were gone, then I crept out. Strands of faint music floated down the darkened corridors, dragging me along. I slipped onto the balcony lining the ballroom.

I was entrenched in shadow and high enough up that any guest would have difficulty seeing me hovering by the red velvet curtains. I drew one back and leaned against the polished balustrade, sweeping the gathering with my gaze. Gentry from all over the country had come to attend this celebration—it wasn't every year that the seventh son of the Lord of Sídhetír came of age. Though the queen and prince regent hadn't accepted the invitation Lord and Lady

Byrne had extended, which was hardly shocking; they rarely attended functions.

This was history in the making, but more than that, this was an opportunity to sway the soon-to-be lord in their direction and rub elbows with fae and other people of distinction.

Sídhetír was where the fae realms and the human world connected through a single gate. Centuries ago, Lord Rhett had made a deal with the fae royals to end the fighting between our species. Now the fae could only enter the mortal realm by the gate in Sídhetír, and humans, besides the current Lord Byrne, didn't know its location—though the occasional human found the hidden gate and wandered through.

After their twenty-first birthday, the heir chose which court to align with—Day or Night. Light or dark fae. When he chose, the gate moved to the court's lands, allowing them access to the mortal realm, which lined their pockets from trade and strengthened their magic.

A huge choice rested on Oren's young shoulders. When he picked which court to align with in the coming weeks, signing the contract in blood, Lord Jonathan Byrne would lose his hold on the land, and Oren would be the Lord of Sídhetír until his seventh son turned twenty-one.

I easily spotted the fae representatives among the masses. Their great height and elegant beauty outshone every human present. The Day Court's nobles were all similar in appearance. Light skin with golden undertones. Brown hair like soil or golden like the sun or red like fire. Pale eyes from blue to green to gold. Forms broad and features soft. They seemed more human, even with their unnatural beauty and tapered ears.

The Night Court nobility was their opposite. Gray skin with a purple undertone. Hair colors from black to white to gray. Eyes like gems. Forms lean and features sharp. They had a feral countenance and an otherworldly air that made humans shy from their presence.

Living in Byrne Manor, I had seen fae all my life, though I'd never been introduced to one. They were not important at the moment. I sought Oren. He was what mattered.

Back and forth, I scoured the full ballroom, taking in the musicians playing lively tunes, the refreshment tables full of delicacies, the windows and doors to the balcony open, the elaborate decorations in golds and greens, and the many people. Still, I didn't see what I sought.

Where is Oren?

Had he left? So quickly? I could easily imagine him escaping his mother's hold and hiding in the library.

A flash of almost white hair drew my attention. Oren stood in the middle of the horde of his brothers. The Byrne brothers aged from over thirty to Oren's twenty-one, resembling each other decently despite having three different mothers. Lord Byrne's first two wives had died, and Lady Hester had finally given him the much-needed seventh son.

The eldest, Thomas, seized Oren around the neck and drew him close, grinning. He would take care of Oren and shepherd him through the political quagmire.

Duty done and worries soothed, I left the manor. It wasn't often I was granted a night of leisure without one of the Byrnes poking into my affairs. The manicured grounds sprawled in front of me. The hedges lined the estate's iron fence, forming a green boundary.

I darted through the hedge maze, checking each corner prior to rounding it. Lovers often sought the privacy the maze lent for a secret liaison. On more than one occasion, I'd come upon people in the throes of passion.

Never a pleasant experience for either party.

Sneaking out of the side of the maze, I moved to the gate hidden among the hedges. No one, to my knowledge, knew of this exit. I'd found it after I became a ward of Lord Byrne, a young boy of eight. One day I'd been exploring the grounds and a heavy iron key had fallen from the ivy climbing the side of the manor. Some days later, I'd come across the gate buried in the hedges.

It was my secret—one I didn't intend to share.

The wrought-iron gate swung open with nary a sound. I slipped out and headed to the dirt track rather than the main graveled road. The hour was early for anyone to be leaving the party, but I didn't want to chance someone seeing me—not that any of the gentry would take note of a random person in the growing twilight. Nevertheless, if they did, I didn't want anyone to know where I was going, or word of my leaving to reach the ears of the Byrne family.

My feet left the dirt trail and took me across the grassy hills dotted with late-blooming flowers and weeds. A lone sheep bleated at me; a careless shepherd must have left it behind by accident. I patted its head, and the creature ambled after me as I walked straight to the looming forest in the distance. As I stepped under the branches, the straggler screamed as only a sheep could, racing back to the hills.

As children, we were warned away from the woods. The gate between worlds resided somewhere in here, and fae often lingered among the boughs. Not all fae were like the nobility of tonight. Some were mindless animals. Others had no humanoid appearance, and devious intentions. Some were merely looking for a new place to call home. All fae, no matter their appearance, were dangerous.

The noble fae were supposed to control who came through the gate, but some still wandered into our realm without permission, hiding in the woods or escaping to other parts of the country. Supposedly, noble and royal fae tracked the wayward fae down, but I'd never seen evidence of that actually occurring.

Mother had spun stories of the monsters hiding in the darkness, but even the threat of death wasn't enough to keep me from the trees. Something about the shadowed forest drew me in like a moth to a flame. I couldn't keep away, much to my mother's, and now, Lord Byrne's chagrin.

I navigated around the massive trees, avoiding the exposed roots, while far-off lights glimmered and whispers rattled through the dying leaves. The cajoling voices called my name, beckoning me to follow them. Wisps. They would lure travelers away from their destination and to their deaths.

I paid them no mind. I'd seen them since childhood. I'd even followed them once, but they'd simply taken me to a glade and bobbed around me in a cloud.

Finally, I spotted what I'd come for—a house with a steep pitch, stone walls, and a water wheel on the side that fed into a small lake. I walked over an arched stone bridge and moved to the rough-hewn door. Using the brass knocker, I pounded on the wood.

"Iris."

Nothing but silence greeted me.

"Iris," I called again. She rarely left home. I could count on one hand the times I'd come to visit her and she wasn't here.

The door cracked open, and a single amber-brown eye stared at me. Opening the door the rest of the way, Iris smiled as she shoved a long brown braid threaded with gray over her broad shoulder. "Aidan. I didn't think you'd be here with the festivities happening tonight."

I waved the comment away. "Like they need me."

"Hmm," the woman said, crossing her arms as she leaned against the door jamb. "Mr. Oren Byrne probably wanted you to come."

"Probably, but it's not appropriate." I was a former ward. I had no place there. I had no place anywhere.

"Bah." Iris stepped inside, leaving the door open for me. "Appropriate things are rarely fun."

I ignored the comment. "He does have his brothers."

"All of them?"

"Yes."

"Hmm." She moved to the fireplace on the back wall and snagged a kettle from the flames. It was much too warm for a fire at the beginning of autumn, but Iris always had a flame going, cooking her potions and concoctions to sell at the market. Being a hedge witch didn't bring much fortune, but she joked it gave her plenty of solitude and an excuse to act crazier than she truly was.

As she placed a cup of tea in front of me, Iris sat down at the lone table in the one-room cottage. "No interest in watching the fae court Oren?"

"Not really." If I watched, I would feel guilty about Oren's terror. I had no way to fix my friend's problem or ease his fear, but logic didn't temper my emotions regarding Oren. I wanted him to be happy, and he never would be as the Lord of Sídhetír. He wanted to go to Wellington University to study—that would never happen.

"No interest in the fae?"

I took a sip of the floral tea. Rose, perhaps. I opened my mouth to say something, then paused, contemplating my words. "I've seen plenty of fae."

"I hadn't thought of that. Living in Lord Byrne's household does have its benefits."

Scoffing, I asked, "Seeing fae is a benefit?"

"Many would wish to be in your position."

"Jealous?"

Iris laughed as she leaped up and snagged the twig broom from against the wall. She started to twirl, her braid flying. "Oh, to be pushed around the dance floor by a handsome fae. Who wouldn't want that?"

I shook my head at her ridiculousness. Iris appeared to be in her forties, but she often acted like a young girl. The broom fell to the stone floor with a clang. She seized my hands and yanked me into a dance before I had a chance to refuse her.

Chapter 2

"If you come across a fae in the wild, run and hope they do not follow you, for they will trick you into staying."
– Lord Keegan, Fourth Lord of Sídhetír.

"You disappeared last night," Nevan said as he sprawled with his twin brother, Neil, by his side. The two were perfect reflections with black hair, deep blue eyes, and long faces. They were closest to Oren in age, at twenty-six.

All of Oren's brothers and I were lounging on a balcony at the back of Byrne Manor. I never understood why, but Thomas had always included me in their schemes or when they all gathered like this, even as a young child. By the time he and his immediate younger brother, Whitaker or Whit, left, it was natural that I be included with them.

Sevrin grinned, lifting a wine bottle to his lips as he crossed his legs. "Does Aidan have a lover? Someone in the village perhaps."

I frowned, and Sevrin continued to grin, his brown eyes twinkling in mischief.

Whit draped a massive arm over my shoulders and shook me. "Little baby Aidan has a lover. Who would have thought?"

"Look, his face is as red as his hair," Thomas teased, and Whit poked my cheek.

I slapped him off, wishing his wife, Frances, would take him away, but she'd remained at home. So had Thomas's spouse, Georgie, which in this case was a good thing. Georgie would have teased me as much as the Byrne brothers did.

Oren laughed. "Who? Who is it? Are they pretty?"

I crossed my arms, refusing to talk. Iris, who was not my lover, didn't want people to know about her. She didn't even sell her goods directly to people; instead, she went through a vendor. I wouldn't betray her trust. I'd found her home not long after my mother had passed, and Iris had always allowed me to visit her whenever I wanted. Her home had become my sanctuary.

Phineas, the third eldest, spoke up, his voice even, "Leave Aidan be." He looked directly at me with those pale green eyes that matched his father's. "You don't have to tell us."

"Thanks."

He smiled. "Doesn't mean we won't tease you."

I frowned again, and all the brothers laughed.

Thankfully, the conversation veered away from my *supposed* lover to Oren and the fae nobles who were vying for his attention.

"The Day Court representative, Lady Blodwen, is gorgeous," Sevrin said, running a hand through his coal-black hair, his hard features appearing even more gaunt in dying light. "Much better than Lord Abnus, the Night Court representative."

I hadn't met either of them, so I didn't offer an opinion.

Oren drew his legs to his chest. "They keep attacking me."

"What?" I asked, sitting up straight.

In the distance, thunder rumbled as an autumn storm began to build. I turned toward the swelling clouds, then back to Oren. The Sídhetír Memoirs said that when the heir came of age, the land responded to his call. He was tethered to the land and it to him. Oren must be more upset than I thought.

"Not truly," Thomas said, placing a hand on my arm before he pulled Oren into a hug. "All day, they've popped out from behind corners, trying to talk to him."

Oren's worst nightmare. He didn't like new people and struggled with basic communication when it came to strangers.

"Why didn't you summon me?" I'd been around all day, but Oren had told me this morning he didn't need me. Normally, I spent the day with him. Talking to others. Taking notes. Answering questions.

He peeked at Thomas and Whit from behind the curtain of his hair. Thomas nudged Oren, who said, "Father told me I needed to do this on my own. Without you."

A sharp needle of pain punctured my heart. It was a steady reminder; while the Byrne brothers treated me like one of them, I wasn't. I belonged to no one. I had no place. I had no home.

"I see."

Whit snagged me around the waist, hauling me to his side, while Phineas shifted closer, his knee brushing mine. Sevrin took a drink of wine, then said, "He was wrong, Aidan. You and Oren are best friends. If he wants you around, then you should be. Father just wants to control everything while he still can."

"Too true," Nevan said, and Neil silently toasted their brother.

I didn't know if that was accurate or not. I didn't know Jonathan Byrne well.

Oren smiled at me, but it was tense. I could easily read his thoughts because we had been by each other's sides for as long as I could remember. Even before I became a ward, we'd played together almost daily, unable to stay away from each other.

He wanted to defy Lord Byrne, but he wouldn't. I gave him a returning smile to let him know it was fine.

The distance between me and the Byrnes would never lessen. I wanted it to. I wanted to be one of them, but it would never be.

Keeping his arm around my waist, Whit kissed the top of my head. "We'll protect you. Don't worry."

I didn't need their protection, but I would allow such thoughts if it pleased them.

After Oren's valet helped him dress for the day, I stood from the sofa and moved in front of him. His skin was pallid and dark circles ringed his eyes. Shoulders slumped, he stared at the lightening window.

"I can come with you and Sevrin," I said.

Today, Oren was to tour Sídhetír with his fae guests. Sevrin, the horseman of the family, was going with him. The Byrne brothers had made a pact to never leave Oren alone with the fae, which was wise.

The Night Court hadn't been chosen since Lord Jonathan's grandfather's time. They had to be desperate to increase their standing and power within the fae realm, so Lord Abnus needed to be watched. Fae couldn't lie, but they did bend and twist the truth until it was unrecognizable.

Though bound by their word not to hurt Oren physically, the Night and Day Court representatives could take advantage of him.

Oren shook his head, straightening, though his shoulders remained rounded. "Father specifically told me you couldn't come. He and Thomas fought, but Father wouldn't relent. He wants you to make yourself scarce."

Why was Lord Byrne banishing me? Sometimes I helped Oren speak to people or answered questions, but that was it. Lord Byrne had always kept me from the fae in the past, and I'd never thought much of it. I'd been his ward, a peasant one at that.

Forcing myself onto this expedition would accomplish only one thing—irritating Lord Byrne. He would unleash said irritation on Oren for not being strong enough to do this without me.

"I will visit my mother."

When I reached the door, Oren whispered, "I'm sorry for being weak."

I replied in a hard voice, "You are not weak. Do you hear me, Oren? You are not weak. Your strengths are different than Lord

Byrne's, but that does not make you weak. You are perfect the way you are. I and your brothers would never trade you for another or wish you to be different."

He swallowed, eyes glassy. "Thank you."

"You can do this."

Oren didn't need me, even if he detested the situation. I squeezed his shoulder before slipping down the corridors and wound through the manor, nodding at the people I passed.

When I stepped outside, the late autumn air held the promise of the coming winter. Leaves rattled on the trees, and the crisp air raised pebbles of gooseflesh on my arms. Tucking my gloved hands into my pockets, I headed to the main gate of the estate.

The footmen at the gatehouse watched me leave, not acknowledging me with more than a nod, which I returned. The main road was well-kept, allowing the walk to the nearby village of Elmbury to be leisurely. Trees hovered in the background, the early morning shadows and fog clinging to their branches.

Elmbury was a gathering of a couple dozen buildings crowded between hills. The wood buildings were a mix of two and three-story homes with steep pitches and turrets. A stone well with a roof sat in the center, ringed by the buildings and vendor stalls. At the edge of the village was a short stone wall, broken and crumbling in places.

As today was market day, vendors hawked food, cloth, and goods of all kinds. I bypassed it, barely glancing at the sellers as I headed to my destination—a modest flower shop.

The wide front windows were framed by planters alive with blooming flowers, even this close to winter. The owners, Connor and Fergus Walsh, lived outside Elmbury with a sizable greenhouse behind their cottage.

I opened the glass door painted with the words *Walsh Flowers*, and a bell chimed. Connor stood behind the scarred wood counter spanning the back of the shop. He pushed his round spectacles up his long nose. Everything about Connor was thin and long, like he'd been stretched. His red hair was a shade or two lighter than mine and freckles decorated his skin, much like my own, though far more numerous.

"Greetings, Connor. How's your husband?"

"Same. Tending the flowers."

Fergus was Connor's almost exact opposite, blonde and broad. He preferred to tend the fields while Connor cared for the shop.

"Your usual arrangement?" Connor asked as he began to gather white roses.

"Yes. Ma's favorite." I only bought flowers when I visited her grave.

He nodded, not responding. Connor was a quiet one, while his husband was always good for a laugh, but Fergus didn't come to Elmbury often.

Once the bouquet was ready, I slapped a few coins on the counter.

When I reached the door, Connor said, "Be careful."

"What do you mean?"

Sídhetír was safe. The local magistrate kept highwaymen and any other human threats at bay. Since Lord Byrne was tied to the land, any fae in Sídhetír could be banished by his will if they caused trouble, which was why many fae stuck to the woods. He could not sense them there.

"More fae have come through the gate because we're in the transition, and you'll be walking near the woods. Watch yourself," he responded.

He was right. I'd quite forgotten. During the transition of power, Lord Byrne couldn't sense the fae nor cast them out. "Thank you."

My feet moved along the track, leaving Elmbury for the church outside the village. As it wasn't Sunday, there would be few parishioners, only people visiting the dead.

On the side of the dirt road, with nothing nearby, stood a building with a tall bell tower at the front. Its arched door was closed and the windows dark. The church backed up to the woods and graves dotted the surrounding area, all framed by a low stone wall. I spotted a few others paying their respects, but I paid them no mind, and they gave me the same courtesy.

A man peeled off the wall of the church like a shadow, and I stifled a groan. Eilis Duffy, the caretaker for the church grounds. He was convinced that every time I came to the graveyard, I was here to cause trouble. His suspicion stemmed from an incident about six years ago when Neven, Neil, Oren, and I had broken into the church to drink the sacramental wine. We'd gotten drunk and passed out in the sanctuary, where Mr. Duffy had found us.

"Mr. Ryan," he said in a grim voice. The man resembled a skeleton, with shockingly white skin, deep-set eyes, and black hair; he was thin as a rail with no meat clinging to his body. He pounded the base of his walking stick into the ground. "Come to disrespect the dead."

"No, Mr. Duffy. I came to see my ma."

He grunted, bony hands clutching the gnarled wood of his walking stick tighter. Mr. Duffy stared at me for several long breaths before he slunk away, leaving me alone.

Leaves from the large elm tree crunched under my feet as I wound between the graves. Crouching, I cleaned the leaves and moss from the gravestone. I laid the flowers down and traced the name, *Vis Ryan*, with my fingertip.

"Hey, Ma. Sorry, it's been a while. I've been busy with Oren. He's about to become Lord of Sídhetír. Can you believe it?"

I almost pictured her smiling face. Her red hair the same shade as mine. Her soft blue eyes, to my light green ones, crinkling with her mirth. Her booming laugh. God, I missed her. It had been thirteen years, but I missed her every day.

Words caught in my throat. I wanted answers she wouldn't give, even if she had been here. Ma had never talked about her family. Ever. I never knew them, or where she was from. Ma had never told me who my father was, only that he was as good as dead to me.

I rested my hand on the grave. "I wish you'd told me. I see Oren and his brothers, and I want that."

My only response was the wind.

The dead had no answers, and it was foolish to want them.

I left the grave and my frustration behind. My life wasn't bad. When I was orphaned, Lord Byrne could've abandoned me, but he'd kept me in the manor, away from the worst of the world. I had a job as Oren's aide. Money. Food. A place to live. Friends. There was nothing more I could ask for.

My boots crunched on the rocks in the dirt road as I paced along the woods. The wind whistled through the leaves, setting off a cacophony of whispers, and brought the damp smell of earth. The hour was early, and Oren would be with his guests. With no need to return, I strode in the general direction of Iris's cottage, staying on the road.

Something always drew me to the trees. A need to be under them, to touch them, and to bask in their presence. I gave into the longing and strolled into the forest.

Twigs snapped under my boots as leaves squished. The fragrance of wet, molding leaves mixed with that of moss and plant life. I took a deep inhale, allowing the air to expand my lungs to their fullest.

No lights glimmered from wisps, but I kept my eyes peeled for fae. Usually, one or two smaller ones were out and about. Most often pixies. They would play tricks, bite me with their needle teeth, or tug my hair. But all in all, they were harmless, unless I approached their nests.

Screeching and flapping tore through the silence as a flock of birds rushed over me. I jerked up, looking around the dimly lit forest. Something had startled them, and I didn't want to meet whatever it was. Picking up my pace, I strode toward Iris's cottage in a more direct route.

From one second to the next, I was walking, then crumpled on the ground. I swore, palms stinging through my gloves and back protesting. My legs were tangled on something solid. Something that had tripped me. I scrambled off, kicking whatever it was, and turned around.

The very blood in my veins froze as my breath turned harsh.

A man was sprawled on the forest floor, blood leaking from his stomach. His tapered ears poked through his white hair. His gray skin was frightfully pale. His sharp features slack.

A dark fae. An injured dark fae.

Chapter 3

"Do not let the fairness of face trick you into believing it equates to the fairness of heart." – Lord Ian, Sixth Lord of Sídhetír.

I stood, locked in place. What the hell was I supposed to do? Fae were unpredictable, especially when injured. If I tried to help him, he could attack me, not understanding. Or perhaps this was a trick. Some fae enjoyed tricking humans for whatever reason. But could I leave him behind? Bleeding?

"Fucking hell." I grabbed his arms and pulled.

He barely moved. The dark fae was tall, taller than me, which was a feat because I was taller than most. While lean, he was dense with muscles that his black shirt and tight trousers didn't hide.

"Well, shit." I placed a hand on my chin and stared at him. How was I supposed to get him all the way to Byrne Manor when I struggled to shift him? The answer was—I couldn't. Maybe I could haul him to Iris's cottage. She *had* wanted to meet a fae. It seemed God had heard her bloody wish.

Peeling my gloves off, I hooked my elbows under his armpits and dragged him backward. My arms and back immediately protested, screaming from the strain. This was going to be a long walk.

Step after step, I yanked the unconscious fae through the forest. The heels of his boots left ruts in the dirt, and blood continued to leak from the wound. I hoped I didn't run into whoever had attacked this fae. If they'd injured a noble fae, they would have no trouble dispatching me.

When the cottage appeared among the trees, I almost dropped the unconscious fae in relief. My back throbbed and sweat drenched my shirtsleeves. With loud grunts mixed with swears, I yanked him toward the door. My arms were burning and my legs had turned into jelly. I looked over my shoulder at the short distance separating me from the door, and I truly wondered if I could make it.

I had to.

Exhausted, I knocked on Iris's door, sagging against the cool stone of her home. Sweat dripped down my temple, and I wiped it off as I waited for her to appear. After a moment, I rapped on the door again.

It opened, and Iris stared at me with a creased brow. "Aidan, it's yourself. I didn't think I'd see you today." She paused, taking in my disheveled appearance. "What's wrong?"

"I found him." I gestured to the dark fae in a heap on the ground behind me.

She blanched, backing away. "Why is he here? Why did you bring him?"

"I found him injured." I grabbed the fae again and began to lug him into the house, but Iris blocked the entry. "Are you going to let me in?"

Slowly, she moved out of the way. As I dragged the fae inside, Iris didn't move to assist me. Blood continued to leak out of his wound, and he was barely breathing. I gently lowered him to the floor, then glanced over my shoulder at Iris, who hovered near the open door.

"Are you going to help me?"

"No," she said, clutching her elbows. "You should've left him where you found him."

"Iris, he's dying."

"So?"

"You're the one who wanted to dance with a fae. Well, help me save him and you'll have a chance," I said as I pressed my hands to the wound to stem the flow of blood. Dragging him across the forest hadn't been good for the injury, and I hadn't thought about binding it beforehand. Caring for injured people wasn't something I had experience with.

"I wanted to dance with a common fae. Not a noble one. I say we let him die, and I'll bury him under my roses. He'll feed them, and we'll never talk about this."

My mouth fell open as I peered back at her. "Are you serious?"

"I don't want to be a part of whatever this is," Iris said, waving a hand. "Why do you think I avoid people at all costs? Why do you think I stay in the forest? People will turn your life upside down and dance on the ruins. He has trouble written all over his pretty face. I don't need or want the drama. If he dies, so will the problem."

I eyed the sharp planes of his cheekbones and the strength of his jaw. He was beautiful. All fae were. But it was more than that. He was alive—a living, breathing person who needed help.

"I have to help him."

"He might deserve it," she said.

I didn't believe that. "Help me."

"I'm not touching him. I don't want any part of the hell he will rain down on us," Iris said, which made me glare at her, but she continued. "I *will* tell you what to do, though, you good-hearted moron."

At her direction, I removed his shirt to inspect the injury. The jagged puncture sat deep in his stomach. Blood oozed from the opening. I swallowed my rising bile as ringing started in my ears. Blood wasn't something I was good with.

"Do you think the knife perforated his bowels?" I asked.

Iris stared at him over my shoulder. "I don't know. I'm not a physician. If you wanted one of those, you should've dragged him to Byrne Manor."

"We wouldn't have made it."

"All you can do is stitch the wound and bind it. If the knife nicked something, he's a dead man."

She brought me a needle and thread. I cleaned the wound with some of the potent whiskey before gulping a couple mouthfuls to steady my trembling hands. As carefully as possible, I stitched the ripped flesh together. With each stitch, I thanked my mother for teaching me basic sewing skills, though flesh was a far cry from cloth.

Once the wound was closed, Iris handed me a tin of foul-smelling paste, which I spread over the injury. Finally, I wrapped his waist in clean bandages.

The dark fae still breathed, but I had no idea if he would survive. Fae generally possessed better healing abilities than humans, but I couldn't say if those would repair this damage.

I rested a bloodied hand on his sternum, feeling the even thump of his heart beneath my palm. Hope remained.

My gaze moved to his face, and I jolted. Black eyes met mine. They were as dark as pitch, with no difference between his iris and pupils. All I saw was a pool of black in the white ocean of sclera.

His long fingers curled around my wrist, holding me tight. A scuttling sound came from behind me moments before the door opened and slammed closed. Iris must have fled, and I didn't blame her.

Fear coiled in my stomach as I stared at him. This fae, even injured, could kill me, but he didn't move. His long fingers remained firmly around my wrist, and his eyes flicked over my face.

With my heart in my throat, I laid my hand on his jaw. "You're hurt, and I'm trying to help you."

The fae didn't react, nor did his inscrutable expression change. He continued to watch me with his fathomless eyes. Eventually, they slid closed again and his grip loosened on my wrist, freeing me.

I sagged back, ass hitting the stone floor. Sweet Lord, he had an intense look, but he hadn't attacked me. Maybe he'd understood what I said. I honestly didn't know if he spoke the common tongue. It was possible my words meant nothing to him.

I tucked a pillow under his head and draped a blanket over him, trying to make the fae as comfortable as possible. I sat cross-legged, facing him, and tracked every twitch. I worried for some odd reason that if I glanced away, for even a moment, he would die, which was ludicrous. My will alone couldn't keep him here.

Several minutes passed before the door creaked. "Is he alive?"

"Yes."

"Damnit," Iris said with such feeling that I chuckled. "Is he awake?"

"No."

She came inside the rest of the way and crouched beside me. "I can make some potions to help with blood loss and promote healing as well as an antidote for poison, but I will not promise they'll actually work. They're made for humans, and dark fae are out of my realm of experience."

"Poison?"

Shrugging, she said, "He's acting fairly hurt for a single stab wound."

Maybe poison was the reason he hadn't healed? I didn't know enough of fae to say for certain. "Thank you."

Iris grunted and moved to the fireplace, starting the fire. The cottage was already warm, but after a few minutes, sweat dripped down my back. She flitted around and pulled down jars full of dried herbs, powder, and bits and bobs. With a groan, she put a pewter pot onto the pot crane and swung the concoction over the flames. She mixed the liquid with a wooden spoon, muttering under her breath while casting scathing looks at me and the dark fae.

"Idiot," she snapped at me.

I turned away from watching Iris make the potion, something I'd witnessed several times, and looked down at the fae. His eyes were open again, staring at me. The breath left my lungs. I bent closer, hovering over him, and rested my hand against his cheek. He did not fight against my hold or shift aside.

"Hello," I said, unable to think of anything else.

He blinked at me.

"Can you understand me?"

The fae lifted one of his hands, curling his fingers around my wrist. His skin was cool against mine. His fingertips rested right on my pulse point, so I knew he felt the racing of my heart.

Iris scooted closer to me, holding out the concoction as far as possible. I frowned at her antics. The fae hadn't done anything to warrant her obvious terror.

"Can you drink this?" I asked.

Once again, he said nothing.

I wiggled my hand from his grasp, and he frowned, tightening his grasp, though, after a moment, he let me go. I slipped a hand under his neck to lift him and pressed the cup to his lips.

As he swallowed the liquid, his eyes remained on mine. Heat rushed to my cheeks, and I couldn't say why. I set the cup down and helped settle him back.

"I'm going to check your wound," I whispered, pulling the blanket down. No blood dotted the bandage. I looked over my shoulder to ask Iris if I should take off the wrapping to examine the actual injury, but she'd disappeared. She *really* didn't want to interact with this dark fae.

Now that I wasn't worried about him bleeding to death, I couldn't help but take in the sight of his bare chest. He was hairless and had well-defined muscles, but what caught my attention was the tattoos. Black vines swirled over his chest and arms, appearing so real I wanted to touch them. Blue flowers with long yellow stamen grew on the thorny vines. On the center of his chest was a crescent moon as real as the one that hung in the sky with a single, seven-pointed star that glowed deep red right next to it.

The tattoos hadn't been there earlier; I was sure of it. I'd heard stories about fae changing their appearance to suit humans. Were the tattoos actually there or had he conjured them for me? Was he no longer able to hide his true appearance? Or had I missed the marks in my panic earlier? I lifted my gaze back to his face, and he silently stared at me.

I didn't bother to speak. Instead, I grabbed his hand to offer silent comfort. He slid his fingers between mine.

Eventually, his eyes drifted closed and his hand turned slack within my grasp.

"Is he awake?" Iris asked in a loud whisper.

I peeked over my shoulder and caught a glimpse of her on the staircase leading to the loft. "He's asleep."

She let out a dramatic sigh and shuffled down.

The windows outside were starting to grow dark. I couldn't believe I'd spent the whole day here. It had taken a considerable amount of time to drag the dark fae to Iris's cottage and even more time to care for him. With the coming winter, the days were shorter, which didn't help. I needed to return before I was missed.

I got to my feet to head toward the door, but a figure blocked the way. Iris crossed her arms. "Where exactly do you think you're going?"

"Byrne Manor. It's getting late and," I said, poking at the blood stains on my waistcoat and light brown trousers, "I'm in desperate need of fresh clothes."

"You are not leaving me with him."

"What do you want me to do?" I asked. "Drag him back to the manor? I'm sure when I pull his body inside, the footmen will be like, 'Ah, Aidan, what a lovely fae corpse you have there. Have a pleasant night.'"

Iris giggled, covering her mouth. "That might be a problem."

"So help me out. I will come back tomorrow."

"I am helping you," she said. "But you will not leave me here alone with him. If I had it my way, I'd hit him on the head and bury him in my garden."

"This again," I said, then paused. "Have you actually done that?"

"That's for me to know, and you to never find out." She cocked an eyebrow, and I let the matter drop. I truly didn't want to know if she'd killed wayward travelers and fed them to her plants. Anything was possible with Iris.

I peered at the unconscious fae. I couldn't drag him with me, nor would I subject him to murder if Iris was serious. If she wasn't, she'd probably kick him out into the cold. Pulling off my jacket, I returned to his side.

"I guess, I'm spending the night." No doubt there would be a fair amount of ribbing when I returned in the morning, wearing the same clothes.

Chapter 4

"A fae owing you a debt can be as bad, if not worse, than you owing them a favor." – Lord Quincy, Seventh Lord of Sídhetír.

Early morning fog covered the fields around Elmbury and the road to Byrne Manor. The crisp air promised a pleasant fall day. I buttoned my tailored jacket over the worst blood stains and smoothed a hand down my trousers. I'd been able to get some of the blood off, but with close inspection, someone would notice the rust-colored streaks that would not come free. Not to mention, I'd lost my hat in the woods when I tripped over the fae, and I'd stripped off my gloves at some point, leaving them who knows where.

When I awoke this morning, the fae was gone. The cloth bandage had been wound around my forearm, and when I took it off, I received another surprise—a tattoo. Thorny vines started at my wrist and disappeared up my arm. How far? I didn't know. I couldn't roll up my sleeve far enough to see the entirety of the mark.

Iris had rushed around the cottage like a chicken with its head cut off when she saw it. Claiming I was as good as cursed. She'd lamented my kind heart, for it had led me to certain doom. However, even with her concern, she had taken the time to make several comments about her wisdom in not helping the dark fae.

I scoffed at the thought of a curse. If the dark fae wanted to harm or kill me, he could've done so with far less trouble than cursing me with a tattoo. If there was such a thing. Ridiculous.

I tugged on the sleeve of my jacket. Thankfully, the tattoo was hidden from view by propriety constraints. No one would see me without my shirt, except for if I took a lover. I snorted. I hadn't ever done that, nor did I expect to anytime soon. By the time that particular problem presented itself, I should've managed to fabricate a decent story about why I had a tattoo.

I walked around the side of the estate to the secret gate. I didn't need the footmen at the gatehouse marking my arrival.

With every passing moment, the sun was growing brighter, and with it, the chance of someone discovering my absence increased. The Byrne brothers would know I was gone, because they'd probably looked for me, but the head of staff, Mrs. Kelly, or Lord Byrne would not. Neither would be pleased about my clothes, or the fact I was returning in the wee hours of the morning. While I was no longer a ward of the manor, I had been invited to remain as Oren's aide, and as such, I needed to present myself accordingly.

Thankfully, I didn't have to worry about my reputation or lack of a chaperone as much as if I'd been Oren or any of his unmarried brothers. They were of the gentry and had to worry about such things as well as being forced to wed.

I slipped the black key out of my pocket, thankful the bugger was still there after the vigorous activities of yesterday, and unlocked the gate. My feet knew the way through the maze, and my mind drifted to the dark fae from yesterday.

Over the years, I'd seen many fae due to my proximity to the Byrnes. Most of the fae who came to the manor were light fae. In my relatively short years, I'd only seen a handful of dark fae. How they differed from their lighter cousins, I didn't know.

One major difference I knew was the dark fae drew magic from the moon, unlike the light fae who received their magic from the sun.

An arm snagged my neck, choking me as my focus whipped to my surroundings. Neil stood in front of me, as silent as ever with a wide grin, while Nevan proceeded to ruffle my short hair.

"Where were you?" Nevan questioned, dragging me down since I was a few inches taller than him. "You're wearing the same clothes as yesterday. Did you visit your lover in the village?"

I elbowed him in the gut, and he jerked back with a gasp. Yanking my coat straight, I glared at Nevan and his twin. Both were five years older than I was, but they didn't act like it. "I made myself scarce as Lord Byrne ordered."

"I don't think he intended for you to stay out all night, Aidan," Neil chastised, his voice deep and even as he ran a hand through his dark hair. "We were worried. With this many fae about, Sídhetír is not as safe as normal."

If that wasn't the truth, I didn't know what was.

They all cared about me. I was the adopted younger brother they hadn't wanted or needed, but they took on my care with great aplomb.

"Thank you," I said. "Matters kept me occupied."

"Matters," Nevan repeated, wiggling his eyebrows, and he ruffled my hair again. I shoved his hand away with a frown, which made him laugh. "What *matters* do you have?"

The question didn't need answering, because they would never believe me if I told them I wasn't with this fictitious lover they'd concocted, and I had no intention of telling them the truth. Knowing of the dark fae's existence would only worry them.

My gaze turned to the growing light. I needed to change before either Nevan or Neil took a close look at my clothes. Flecks of blood were visible on my waistcoat that my jacket did not hide. Streaks of rust from wiping my fingers had left their marks on my thighs.

I frowned at the pair for good measure, and Nevan began to sing about me and my supposed lover as I darted to the manor. I slipped in through a side door and up the stairs as fast as possible without arousing suspicion. Nothing drew attention like running through the halls.

The moment I was in my room, I bolted the door. Thankfully, no one had noticed me besides Nevan and Neil. If either of them had seen the marks on my clothes, they would've had questions. Especially Nevan. He could never help but say what was on his mind.

Methodically, I undressed, separating my blood-stained clothes from the rest. I would have to launder the clothes myself and see if they could be salvaged. If the rust-colored marks wouldn't wash free, I would have to make a trip to the tailor.

When I pulled my white shirt off, I stared at my left arm in the full-length mirror. The black vines started at my wrist, wound up my arm, and danced across my shoulder. Some disappeared, looking like they burrowed into my very skin. Over my left pectoral, they formed a ring. In the center rested a crescent moon with a dark red, seven-pointed star, identical to the one that had been on the fae's sternum.

My fingertips traced the marks, lingering on the crescent moon, which appeared so real. The star glimmered with an internal glow that spoke of its magical origin, and the thorny black vines pulsed with the beat of my heart, occasionally moving.

I didn't know what to make of the tattoo. The dark fae had imbued the magic into my skin before he left, but why? What purpose did it serve?

There was no way to answer the questions unless the fae showed himself and chose to explain, but getting the truth from the fae wasn't easy, according to the stories. It was possible I would never know what the mark meant until it affected me. Hopefully, the tattoo wasn't the curse Iris seemed to think it was.

The late afternoon sun hung overhead as I rode beside Sevrin. After my disappearance yesterday, the brothers decided one of them should accompany me in my exile. Originally, Oren wanted to go with me, but Thomas told him the fae representatives were here for him. Oren didn't seem to appreciate the reminder.

Sevrin's choice of activity was taking a leisurely ride around the estate, which wasn't surprising. He was always happiest with horses, whether riding or in the stable. He co-owned a profitable horse ranch with his elder brother Phineas in the southern part of Sídhetír, which Lord Byrne had helped them establish.

Since the estate was entailed to the seventh son, the older sons had to make careers for themself, and each of the Byrne brothers had. Sevrin's career of choice kept him closer to Byrne Manor, though he rarely left his ranch.

"Where did you actually go last night?" Sevrin finally asked.

All morning the Byrne brothers had pestered me about my activities, but I hadn't answered. Iris wanted to be kept a secret, and I felt an unexplained need to not speak of the fae. Besides, the whole scenario would worry them more than necessary. If the time came when the magic of the tattoo revealed itself, I would explain what happened.

"Why won't you accept my explanation? I was doing something I would rather keep private."

He snorted, and his horse tossed her head, making her white hair flop to the other side of her tan neck. "Phineas thinks we should. He said you are allowed your privacy."

"Then let me have it."

"Whit believes we should beat it out of you, and I concur," he said, raising a black eyebrow.

"I don't agree."

"I second that sentiment, human," a soft voice whispered, sending chills down my spine.

Sevrin jerked his horse to face the darkened forest and demanded, "Show yourself."

The voice chuckled. "It is not you who can command me, human."

I swore the vines writhed on my arm, digging deeper as the voice spoke. I commanded, "Come out."

Not a moment later, the dark fae slid out from the trees. His void eyes remained on me as he gracefully strode in my direction, his white hair tickling his waist. The dying sunlight made his gray skin even more pallid than I remembered. My horse snorted, pawing the ground as she took a step backward. I patted the mare's neck in an attempt to soothe her, but the horse would not calm.

Slipping from the saddle, I tossed the reins to Sevrin, who gaped at me. While the fae's black shirt allowed me to see the thorny tattoos matching mine, it didn't let me see the injury—though he seemed healed, if his smooth steps were any indication.

"You've recovered?" I asked.

He came closer, forcing me to look up. "Indeed. You showed great kindness yesterday."

"Aidan," Sevrin said, his voice deepening in warning.

"Aidan," the dark fae repeated. "Is that your name?"

I hesitated for a single breath. Fae were said to be able to control people with their true names. I was human. I had no true name. Besides, Sevrin had already told the dark fae my name. "Yes."

"Aidan," he said once again. He placed his long fingers on my cheek, and I swallowed. He brushed featherlight touches over my skin, making shivers slide down my spine. He bent closer, his breath on my ear, as he whispered. "You may call me Cethin."

Rubbing my ear, I tried to banish the unexpected tingles. By the way he phrased it, I assumed Cethin wasn't his name—not that I expected him to give me his true name just because I'd saved his life.

Cethin smiled at Sevrin. It was not a kind gesture. The wide stretch of his lips showed off his impressive canines and made him appear feral. "I will be borrowing Aidan."

"Let him go," he ordered, drawing a pistol as Cethin hooked an arm about my waist.

I tried to step forward, but his hold was made of iron. Cethin drew me into the forest, and Sevrin started to charge after us, but his horse wouldn't go beneath the trees. He dismounted, and my stomach dropped. No one was safe within the forest. It had spared me time and time again, yet here I was ensnared at last. Sevrin couldn't follow us or risk losing himself.

"Stay back, Sevrin."

He hesitated, pistol leveled at Cethin, who continued to pull me along. "I will get a search party together."

Before I could tell him not to, we rounded a tree, and the view of Sevrin and the sloping hills vanished.

Chapter 5

"Magic always exacts a price. What? You'll never know until much later." – Lord Edmund, Second Lord of Sídhetír.

Cethin kept his arm tight about my waist, as if he feared I would run the second I was granted freedom. It was an accurate worry, if the fae had it, because I *would* undoubtedly run. I would run like I should have when I saw him unconscious yesterday. I would run like I should have when his voice whispered through the leaves. I wouldn't make the same mistake again, and yet... I felt myself wanting to stay to ask questions. Foolish.

He kept walking, steering me around fallen trees and underbrush with ease, until we reached a glade I'd never seen. A run-down cottage abutted the trees covered in red and orange leaves, and a creek rushed past. The only way across the water was a row of moss-covered stones I was not about to step on. I'd already ruined one set of good clothes, and I wasn't going to ruin another.

"Where are we?" I asked, arms crossed.

"Where I will be staying for the foreseeable future. Now you can find me, should you desire it."

"Why would I want to find you?"

"Why wouldn't you?" Cethin smirked, head tilted, which sent his starlight hair tumbling over his shoulder.

I shoved my jacket and sleeve up as far as they would go. "What is this?"

"A tattoo. Surely Sídhetír is not so remote that you've never seen one?" Cethin started toward the cottage, easily hopping across the stones to reach the other side of the fast-flowing creek.

I rushed after him, hesitating momentarily at the edge. I should run away. If I did, I would never get the answers I wanted. Swearing, I placed a foot on the closest stone. My boot slid a bit before I gained traction. The creek gurgled past me, and I caught a glimpse of a fish in the water's depths.

Cethin stood across the creek, tracking my every movement. Every wobble and twitch made his hands stretch out like he intended to grab me. I stepped onto the next stone and leaped to the last one before hopping to the other side. I landed not far from Cethin's side. He stared at me for a single moment, which stole my breath and I couldn't say why, then he headed further into the glade.

"What does the tattoo mean? And why did you give it to me?"

"Must there be a reason?"

"Yes."

I followed him straight to the cottage. He opened the door, and I went after him, pausing at the entrance. Perhaps this was not the wisest decision.

The cottage was small with a bed off to the side, a fireplace on the back wall, and a single cabinet. Cethin sat on the threadbare rug in front of the empty fireplace and motioned to the space across from him. Frowning, I took a seat.

"There is a reason," he said. "But must you know it? Does it truly matter?"

I rubbed at the skin of my wrist. It felt no different with the tattooed vines embedded in it, yet I expected to feel the sharp bite of the thorns. "Why did you do it? Is it permanent?"

"Even more questions. Are you always so curious, Aidan?"

Yes, I was. Having a strange dark fae marking me with a magical tattoo had increased my usual curiosity. Shocking.

I blinked as a thought came to me. "I saved your life."

"You did."

He said the words without even trying to obfuscate, leading me to believe it was the truth. I shoved up my sleeve again and traced the vines swirling up my arm. He followed the movement, his black eyes growing bright as if a fire burned within them.

"Did you do this because you owe me a debt?" I asked.

Leaning back on his elbows, he said, "You could take it as such if you wish."

"*Do* you owe me a debt?"

"I owe you everything," Cethin answered, his silky voice deepening. "And as such, I will be here should you have need or want of me."

Pulse racing, I gaped at Cethin. What was I supposed to say? I opened my mouth to refute his claim, but the words caught in my throat. I *had* saved him. I wouldn't say he owed me everything, though.

The silence grew between us. I tried to parse through my response in my head, and Cethin appeared content to stare at me. His gaze traced over me, back and forth, lingering on the base of the tattoo that was exposed near my wrist.

I pushed down my sleeve, and he smirked.

"Tell me about yourself," Cethin said.

"Why?"

"Why not?"

I frowned at him, and Cethin raised his eyebrows. I saw no reason not to tell him. "I was ward of Lord Byrne. My mother died when I was eight. I've been living with them since. I'm Oren's aide now. He's the heir."

"Hmm."

"All of the Byrnes have become like older brothers to me. Of a sort."

"Are they your only family?"

"They're not exactly family, but yes. You?"

"Parents, younger sister, two uncles, aunt, and cousin."

I'd always wanted a family like that. The Byrnes had each other and innumerable amounts of uncles, aunts, and cousins. Every summer, the *entire* Byrne family, or as many of them that could come, would gather for a fortnight. The amount of people was staggering.

"Tell me more," he demanded, and I found myself doing just that.

Cethin led me to the edge of the woods before vanishing amongst the trees. I walked as fast as I could toward Byrne Manor, thankful I tripped less often than I thought I should on the uneven ground. The moon was high and illuminated the grass, turning it a silvery hue, but it wasn't bright enough to truly see by. The outlines of the trees and the distant buildings of Elmbury, which disappeared as I dipped down a hill and reappeared as I started to walk up another, framed my walk.

Sevrin had no doubt done as he said, forming a search party for me. Lord Byrne wouldn't have sensed me or Cethin among the trees, even if his power hadn't been waning. To find people in the woods, we had to look in person. On more than one occasion, Lord Byrne, his sons, some locals, and I had gone into the woods to search for curious children or hunters who went missing—something we only did when absolutely necessary, due to the inherent danger.

With the transition, the woods were far more dangerous than usual, because in the fae realm, the gate had moved to the stretch of land connecting the Night and Day Courts. Fae could easily enter, and Lord Byrne was helpless to stop it, making me wonder if he *would* search for me.

As I crested a hill, I faced Byrne Manor, which was alive with lights glimmering in the distance.

"Shit," I muttered.

Even with no particular regard for me, it seemed being Lord Byrne's former ward was enough for him to not let a dark fae abscond with me. Or it could be because a Night Court representative was in the manor, which helped guarantee my return. Or the Byrne brothers simply hadn't given him a choice.

Leaving off any show of propriety, I raced to the estate. A hitch in my side started, and my feet burned. The boots I wore were not made for this; they dug into my soles and restricted my ankles. I had to halt long before I reached the manor. I clutched my side and took heaving breaths, then started once again.

The journey took much longer than I would have liked. Honestly, I probably would've reached Byrne Manor faster if I'd walked, but I wasn't going to admit that to anyone.

I approached the gates, and one of the footmen yelled, "He's back. Tell Lord Byrne."

The wrought-iron gates swung open for me before closing with a loud clang.

So much for not worrying people.

The double doors of the manor loomed in front of me. Impassive. Solid. Oddly enough, I had the perverse urge to run back to the forest and Cethin's cottage. Surely the dark fae was better than Lord Byrne and all his sons.

Out poured all of the Byrnes, giving me no chance to flee.

I was seized by Oren first. I returned his hug. "I'm well."

Thomas grabbed me next, but he barely squeezed me prior to Nevan and Neil snagging me from his grasp. I was passed one by one to all of the brothers—even Lady Hester took a turn and placed a kiss on my forehead—before I ended up right in front of Lord Byrne.

His light green eyes stared at me as a stern frown flattened his already thin lips. The age was obvious in the wrinkles on his brow and the deep lines by his mouth and eyes. His blonde hair was cut to the current fashion, but it was threaded with silver. But, despite being close to sixty and having lost two wives and raising seven sons, the lord had kept his respectable appearance and strong build.

"Aidan Ryan," he said. "You caused quite a stir."

"Yes, my lord."

He faced the manor and ordered over his shoulder, "Come."

I followed after him, and Oren sidled up to me. I raised an eyebrow. Lord Byrne hadn't excluded him per se, yet I doubted he wanted Oren present for this conversation.

Oren tightened his hold on my arm. "I'm going to be the new lord in a matter of days; he cannot order me away. I want to hear what happened, anyway."

I had no idea what I was going to tell them. The truth I supposed was the only real answer, and yet, I didn't want to share everything. Iris and her hedge witch status. Cethin marking me or his cottage. I shook my head. I would have to tell Lord Byrne enough to satisfy him without lying.

Lord Byrne sat behind the gleaming desk in his bookroom with steepled hands. Bookshelves framed the wall behind him from floor to ceiling. Oren and I sat in the two chairs facing the desk.

"Oren," Lord Byrne said, "I don't believe you were invited to this conversation."

"I'm about to be Lord of Sídhetír," Oren said, but the quiver in his voice betrayed the nerves he tried to hide.

Lord Byrne stared at his youngest child. "You are not lord yet. Leave."

I whispered, "All will be well enough."

With a glance at me, Oren left the room, closing the door behind him.

Lord Byrne sagged back, running a hand through his hair and tousling the artful hairstyle that hid its thinning. "What am I going to do with you, Aidan?"

"What do you mean, my lord?"

He moved to the window on the left wall. I adjusted in my chair, making it creak, as I followed his movement. He placed a hand on the pane, the clean glass reflecting his grim expression. "What happened?"

I chose my words carefully. "I stumbled upon an injured dark fae in the woods."

"Why were you even in the woods?" He turned toward me, hands clasped behind his back. "This is a dangerous time, and you shouldn't be in there regardless."

"I like the trees," I offered. It wasn't much of an explanation, but it was the only reason I possessed.

"God preserve me." He took a deep breath. "Continue."

"I saved him. That's where I was last night."

"Last night?" he asked.

I winced. "I see your sons didn't tell you."

"No, they did not."

"The fae spoke with me. Perhaps he wished to thank me without explicitly saying so," I finished. Fae did not thank people as a rule—it created a debt that had to be honored.

"That could have ended much worse, Aidan. Fae are unpredictable and cannot be trusted." Lord Byrne moved to lean against the front of the desk. "I want you to stay away from the fae."

My jaw clenched, but I didn't reply. I already knew I was going to defy his request. Eventually, I would wander back to Cethin. I was curious, and he was an easy source of knowledge. His unwavering gaze floated through my thoughts. I had talked and talked, more than I normally would, and Cethin had listened, asking questions and remarking, but never acted like he wanted me to stop. In fact, when I took a breath, he'd asked more questions.

"Damnation, Aidan, I'm trying to protect you."

I met his earnest expression. Lord Byrne had helped raise me. A distant figure in my childhood who checked on me and monitored the progress in my studies and whatnot. He was attempting to protect me, but I didn't want or need it, at least in this instance.

"I know, my lord."

"You're not going to listen to me, are you?"

"Whatever do you mean?"

He shook his head, straightening. "You never listened to me when you were young. Why would you now?"

"I heeded all of your commands that I could."

"That you could," he repeated with a smile that reminded me of Phineas. Out of all of his seven children, Phineas resembled Lord Byrne the most. They shared the same blonde hair, strong build, and soft green eyes. The rest of his sons took after their respective mothers.

"That I could." I nodded.

Lord Byrne brushed a hand through my hair, smoothing the red strands back. I swallowed at his touch, tensing. I could count on one hand the times he'd been physically affectionate with me. He'd never gotten mad or struck me, but he'd never shown much interest in my care either.

"Be safe, Aidan. The fae will trick you in ways you cannot predict. I cannot protect you if you do not listen to me."

That might be so, but I would see Cethin again if I desired.

Chapter 6

"The future Lord of Sídhetír should expect trickery from both the light and dark fae, for they want the same thing—power." – Lord Louis, Third Lord of Sídhetír.

I stood behind Oren's chair with my arms crossed, listening to the report. Lord Byrne was at the head of the table, with Oren at his right hand and Lady Hester on his left. The rest of the rectangular table was filled with the Byrne brothers.

On a normal visit, they would've returned to their usual pursuits, leaving the manor behind after a few days, but this time, they would remain until Oren chose which court to align with and took the mantle of lord. Thomas and Whit were the only ones married and with children. Remaining longer presented more difficulties for them, but they wanted to stay.

"The Hillridge Farm was destroyed, my lord," Colonel Tarrah Fletcher said, standing at the other end of the table. She was the head of the regiment currently stationed in Sídhetír for the duration of the transition. Fletcher looked minuscule next to the large door and all of the Byrne brothers, but I knew her to be a fierce fighter. A scar sliced down her tan cheek, catching the edge of her full lips, and continued down her chin, giving her a rakish air. Her shorn brown hair assisted in that appearance.

"What happened?" Lord Byrne asked.

"We don't know yet. We received reports of a fire, but when we arrived, everything had burned. Very little is left," she reported.

"What of the people living there?" I asked, ignoring the glance Lord Byrne threw my way. I'd always been allowed to attend meetings with Oren, but Lord Byrne didn't like it when I spoke, though I rarely did.

Captain Fletcher faced me. "Neither I nor my soldiers found anyone or their remains."

"Magic?" I asked.

"We don't know, Mr. Ryan."

Lord Byrne should've known if fae magic was performed on his lands. The human variety of magic was different. It was of this realm and hid among the natural ebbs and flows. Fae magic could not. If the fae remained in the forest, he didn't feel their magic because the land was saturated in fae magic and the trees held it close, maintaining it. On his own lands, though, it should have been easy to sense.

Lord Byrne met my gaze. "The transition of power is already happening. I cannot perceive the land like I once did."

"I didn't feel anything," Oren said.

"You probably won't until the transition completes," Lord Byrne remarked. He rested a hand on his chin and focused on Colonel Fetcher, who'd watched the exchange with a bland expression. "I will survey the damage and see what I can feel. Perhaps the fae representatives will accompany me."

"Very good, Your Lordship," she said with a bow.

Lord Byrne dismissed her, then faced us. "The first wave of trouble."

"Indeed," Thomas said.

According to the stories, attacks became more common during the transition of power because the creatures could wander into the mortal realm with ease. Deals with noble and common fae became usual as well. It was a time that reminded us humans of what it was like prior to the contract—before the tide of bloodshed was stemmed.

"You need to choose, Oren, so we can put this all behind us," Lord Byrne said.

"That is hardly fair, Jonathan," Lady Hester said. "It's been only a few days. This is not a decision he can or should make lightly, as it will affect the rest of his and our lives."

"You don't think I know that?"

My gaze turned to Thomas and Whit as Lord Byrne and Lady Hester glared at one another. They normally got along, except when it came to Oren. Thomas caught my eyes, then looked at Oren, who sat tensely with his hands curled around the arms of his chair. Whit lifted an eyebrow, and Thomas stared at me like he expected me to do something about the situation. What? I didn't know.

I laid a hand on Oren's shoulder. "You don't have to choose until you're ready. No one can force you."

Lady Hester sent me a smile; whereas, Lord Byrne glared at me. It wasn't my place to interfere, but I felt Oren steady beneath my hand.

Oren said, "I will go with you to see Hillridge Farm."

"Good," Lord Byrne said. "Shall we ask if the fae representatives want to go together?"

"Yes," Oren answered. "Thank you."

Lord Byrne looked at each one of his sons and then me. "No one is to go anywhere alone. Thomas and Whitaker, you will come with us to the farm, if that is acceptable, my dear?"

"I'm perfectly fine with that," Lady Hester replied.

"I will take Sevrin and speak to the locals about any fae sightings," Phineas said, and Sevrin nodded.

Nevan spoke for himself and Neil when he said, "We'll patrol the area around the estate, keeping watch for fae."

"Keep your wits sharp, my sons. There may be fae who want the contract to end, and the only way that will happen is through Oren's death."

"That will never happen," Whit said.

I tightened my hold on Oren when a tremor slid down his spine. I wished he could be spared from the fate of being Lord of Sídhetír, but his fate had been written in blood, and only blood would wash it away.

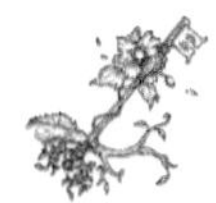

The preparations for heading to Hillridge Farm had commenced. Both of the fae representatives had agreed to go once they heard Oren was going. According to Sevrin, they'd expressed dismay about the destruction of the farm, but he didn't believe them.

I was ambivalent about their responses. Humans mattered little to beings that lived for eons. We were a source of entertainment, profit, and in some cases, sustenance.

It was decided they would go the following morning. While the fae courted Oren for his endorsement, Whit and Sevrin stuck close to him. Thomas and Phineas did the same with me.

A week had passed since Cethin had absconded with me, but none of the Byrnes had forgotten it. They all watched me like they feared I would vanish from beneath their very noses.

Lord Byrne still wished me to remain away from Oren and the fae, even though he'd told the fae of my abduction when he formed a search party for me. I truly believed he wanted to keep me away from Oren, so Oren would be forced to speak. When I was there, Oren retreated behind me like I was a shield. I didn't mind protecting him, but this path was one he had to walk and I couldn't follow him.

Phineas whittled carefully, sitting on the damp grass, heedless of his white trousers or the cold emanating from the ground. His movements were slow and even from years of practice. I'd grown up watching those steady movements. Scrape after scrape, a figure took shape. As a child, I had several toys carved for me by Phineas. They'd been some of my most treasured possessions.

Thomas sat right beside me on the garden bench, arms crossed and head back, as the autumn wind rushed over us, rattling the leaves and flaring his hair. As the eldest of the brothers, Thomas often acted like it was his purpose in life to keep his siblings safe. I often fell into that category.

"Must you guard me?" I asked.

"If we left you alone," Thomas said, "the dark fae might steal you to their realm, and we'd never see you again. We'd never recover from such a loss."

Dramatic, really. All of them were so dramatic. Cethin hadn't even hurt me. All he'd wanted to do was talk.

"You heard Father, Aidan. None of us are to go anywhere alone," Phineas said, carving the delicate curl of a goat's horn.

"He was speaking to you lot, not me."

Thomas scoffed. "He looked directly at you. None of *us* have been tempting fate. It's like you're asking for the good Lord above to take you."

"Not so," I protested.

"You're stuck with us, so do stop complaining," Phineas said. "We can do something more interesting if you don't wish to laze about. Perhaps we can retire to the library or Father's bookroom?"

I didn't possess much interest in reading. When the weather was fierce, I didn't hate passing the day with a book, especially the tomes of the previous Sídhetír Lords, but when the weather was nice, I preferred to be outside. My hands in the grass. My feet on the land. My heart free of the walls.

My thoughts turned to the burned ruins of Hillridge Farm. I almost saw it in my mind's eye: the barns, the house, the fields. All of it was clear to me, but altered, burned. I didn't know who could have done it.

A cruel thought popped into my head. Perhaps Cethin had done it. He was alive and able. I couldn't say if he had the necessary magic to burn a farm to the ground and corpses to ash, but he was a noble fae. Of that I was sure—he resembled the other Night Court nobles who'd come—so he had to have *some* power.

Would he answer me if I asked him? He might. Cethin did owe me a debt.

A restlessness built in my legs, making me twitch. I wanted to see the damage for myself. I wanted to see what had become of the land. What about the Hillridges and their young daughter and heir, who wasn't even ten? Nancy's smiling face framed by blonde braids grew in my mind as my heart thrashed against my ribs. I had to see Hillridge Farm, which meant escaping Thomas and Phineas's watchful gazes.

Thunder rumbled in the distance, making me blink. Storm clouds started to form in the north, dark and looming. A crash of lightning struck, and after a few breaths, the grumble of thunder came again.

"Storm," Phineas said.

Thomas glanced at me. "Seems so."

"Perhaps Lord Byrne or Oren is upset?" I offered.

"Perhaps," Thomas said, eyes not leaving my face.

I peered over my shoulder as I snuck toward the secret gate. Thomas and Phineas had been momentarily distracted when one of the fae representatives had wandered through the garden, searching for Oren, who'd disappeared. They'd both moved to block me from Lord Abnus's view, and I'd rushed away without a backward glance. I wasn't worried about Oren. He'd probably curled up in a nook with a book as he tried to hide from everyone and everything.

The gate was perfectly quiet as I snuck out. I hovered near the hedges and kept my eyes peeled for even a hint of a footman, servant, or one of the Byrne brothers, but as I rounded the north side of the estate, I didn't spot anyone. Hurrying, I headed to Hillridge Farm.

My eyes darted continuously between the uneven ground and the surrounding area. I didn't want to twist my ankle in a hole, but neither did I want to come upon a fae. The fields remained blissfully empty, except for a herd of sheep and a few cows.

The acrid stench of char mixed with the stinging feel of something I didn't recognize was the first warning I was close to my destination. My steps slowed and my pulse quickened as I approached the blackened ruins.

A ring of charred buildings stood in the middle of the desolate farm. Burnt support posts stuck up in the air, broken, like bones of the buildings that were once here. The barn, silo, coop, and outbuildings were all destroyed. Burnt and reduced to rubble. The only thing standing was the stone fireplace and chimney from the farmhouse.

Everything else was gone.

Horse hooves and boot prints marred the ground. I didn't know if they were from the attackers or the soldiers who'd come to check on the fire. I scoured the remains, searching for bodies. Hillridge Farm was decent-sized. There should've been several farmhands as well as the family, but there were no bodies. No animals. No humans. Nothing.

"Why, if it isn't Aidan, completely alone. How intriguing."

Tattoo writhing under my sleeve, I turned, unsurprised to see Cethin leaning against the chimney of the destroyed home. His long white hair hung around his lean frame. He was in a black long-sleeved shirt with a plunging neckline, which exposed the tip of his crescent moon tattoo as well as making me gape at the miles of bare skin, and a pair of obscenely tight black trousers tucked into calf-high boots.

Only a week had passed since I'd seen him, but part of me believed I'd fabricated him, even with the tattoo on my arm. He was as otherworldly as I remembered, and, unfortunately, as lovely as I recalled.

"Cethin."

"So you *do* remember the name I told you."

"Why wouldn't I?"

Cethin pushed off the chimney and stalked in my direction. My spine straightened, and I fought back the urge to take a step back. His predatory movement awakened some deep prey instinct to run.

"It's been a week. You haven't come to see me or called for me."

"*Called*?" I asked. He stopped right in front of me, forcing me to look up. "If I said your name, would you appear?"

"Yes, Aidan." Cethin's black eyes burned into me. "I will come if you call for me."

My throat closed and my stomach swooped. Warmth swelled up my spine, at odds with the cool autumn temperature. What the bloody hell was he doing to me? I'd heard stories of fae enthralling humans, but I'd never believed it, because I'd seen no evidence of the like. I also figured if they could enchant humans, why didn't they do it all the time, but then again, what was *happening* to me?

With a step back, I took a deep breath, trying to clear my mind of his light floral fragrance, which evoked an image of moonlight kissing a field of flowers. "Why are you here?"

"Why wouldn't I be here?"

I frowned. "Can you answer my question?"

Cethin smirked, head cocking. "I could, yes." When I continued to frown, he said, "I am here because you are."

I didn't understand why my presence would draw him here, so I remained silent and started walking among the burnt buildings. A sizzlingly hot feeling I couldn't place raised the hairs on my arms and stung my nose like I had a bleed. I rubbed my nose with a handkerchief, but the white fabric came back clean.

"Magic," Cethin said.

"I beg your pardon?"

"That's what's bothering you. Magic burned these buildings."

"You?" I asked.

"Why would I burn human dwellings?"

That was not an answer. "Did you do this?"

"No," he said evenly. "I did not burn these buildings or take these people."

"Do you know who did?"

"No." The black thorny vines of his tattoo on his neck and hands began to glow brighter. "Light fae."

My first instinct was to believe him, but I stalled. He'd merely said light fae. That could mean anything or nothing. "And I should believe you?"

"You do not have to. Why don't you ask whatever-you-call-him in the manor to ask his fae representatives and see what they say?"

"Lord Byrne?"

"You can call him that."

"That's his title."

Cethin shrugged.

As I faced the ruins, my hands curled into fists as impotent rage simmered in my gut. I wanted to do something. I wanted to help, but I didn't know how.

"I wish it was summer," Cethin commented.

"Why?" I asked. Where had that come from?

A smile grew on his lips and his eyes glimmered in mirth. "Then I could see the entirety of your tattoo. I have yet to lay eyes on it."

Laughter spilled out. "It wouldn't matter if it was boiling hot—you still would not see it. The confines of modesty and propriety don't allow me to walk around shirtless."

"Pity. I should like to see it." His eyes drifted over my body in a way that sent heat to my cheeks.

Face on fire, I stared at the ruined farm. “Do you know what became of the Hillridges?”

“Shall we find them?”

“What?”

He held out a hand. “I will help you find them, Aidan.”

“Why?”

“Because you want to.”

Chapter 7

"The transition is an exceedingly dangerous time. As humans, we have forgotten what it is to have fae among us. They have not." – Lord Ian, Sixth Lord of Sídhetír.

I stared at his waiting hand—the open invitation to go with him. Disappearing with a dark fae didn't seem wise, yet I wanted to place my hand within his. I was curious, undeniably so. If Cethin wanted to harm me, he'd had ample opportunity to do so. I didn't think he would kill me, as idiotic as that notion was. Going with him was foolish, but the temptation overcame my sense.

Out of nowhere the dark clouds overhead opened, and water poured in heavy sheets, drenching me. Cethin glanced up, rain sluicing down his cheeks, his hand hovering in the air.

"You must decide, Aidan. The water will wash away any magical trace, and I will be unable to find your humans."

Nancy's grinning face appeared in my mind. The young girl liked to follow me about Elmbury when her parents were in town. I had no idea why, but she would take my hand or chase after me, usually calling me "pretty" because of my red hair.

"Let's go." I didn't take his hand; instead, I buried them deep into my pockets and moved to his side. Cethin raised an eyebrow but didn't remark. When he strode north, following a path I couldn't see, I asked, "Where are we going?"

"After the light fae who stole your humans. I have no idea where they went—hopefully, not to the fae realm. If they did, your humans are lost."

"We must hurry."

The rain didn't lessen as time passed but rather increased. Soon, my boots were squelching in the mud and shivers wracked my body.

Cethin's longer stride slowed to match mine. "Are you well, Aidan?"

"Why?"

"You're shaking. You shouldn't fear this light fae or any other. No matter who or what they are, I will not allow them to harm you."

"Do you mean that?"

"Yes," he said, staring directly at me. "I will kill anyone who tries to hurt you."

My stomach swooped and my mouth went dry. I forced myself to look away from Cethin. Clearing my throat, I said, "I'm shivering from the cold. Not fear."

"Ah. I apologize. I'm not well acquainted with humans or their needs. I shall learn. Fear not." His head tilted back. "Will this rain make you ill?"

"We need to hurry."

"Then hurry we shall. I very much doubt I would like you being ill."

I struggled to find something to say. Cethin didn't wait for a response; he gripped my elbow and started to walk faster, hauling me along. We rushed over the marshy hills. Mud splattered my trousers, and my wet clothes clung to my skin. I couldn't see more than a few feet in front of me, causing me to stumble every so often. Cethin's firm grip kept me upright, but he never deviated from the unseen path.

We stepped under a lone tree, which provided some shelter from the autumn storm. Water ran down my neck, and my hair stuck to my face. Cethin was no better. His long hair dripped water everywhere, and his wet clothes hugged his lean muscled body, giving me a scandalous view.

I peered around. "Where are the Hillridges?"

"The trail has washed away with the rain."

"We can't give up." I started to head back into the rain, and Cethin snagged me around my waist and drew me back into the shelter of the tree, my back pressed against his front, sending a pulse down my spine. It felt oddly right to be in his embrace—like I belonged there.

"You're shivering, Aidan. You need to return to the manor."

"I need to find the Hillridges."

"I shall get them. Go back."

I glanced in the direction of Byrne Manor. It was a long walk back in the torrential rain. Thomas and Phineas would be upset about my absence, to say the least. If they told Lord Byrne, he would search for me, and I would receive another lecture. Either way, the Byrnes would never let me out of their sight.

"You will get them?" I asked Cethin.

"I will do my best to retrieve your Hillridges."

I took a single step toward the manor and out of his arms, then paused as a thought wandered through my head. "Cethin, do you know where the Hillridges are?"

"Why do you ask?"

"You do, don't you?"

"Aidan, go home."

"Answer my question."

"I believe I know where they are," he said in a strained tone.

"Liar."

"Hardly. I cannot lie. I merely told you the path had disappeared, which it has." Cethin moved to stand right in front of me. His claws scraped on my cheek as he tucked my hair behind my ear, his fingertip tracing the shell. "You are very clever."

I refused to let his presence distract me. "Why are you trying to send me away?"

"I smell human blood and fire. I do not know whether your humans are alive or not. Also, I don't want you to watch me slaughter the fae, for I will. They are a threat to you, and they must die."

"I'm going with you."

His eyebrows drew together.

"Where are they?" I asked in an unyielding voice. I would not abandon the Hillridges to their fate, nor allow Cethin to face this threat alone—though I wished I'd brought my iron dagger, so I wasn't entering this fray weaponless.

Cethin started off once again, not arguing, and I trailed behind him, unease curling in my stomach. The Hillridges and their farmhands might be dead. Bile began to climb my throat, making me cough. I'd never seen a dead body. Death wasn't something I'd been exposed to. Even when my mother passed, I hadn't been permitted in the room or allowed to see her body afterward.

Straightening my spine, I was resolved to see this through, regardless of what lay at the end. Cethin remained close to me as he walked toward a cabin in the distance, not far from the looming trees of the forest.

I swiped the hair off my forehead, but the rain plastered it to my skull, making the strands slide in front of my eyes yet again. "Is that it?"

"I believe so. I smell copious amounts of human blood."

"Let's go." When I moved past him, Cethin snagged my wrist and drew me back. "What?"

"I will go first. Stay behind me and retrieve the humans while I deal with the fae. Do you understand?"

"Fine."

We started in the direction of the cabin with Cethin in the lead. He slowed as we approached, his steps silent in the pouring rain. But the water and wooden walls of the cabin didn't block the agonized screams coming from inside. My heart thrashed as I raced to the building. I had to help them. Thunder rumbled and lightning crashed into a tree, setting it on fire. The rain, if possible, grew heavier.

Cethin smoothly moved in front of me, forcing me to stop. "Calm yourself. A frantic mind will not help this situation."

I took a deep breath in an attempt to slow the rapid beat of my heart.

"Again. You're not ready."

"Cethin, we don't have time for this," I snapped, struggling to keep my voice low.

"When you get inside, do not try to help me or attack the fae. Do not be distracted by what you see. Get the humans who are alive and run. Do not look back. If all the humans are dead, leave and return to the tree."

"I understand."

His eyes met mine in a calculating glance, but he said no more. Cethin thrust out his left hand, and shadows, glowing with stars and blue flowers like the tattoos on his skin, flowed down his arm and began to take the shape of an obsidian sword. He gripped the silver hilt and looked at me.

I had to help whoever was still alive. The screams coming from inside the cabin had to end, and I had to be a part of the solution.

In one smooth motion, Cethin opened the door and stepped inside.

Chapter 8

"I hope you never witness the atrocities I have. If you do, I hope you'll understand why I did what I did. I had to protect us all from the fae. Balance the carnage on both sides." – Lord Rhett, First Lord of Sídhetír.

Two fae jerked up from in front of the sprawling fireplace. They were massive like mountains, but unlike any fae I'd ever seen. Their skin was leathery and two horns curled from each of their heavy, protruding brows and shaggy brown hair hung around their round faces. They snarled, revealing stained, jagged teeth.

Mrs. Hillridge sat in the corner, trying to shield Nancy with her body, shrieking while her husband roasted alive on the flames. He made little to no noise, but his skin was melted and blistered as he writhed on the red-hot coals, mouth opening and closing.

Bile rose up my throat at the scent of burning flesh. Not far from the fireplace was a haphazard pile of greasy bones with scraps of meat clinging to them.

Mr. Hillridge hadn't been their first victim.

I could not look away. I was frozen in place, watching Mr. Hillridge being cooked over the flames.

The fae didn't have the same problem. They launched at Cethin with surprising speed and grace for their bulky frames. "These humans are ours!"

Cethin deftly moved out of the way. He slapped one of the fae's outstretched hands with the flat of his blade. The creature grunted, and the other tried to seize him. Cethin ducked and sliced the second fae across his bulging gut. The hulking beast didn't even wince. The blade had cut through the fabric of his rough brown shirt, but the leathery flesh underneath was unmarred.

"Move, Aidan," Cethin snarled.

Lurching, I jerked toward Mrs. Hillridge, Nancy, and the single farmhand that huddled in the corner. Their hands were tied behind their backs and their ankles were bound together. I raced to the modest kitchen, trying to ignore the sounds of the fight and Mrs. Hillridge's cries. I ripped through the cabinets and drawers, searching for anything sharp.

I seized a knife, the blade nicking my fingers in my haste, and dashed to the hostages. As I bent down to slice through Mrs. Hillridge's bindings, Cethin crashed into the wall not far from me, splintering the wood. Right on his tail was a sphere of fire.

"Cethin," I screamed.

He held up his hands, grabbing the flames. "Fuck." Black magic mixed with silver stars encased his hands, and he slammed his palms together, quenching the fire. "I'm fine," he said, pushing off the wall. "Get them outside."

I sliced through Mrs. Hillridge's ties first, and she rushed to her husband. I didn't try to stop her, but turned to Nancy, who stared blankly at her surroundings, unmoving. Once she was free, I shifted to the farmhand, who was muttering under his breath and had tears coursing down his tan cheeks. He didn't even move when I cut his ties. I glanced at Mrs. Hillridge who, heedless of the flames, tried to drag her husband out of the fireplace, but his skin slid off his bones at her grasp.

I couldn't get them all by myself. Nancy would have to be carried. I grabbed the collar of the farmhand's shirt and slapped him soundly across the face. He jumped.

"Grab Nancy and run."

He froze.

I shook him and bellowed, "Now!"

The farmhand snatched Nancy, who didn't even squeak, and ran into the pouring rain.

Heat scorched my back, and I dropped to the floor a single moment before a ball of flame hit the cottage wall. The wood sparked and caught alight.

"Shit," I growled. This *was not* the place for a fire fight.

Cethin moved in front of me, shielding me from another fireball headed in my direction. He caught it and tossed it back at the fae. The massive creature didn't move out of the way. The flames burned their clothes, but did not harm them.

Ignoring Cethin and the cabin burning around us, I went to Mrs. Hillridge, who was still trying to retrieve her husband. The closer I got, the worse the stench became. The man was not dead yet, but he wouldn't survive. His skin was ruined and the inside of his lungs had to be scorched from the heat of the fire. I doubted even magic could save him.

I wrapped my arm around her waist and dragged Mrs. Hillridge to the door.

"No," she screamed, clawing at my arms. "I can't leave him. John!" She kicked my shins, but I didn't slow, and her shrieks didn't quiet. I dragged her out of the cottage, leaving Mr. Hillridge behind.

Steam came off the cabin in waves, and the fire continued to grow, consuming the entire structure. The smoke stung my eyes, and my legs ached from the repeated kicks, but I didn't release Mrs. Hillridge. She fought me every step of the way. If I let her go, she would run to her death. Nancy had already witnessed the horrific death of one parent—she couldn't lose her mother as well.

I stopped near the farmhand, who clutched Nancy to his chest a good distance from the cabin. I chewed on my lip as my heart thrashed against my ribs. Where was Cethin?

He was still inside. He'd told me not to come back for him, but every instinct commanded me to find him.

"Let me go," Mrs. Hillridge yelled, savagely kicking me again. "I have to save John."

Turning her around, I gripped her upper arms. "He is dead. If you go in there, you are going to die."

"Then I will die with him." She writhed in my hold.

"So you will leave Nancy alone?"

She froze, and for the first time, she looked at her daughter, who was motionless, her expression slack. Mrs. Hillridge glanced back to the burning building, obscured by the heavy rain. Her face scrunched as she panted, but she turned away from where her dead husband was, grabbing her daughter and holding her close.

My gaze returned to the fire, trying to catch a glimmer of Cethin. I couldn't hear anything over the rain, but the flames had swelled, glowing brightly in the dim light.

"Please," I whispered. Cethin was only in there because I'd wanted him to find the missing people. The thought of losing his mischievous smile, or the way he stared at me as I talked, created an unexplainable ache within my chest.

A tremor went through the ground a moment before the cabin exploded, knocking me off my feet. Mrs. Hillridge and the farmhand landed on the mud right behind me. My back throbbed, and needles pricked my lungs with every breath. Dots danced in my vision as I struggled to get my lungs to work. I shifted, despite the pain, trying to catch sight of the cabin.

All that remained was a smoldering mass.

Surging to my feet, I shouted, "Cethin!"

My screams were drowned out by the rumble of thunder and the crash of lightning. I ran forward, heedless of the danger. Burning debris littered the ground and sputtered in the heavy rain. Mud splattered my legs as I tried to find Cethin.

With a grunt, I fell to the ground when the toe of my boot got caught in a hole. I landed on my hands, the impact reverberating up my arms. My palms stung, and my ankle throbbed, but I ignored it all and jerked up.

"Cethin." He told me he would come if I called. He had to.

A figure appeared out of the darkness, and my breath stalled. Smoke curled around Cethin as he walked in my direction, sword in one hand and both of the fae's heads swinging from their brown hair in the other hand. Blood dripped from their severed necks, their mouths agape and eyes wide.

Cethin did not look like he usually did.

A feral grin split his face, and massive leathery wings stretched out behind him like a dragon of old. Two black horns curled back from the top of his head, adding to his towering height. His features were sharper, and his eyes harder. All semblance of humanity had been burned away.

Cethin's true form—one without a glamour to soften him.

He threw the heads down in front of me with a smile like he expected a response. When I gaped at the putrid blood leaking from the necks of the severed heads, bile creeping up my throat, Cethin said, "You called for me."

"H-how?" The fae had been beating him before I left.

"You got the humans out, and I no longer had to worry about hurting them with my magic."

"Your magic?" I asked, my thoughts moving slowly.

"I would not have harmed you, under any circumstances," he said, crouching. "But the others, possibly."

My gaze locked onto his hands. Burns covered his long fingers from where he'd caught the balls of fire. The image of Mr. Hillridge cooking on the flames formed in my mind. Unable to contain my stomach, I vomited, again and again, nose running and eyes watering, until there was nothing left.

Cethin stroked the back of my head as I panted on all fours. "You were very brave."

I hadn't done anything. Cethin had killed the fae and protected us.

His fingers slid through my hair as the rain dripped down my face in rivulets. Every ache rushed to the forefront of my senses. The nicks on my fingers from the knife. The bruises on my shins, and the scratches on my arms from Mrs. Hillridge. My skinned palms. My twisted ankle.

Shit, I wanted to lie down, but the rain had not lessened and I was shivering in cold and strain. Cethin continued to pet my hair as I breathed heavily through my nose. The strong odor of bile and blood clogged my nostrils, and my stomach threatened to escape again.

Gently, he cupped my chin and lifted it until I met his pure black eyes. "I need to take you and the other humans to the manor. You're cold and injured."

My fingers wrapped around his wrist and drew his hand down so I could examine his palm. Blisters and raw, red skin filled my vision. "I'm not the only one injured."

"I will heal quicker than you." He looked at the decapitated heads and asked, "Do you like the gift I brought you?"

Words lodged in my throat. No. I did not like them. Why would I want two fae heads? They were disgusting. Somehow, I assumed, he would not appreciate that sentiment. "I appreciate you saving me and the other humans."

A smug smile tugged at the corner of his lips. "You saved me first."

"We're even now, I suppose."

His smile died. "No. You are not free of me."

I tightened my hold on his wrist. Did he wish to be free? For some reason, that thought didn't sit well with me. Cethin cupped my cheek with his free hand, his thumb brushing over my cheekbone. At some point, his sword had disappeared back to wherever it came from. I couldn't think about the sword's location, because the entirety of my focus was locked onto the feel of him touching me and my fingers on his cool wrist.

After a minute, Cethin helped me to my feet. He gripped my elbow, ignoring his burns. "Let me help you and your humans to Byrne Manor, lest you sicken."

I nodded as warmth seeped under my skin. What was happening to me?

Chapter 9

"Remember, the fae do not think as we do. But their differences can ensnare us easily, for they are like a flame that we inevitably want to burn on." – Lord Edmund, Second Lord of Sídhetír.

I leaned against my headboard, staring at the people gathered around my bed. Every single one of the Byrnes, including Lord and Lady Byrne, were in my room.

Cethin had left me, Mrs. Hillridge, Nancy, and the farmhand near the gate of the Byrne Manor. The footmen had taken one look at me covered in muck and blood, then at the people behind me, before they issued shouts for Lord Byrne and ushered us all inside.

Mrs. Hillridge had burns on her hands from where she tried to save her husband, but the other two had survived with only mental and emotional wounds, though I doubted those would heal any time soon, if ever.

Once my injuries had been tended to, I was led to my room. No one questioned me then because the second I was out of public, tears coursed down my cheeks and I vomited until bile burned my nose and I shook in strain. I couldn't rid my nose of the stench of Mr. Hillridge's burning flesh, or free my thoughts of his ruined form on the flames. Even Cethin, holding the decapitated heads, haunted me.

But now, two days after the incident, I had to answer the questions everyone had held off asking. My fingers drifted to the tattoo on my left arm. The physician, Ilene Maher, had seen the base of it, but I wouldn't allow her to investigate further, even when she tried. I'd told her she didn't need to concern herself with it, but I didn't know if she agreed because she gave me a loud, "Mmmhmm."

Oren tracked my movements, eyes narrowed. I yanked my hand away from my wrist lest he become suspicious. The tattoo was yet another question I didn't know how to answer.

Lord Byrne was the only one with a calm expression. The others ranged from worry to anger. Even Lady Hester appeared annoyed with her pinched eyebrows and downturned lips.

"What exactly happened after you defied my order, Aidan?" Lord Byrne asked.

"I left Byrne Manor to see Hillridge Farm."

Thomas glared at me, arms crossed. He'd been watching me when I gave him the slip. Well, him and Phineas. My eyes flicked to Phineas, and my shoulders hunched clear to my ears. His expression mirrored his eldest brother's, but his eyes were alight with betrayal.

Lord Byrne rubbed his forehead. "Why?"

I had no answer. I'd needed to see it. The urge couldn't be explained or denied.

When I remained quiet, he asked, "What happened after you left Thomas and Phineas?"

I wanted to frame the story carefully to say as little about Cethin as possible. I thought through my response, choosing each and every word. "When I arrived at the farm, it was ruined, and I found no trace."

"Then how did you come back with Mrs. Hillridge, Nancy, and one of their farmhands?" Sevrin interrupted.

"The dark fae."

"The one that stole you?" Oren questioned.

"He came, and he was the one who found them."

"Probably because he burned the farm down in the first place," Whit muttered.

"No," I snapped. "He didn't do it."

Whit blinked, mouth falling open. And he was not alone. The brothers all stared at me, and Lord Byrne frowned. Lady Hester's face scrunched before a knowing smile tugged at her lips. Whatever she saw in my fierce expression amused her.

I cleared my throat, fighting a blush from my outburst. "I asked him directly and he, with no obfuscation, said he didn't do it. He did find them and killed the fae who took them."

"Why?" Lord Byrne asked.

"Why what?"

"Why did he help you?" Lord Byrne reiterated.

"Because I wanted them found."

Lord Byrne studied me, and I looked away, my gaze landing on Oren. His eyes were wide and his mouth was slightly open. He quietly asked, "What's your relationship with the dark fae, Aidan?"

It took every ounce of my control not to blush. "I saved his life."

Lord Byrne said, "You are not to leave the manor again, Aidan, until Oren has accepted his mantle. Do you understand?"

"Yes." I understood, but I wasn't going to obey that order.

Oren lay on the bed next to me, his head supported on his hand. "You have feelings for that dark fae, don't you?"

I glared at Oren, and he lifted his pale eyebrows. He'd always had a way of knowing my thoughts. I closed my eyes, and Cethin's face appeared in my mind, though, after a second, his fine form and sly smirk was replaced by Mr. Hillridge. My eyes shot open, and I swallowed the surging bile.

My dreams had been plagued by images I desperately wished to forget.

Oren grabbed my hand, startling me. "Aidan?"

"My apologies. I was thinking about what happened."

His grip tightened. "Was it horrible?"

"Yes," I said, voice strained. Whitaker had tried to talk to me. He'd been in the navy before he'd met and married his wife and had spent his life seeing and doing things he would rather forget. But when he tried to speak with me, I'd changed the subject. I didn't want to talk about it. With anyone.

"Back to the fae," Oren said, probably sensing my hesitancy. "You like him."

"He's attractive."

"All fae are."

I sighed and finally admitted, "I'm attracted to him."

"I thought so." Oren beamed at me. "I find the whole situation highly romantic."

"How so?"

"You saved his life, and he saved yours."

"Do not pin too many of your romantic hopes on this, Oren," I said. "He's a noble dark fae, and I'm a former ward of Lord Byrne. We will never be together. He will most likely vanish once you choose who to align with."

"Then I won't choose."

I laughed and rolled to my side to face him. "That is very kind of you, but this should not go on indefinitely."

"I suppose not. Father says I will feel the urge to bond with Sídhetír, but I don't. I don't feel anything, so I haven't picked yet."

"If Lord Byrne says it will happen, then it should," I said to soothe him.

Oren shrugged as if he couldn't care less and scooted closer, whispering, "Are you going to sneak out to see him?"

"Not at this exact moment," I said. "I imagine if I did, it would infuriate Lord Byrne and your brothers. One of them is probably outside my door."

He nodded.

"I'm not surprised."

"Do you want me to sneak him in?"

My lips opened to form the word yes. For an unexplainable reason, I wanted him. Cethin probably didn't care one way or another if he saw me, but I desired to see him, to hear the soft rumble of his voice, and to feel the cool touch of his fingers on my skin. I wanted to talk to him. Not about what happened, but about him. What did he like? What didn't he like? I wanted to know more about who he was, and I refused to think about why I felt the need to learn about him.

Swallowing my response, I said, "That would not be wise."

"No, but if you want it, I will do it."

"You're too kind to me, Oren."

"Not at all. We're best friends. Brothers, basically."

My thoughts froze on the word brother. God, I wished that was true. While I didn't want to be a Byrne, I wanted a family. Mine was gone, and I wanted somewhere and someone to belong to.

"Thank you," I said simply, because I couldn't think of another reply.

Oren left after a couple of hours, but not before I secured a promise from him not to search for Cethin. When he left, I leaned back in my bed and tried to sleep, but rest would not come. Instead, my thoughts circled round and round, reliving every horrific moment. I wanted to think of something else, but every time I did, my thoughts would inevitably return to what had occurred in the cottage near the woods.

Perhaps Iris would have something to help me sleep? But that would mean leaving Byrne Manor. The iron key to the secret gate had made it through the incident, so I could sneak out, but I didn't think my door would stop being guarded anytime soon.

I rolled over and my thoughts returned to the stench of the flames, the sight of Mr. Hillridge, and the sounds of Mrs. Hillridge's screams. I flopped to my other side. No matter how I turned or what I thought about, I always returned to the cabin. I tried to recall Cethin stroking me in soothing motions. The way his fingers had moved through my sopping hair.

My breath eased for a single moment until I remembered the burns on his hands. Was he alright? Cethin was a fae, and he healed faster than humans. But when he'd been stabbed, it had almost claimed his life. What if the burns got infected?

He will be fine, I told myself sternly. Besides, why did I even care? He was a dark fae who I barely knew.

Stomach churning, I threw the blankets off. I paced over the plush rug in my room, wearing nothing but my nightshirt. I should've asked Oren to bring Cethin inside. Then again, how was Oren to find him? Oren couldn't wander the woods, randomly calling for Cethin. I hadn't even told anyone Cethin's name.

I peered out the window. The late afternoon sun lit up the manicured gardens. The storm had passed over while I was recovering, but the rain had left everything greener and the air cleaner than normal.

I wanted to go outside. I hated being forced to remain indoors. Even if I'd been allowed to venture out, escape wouldn't happen.

My eyes flicked over the garden and paused on the balcony two windows away from mine. Thick vines wrapped around the stone railing and down the pillars to the ground. I focused on the thin ledge that ran along the side of the manor, leading to the balcony.

I could shuffle along the wall to the balcony and climb down. I'd never done it, but it didn't appear impossible. Though I was four stories up. If I fell, the damage would not be pleasant.

I stripped off my nightshirt and quickly donned some clothes, then arranged the pillows under the blanket to give the appearance of my sleeping form. The window opened with the slightest squeak. I peeked over my shoulder at the door. I was unsure which Byrne brother was guarding my room, but Whit and Sevrin had ears like wolves.

My muscles tensed, and I held my breath, waiting. After a couple of moments of silence, I released a long breath.

I threw my leg over the sill and grabbed the frame, leveraging myself out. I looked down and tightened my grip. *What the fuck am I doing?* This was so reckless, and not something I would normally do. I was usually so controlled and followed the rules, for the most part. For all of one second, I thought about slipping back inside, but I couldn't. What if Cethin's injuries had gotten infected?

With careful movements, I hugged the side of the manor. I shut the window and began to slide along the ledge.

As I reached the next window, I peered inside to check there was no one within sight. I did this at the next window too, then climbed over the railing. My breath was not even harsh when I stepped onto the stone balcony. It felt as easy and natural to walk along the ledge as on the ground.

I pressed against the wall and peeked inside the glass doors that opened into a family parlor. No one was inside. thankfully, or I would've had some uncomfortable questions to answer.

I climbed over the railing. The vines were easy to grip as I clambered down, but the leaves were slick with moisture. I had to be careful, but a solid vine was always within reach.

The moment my boots hit the flagstones, I raced to the hedge maze. I slipped inside and turned a corner, looking over my shoulder at the manor to check for pursuers, and collided with someone. I staggered backward. Oren stood in front of me, eyes impossibly wide.

"The incident has been handled. It appears to have been two rogue light fae," Lord Byrne said, his voice approaching.

Oren shoved me in the opposite direction, and I hid around the curve. "Father," Oren said in a high-pitched voice, "we should offer our guests tea."

"Indeed," Lord Byrne said, but I heard the surprise in his tone.

I peeked around the corner as the fae strode by. The light fae followed right behind Lord Byrne with a serene smile on her round face, long brown hair hanging down her back. The dark fae walked past where I hid and paused, his head cocked. He was dressed to the nines in a tailored jacket and tight trousers, all black, and his short black hair hung to his sharp jaw. He started to turn to where I hid, and I pressed against the hedges, peeking through the branches.

Lord Abnus's dark purple eyes locked onto the exact spot where I was hiding. His nostrils flared when he took a deep inhale. "Curious." The fae took a single step toward me, and I knew this was it. I was going to be discovered, and Lord Byrne would never leave me alone ever again.

"Problem?" Oren asked, appearing behind the fae. The man turned, towering over Oren's slight frame.

"I do not believe so." The fae glanced over his shoulder.

Oren slid his hand into the crook of Lord Abnus's elbow and said, "Come along. I acquired a new tea for you."

"How very kind," the dark fae said. "You must take care not to burn yourself this time."

"I will," Oren replied with a laugh. "You can tell me more of your aunt, Queen Eilidh, as we sample it."

As they exited the hedge maze, Oren winked at where I hid.

Without a backward glance, I dashed to the gate.

Chapter 10

"I often write of the evil of the fae, but there is just as much good in them. Their magic can heal, protect, and bring enjoyment. They are like us, a mix of good and bad. But their dark acts often drown out any of their light."
– Lord Rhett, First Lord of Sídhetír.

"You're a fucking idiot," Iris said, handing me a cup of lavender tea.

"I beg your pardon?"Iris sat down across from me, wide hands wrapped around her delicate teacup. "You went off with a dark fae. He gave you an excuse to leave, and you charged into danger. And now you've left Byrne Manor after the lord explicitly told you to stay. All marks of stupidity."

"Those might not have been my wisest decisions."

She laughed. "They were stupid, but your intentions were good. I suppose that counts for something. Not much. But something."

I took a sip of tea, and the floral flavor rushed over my tongue as warmth settled in my stomach, soothing me. I leaned back in the chair as all of the tension fled my body.

"I will send plenty of tea home with you. It will help you sleep."

"Thank you."

"A good fuck would also help you sleep."

I jolted and hot tea splattered my hand. Swearing, I dried my hand and dabbed the thigh of my trousers with my handkerchief. "Must you, Iris?"

She lifted her eyebrows. "What? It would help."

"I'll stick with the tea."

"Your choice," she said with a shrug.

Eyes on the stain on my trousers, I asked, "Do you have anything to help with burns?"

"Were you burned?" she asked, chair scraping on the stone floor as she stood.

"No. The fae was."

Iris snorted, but she wandered over to a shelf and chucked a tin at me; I instinctively snatched it before it hit me in the face. She sat back down and crossed her legs, foot bouncing. "I'm sure he's healed, but spread this on the burn and it will dampen the pain, reduce infection, and promote healing. Not that you should want to save him. It would be better if he died."

"Thank you."

"Maybe he will fuck you to sleep? He might as well be useful if he can't fertilize my roses."

I frowned at her, and Iris simply raised her eyebrows.

My feet followed an unseen path through the woods. Lights flashed in the distance, followed by whispers, and I smiled. Wisps. It had been a little while since I'd seen them, not that they cared. I kept my eyes on my surroundings, searching for far more dangerous fae. I didn't know what kind of creatures had hurt the Hillridges and their people, but I never wanted to see them again.

Eventually, I came to the creek and Cethin's cottage. No welcoming curl of smoke came from the chimney. Was he gone, or did he not require a fire as the weather cooled? The creek was higher than it had been the last time I was here. Only the very tops of the stones were visible, and they were shiny with moisture.

I heard Iris calling me an idiot as I stepped onto the first stone. My boot slipped, and my arms went out straight, but I managed to catch myself. "Why does Cethin have to fucking live across a creek with no bridge?"

"Because it was empty," Cethin replied.

Jolting, I started to fall backward, arms swinging wildly. Cethin moved so fast, I couldn't track the movement. One second he was across the creek, and the next, he was holding me upright.

"You are far more trouble than I realized you would be," he commented.

"You startled me."

"That I did." Cethin helped me across the creek, but he didn't remove his hand from my wrist. "Are you recovered?"

"Mostly."

"You should be at the manor, then, if you are not well."

"All I have left is bruises and scabs," I replied. "Nothing to worry about. Are you well?"

His head tilted to the side, sending his white hair tumbling. "What do you mean?"

"Your hands." I pulled out of his hold to grab both of his hands. His skin was gray, with its normal purple undertone, and free of blemish. Iris had been right. I skimmed my thumb over his palm, and Cethin tensed at the touch, fingers twitching. I cleared my throat and tucked my hands into my pockets as heat swamped my face. The tin Iris had given me bumped against my knuckles, and her words bounced in my mind.

"I got this for you," I said, handing him the tincture. "I thought you might still be injured."

He held it close, throat bobbing. "That was very kind of you."

My cheeks were still burning as I said, "I should get back before anyone discovers I'm gone."

A light touch on my elbow stopped me. "I will escort you home."

Cethin stayed close as I crossed the creek with no issues this time. As he walked by my side, I was tempted to put my arm through his, much like Oren had done with Lord Abnus, but I didn't. The forest was empty of noise, except for the sound of my feet breaking twigs, crushing leaves, and smashing the underbrush.

When the sunlight hit my face, I released a long breath. The autumn air rushed over me, making me want to lie on the grass. I was exhausted. Hopefully, the tea Iris had given me would help.

Fingers gently brushed my hair. Cethin held the back of my neck, his thumb resting on my pulse point. "The first time you witness something of that ilk stays with you."

How had he known? "I'm having nightmares."

"That's to be expected, Aidan." He tightened his hold and drew me closer until my nose was practically in his shoulder. "They will fade in time. What you witnessed was unpleasant."

"Mrs. Hillridge and her daughter saw far worse."

"That does not make what you saw any less horrible. You are allowed to be upset by it."

"It didn't bother you, did it?" I asked, though I knew the answer.

"It did not. I have seen much in my long years."

"Maybe I will be like you one day, though I won't live as long."

Cethin's hand tightened on my nape. "I hope not. Becoming immune to such sights is not something to desire."

I couldn't speak with Whit or Oren, who I'd known my whole life, but with this stranger, the words slipped freely out of my lips. Why? Cethin's hand slid from my neck, down my back, and settled around my waist. His other arm joined the first to hold me snuggly in his embrace.

"It's fine to be upset, Aidan. It's alright to vomit or have nightmares or grief. Whatever your response is, it's fine."

"Thank you."

He laughed against my ear, which did odd things to my stomach. "I will have to teach you to never say those words to another fae besides me, for they could take it as you owing them a debt."

I stilled. Never thanking a fae was basic knowledge. Most people gave the fae gifts in lieu of saying thank you. Normally, I never struggled to control my words. With Cethin, something was different.

"I know that."

"Good," he murmured, lips against my neck. "If another fae tried to take you, it would not end well for them."

"What do you mean?"

He chuckled darkly. "I will kill anyone who harms you or tries to take you from me, and that is a promise, Aidan."

I swallowed. What the hell was going on between us? We'd only known each other for a few days, and yet I was willing to break orders to see him. I'd never experienced anything even close to this.

Cethin squeezed me before relaxing his hold and taking my hand. "Let us continue. You need to rest."

I left my hand in his grasp as we headed in the direction of the manor. The closer we got, the slower my steps became. I didn't want to go back into the confining walls.

When my pace became as slow as a snail, Cethin glanced at me. "We could have stayed at my cottage." For some reason a blush surged to my cheeks. Cethin rubbed one with a smirk. "Shall we go somewhere else?"

"The apple orchard."

"Lead the way."

Harvest was coming soon, so the trees were laden with deep red apples. I snagged one of the plump fruits from a low-hanging branch and took a bite, juice flecking my chin. I grabbed another and handed it to Cethin. "Have one."

He held the fruit but did not take a bite. "Do you like apples?"

"Yes, they're my favorite," I said, taking another bite. "I love this time of year. The weather, the baked goods, watching the leaves change color." Cethin didn't say anything as I ate the apple and tossed the core away. He still held the apple I gave him. Maybe he didn't eat human food. Perhaps he didn't like apples?

Cethin grabbed an apple from a heavy branch. "Here is another."

"Do you like apples?" I asked, taking a bite.

"Yes."

I looked pointedly at the apple in his hand, but he didn't eat it. "Do you like autumn?"

"I prefer winter. The deep cold and snow. How bright the stars shine. The glow the moon has amongst the clouds. I don't dislike autumn like spring or summer, though."

I nodded, eating the apple as he watched. When I finished, he started reaching for yet another, and I laughed. "I don't want any more."

His head cocked. "That wasn't much food, and yet you're full? Is that a typical amount for a meal?"

"That wasn't a meal. It was a snack."

"Ah. You require snacks as well."

"I don't necessarily require them, but sometimes, it's nice."

He nodded, stepping closer. "I have much to learn but do not fear, I will."

Why did he care? The debt? He bent down and one of his hands rested on my hip, making my heart leap in my chest.

"What are you doing?" I asked as his lips neared mine.

"Kissing you."

"Why?"

"Because I'm attracted to you, and I thought you were to me." Cethin straightened, his fingers tightening on my waist. "Was I wrong?"

"N-no." I'd never kissed anyone. While I didn't know Cethin's age, I knew he had to be significantly older than me, and therefore more experienced. What if I did it wrong or in a way he didn't like?

Cethin stared at me, not moving. He was waiting—waiting for me to decide. Burying my worries, I pressed my lips against his. It was like a bolt of lightning hit me. Every hair on my arms raised, and my heart tried to break free of my rib cage. I grabbed the front of his shirt and held on, afraid he would back away before I was ready.

He did not seem inclined to leave.

His lips pressed against mine, the pressure soft and slow. Cethin pushed me back until I smacked into the tree, sending several apples to the ground with dull thuds. I tried to imitate his movements, but I couldn't seem to get it right. I tilted my head and tried to mesh my lips to his better. I groaned, frustrated, when it didn't work.

"Stop thinking," Cethin ordered, then bit my bottom lip before running his tongue over it.

The jolt of his tongue touching me went straight to my cock. He closed the distance, his body shoving me back into the rough bark. His mouth became so insistent on mine that I lost all track of my thoughts and focused entirely on the coolness of his skin and the feel of him crushing me.

Cethin kissed my mouth open, and his tongue brushed mine. I jumped. He started to pull back, but I yanked him closer. He chuckled against my lips, making me flush. This time when he invaded my mouth, I was prepared. His tongue ran along mine, and I moaned.

Eventually, Cethin shifted back. His breath was ragged, though it was a sight better than mine. He ran a thumb over my swollen bottom lip. I tightened my hold on his shirt, not wanting him to leave. He pressed a gentle kiss to my lips before stepping back.

I slid my hand down his chest, and Cethin's breath sharpened. I took his hand in mine. "I should go back."

Cethin tugged me, and I stumbled into him. "Come and see me, or I shall find you."

"Is that a threat?" I asked, but there was a smile on my face.

"Yes."

Chapter 11

"A fae cannot lie. It is said that if they do, their very magic will curdle their blood. What they can and will do is bend and twist the truth until you believe a lie." – Lord Rhett, First Lord of Sídhetír.

Two days. It had been two days since I'd seen Cethin. But the opportunity had not presented itself for me to escape again. I wondered how long it would take for Cethin to seek me out. I didn't know if I wanted him to come or not. Could he even get inside the manor without anyone seeing him?

I scoffed. Cethin had wings, so I assumed he could fly.

Sevrin glanced at me, and I waved off his concern. The Byrne brothers had, if possible, rallied around me even closer. Sevrin, Whit, and Phineas stuck to my side like burrs.

Thomas, Nevan, and Neil had gone to Elmbury because rumors had reached Lord Byrne's ears of a fae making deals. I'd wanted to go with them, and Thomas actually laughed in my face. They had no intention of letting me out of their sights or off the manor grounds.

Meanwhile, Oren had decided to brave the fae representatives alone today, without even Lord Byrne by his side.

We walked around the gardens while the weather held. The fall wind ruffled the leaves and stirred my hair. I couldn't help but look at where the hedge maze lay. I wanted to return to the apple orchard with Cethin again. His lips on mine. His body pressed against me. His warm chuckle in my ear. I wanted to hear more about what he liked and didn't like. Apples and winter were not enough information.

Shit, I missed him. As insane as that thought struck me, I craved him like I was starving.

An arm appeared in front of me; Sevrin blocked the way. My pulse leaped. Maybe Cethin had come for me. My eyes darted back and forth, searching for a glimpse of him, and instead, I saw Oren sitting on the bench next to Lord Abnus without another soul in sight.

The Night Court fae nodded, expression blank, as Oren talked with a large smile on his face and his hands waving through the air. I'd never seen him like that besides with us.

"He's talking," I whispered. Phineas and Sevrin both grinned. Whit stared at them with an open mouth. "Turn around. Quick before he sees us." We headed in the opposite direction, leaving Oren to continue his conversation undisturbed.

As I got undressed for bed, my mind kept going back to Oren talking to the dark fae. I hadn't gotten a chance to speak with him about it, but the scene warmed my heart. Oren struggled to speak to people, but that conversation hadn't appeared forced. Maybe they were becoming friends? If true, that would ease some of the worry I had for Oren when he accepted the mantle of Lord of Sídhetír.

I grabbed my nightshirt and paused. The thorny vines encircling my arms were the same, but on the inside of my forearm was a blue flower bud. It hadn't been there yesterday. I was sure of it.

I dashed to the mirror to inspect the tattoo. It was the same as ever, the vines growing around and through my arm, and on my left pectoral was the crescent moon and seven-pointed red star. With difficulty, I tried to look at my back. From what I could see, the tattoo only covered my left shoulder blade.

The tattoo was the same, except for the small bud. I stroked it, thinking I would feel the smooth silk of a petal beneath my fingertip, but the flower was the same as the rest of my skin, exactly like the vines. Who knew how the magical tattoo would change? Cethin probably did, but he had yet to share.

I pulled the nightshirt over my head and crawled into bed. My finger traced the bud as I stared at the darkness above me. I wondered where Cethin was and what he was doing. Was he thinking about me like I was him?

Tomorrow might give new opportunities to sneak out. I would watch for any possible way to escape so I could see him again.

I rolled over and snuggled against the cool pillow next to me, which was harder than I expected. I nuzzled it and soft strands fell over my face. The pillow must be old. Fraying. I would have to set it out for the servants to dispose of. Something around my back pulled me closer to the pillow before something soft pressed against my forehead.

With a groan, I opened my eyes. Light filtered in through the windows, showing another pleasant autumn day. I squeezed my pillow, closing my eyes, and my pillow squeezed back.

My pillow was holding me. Pillows did not do that. My eyes snapped open, and I jerked up.

Cethin was beneath me. "Aidan."

"What are you doing here? In my bed?" I whispered, glancing at the door. Someone was still guarding me, though the Byrne brothers allowed a footman to watch my door at night. They didn't trust me to not disappear.

"You did not come for me, so I came for you." Cethin leaned up to press a kiss to my lips. "I told you I would."

I flopped onto my back, blushing. "How did you get inside?"

"Your window is not locked, nor is the frame made of iron."

I chuckled quietly.

He rolled to the side and slung a leg over my hip as he drew me close. I swallowed and tried to think of innocuous things. Cethin nuzzled my neck and rocked into me. My cock twitched.

I frowned at him. "You're doing that on purpose."

"Yes. I am." He pressed a kiss on my neck.

Arousal flooded me, and I bit my lip as Cethin continued to drop kisses along the line of my jaw. I wanted to be with him, and yet, I couldn't suppress the nerves prickling my stomach. I'd never been intimate with someone. What if I did something wrong? What if Cethin didn't like it? Kissing had turned out better than I'd expected, but fucking was different.

Did I even want to? I didn't know Cethin well, but in such a short time, he had created feelings within me that I'd never felt. Perhaps this was too fast. I'd had my first kiss only a couple of days ago. Still, the thought of pulling away was too much. I wanted to get closer to Cethin. I wanted this. I wanted him.

Cethin said, "You are thinking far too much to be enjoying what I'm doing. Shall I stop?"

"No," I immediately protested.

"Then what's bothering you?"

"I've never..." I trailed off.

"Yes?"

"I've never been with someone."

His eyebrows knitted together, forming a divot in between them. Finally, he nodded. "Ah. You're a virgin."

A blush raced to my cheeks at his blatant words, and my gaze slid to the side.

He forced me to look at him with a hand on my cheek. "Why are you embarrassed?"

"Because I've never been with anyone."

"So? Why would that matter? Sex is like any other experience in life. It does not change or define you. Have you dueled someone or leaped from a cliff?"

"No," I said, unsure of where this was going.

"Are you ashamed of not doing those things, or any other activities you haven't done?"

"No."

"Why be embarrassed about not having sex, then?" Cethin asked. My mouth fell open to say it was different, but he silenced me with a harsh kiss. "Virgin or not does not matter. Everyone is ready in their own time, and some choose to never have sex. Do not be ashamed of your lack of experience."

My cheeks still burned, but some of the tension eased out of my muscles while my cock demanded attention. I pressed a kiss to his lips, and Cethin moved on top of me. His lips were firm and insistent against mine. His tongue flicked out, and I opened for him, eagerly meeting him with mine.

My hips lifted to rut against him. Cethin groaned against me, and I felt something hard swell and press into my thigh. Breathless, he said, "I need you to tell me if you want this, Aidan. If you don't, I will not be upset, but I need to stop."

I swallowed as my nerves returned to full force. It wasn't that I didn't want Cethin, because I did, badly, but some part of me refused to relax. "I'm scared."

He smiled at me, thumb tracing my bottom lip. "There's no shame in that." His smile turned mischievous. "How about I make you feel good? No need for you to reciprocate, for I will enjoy this as much as you."

My throat went dry and my hips arched when I gathered his meaning. I nodded.

"I need you to say it."

"Yes, Cethin."

He grinned, kissing me as his hands trailed up my thighs, rucking my nightshirt up. "I am glad I will be your only."

"What?" I asked, but quickly forgot what I was thinking because his fingers stroked my shaft. I grunted, then bit my lip. I didn't want the footman outside to hear me and come in. His fingers slid up and down my cock before circling the head and gently brushing my slit, spreading the liquid gathered there. His hand slid down and cupped my balls and tugged on them, which made a strangled sound come out of my throat. My head pressed back into the pillow as shocks went up my spine.

Cethin's hand disappeared, and my eyes opened as I panted. "Don't stop."

"I'm not." He pulled on the edge of my nightshirt. "May I remove this?"

"Yes." I didn't care if he saw me naked. All I wanted was his hands on me and his lips on mine.

I lifted my arms, and he drew the nightshirt off me. His eyes ran over my body, tracing the tattoo on my skin. His gaze returned to mine, and a feral gleam shone within the black depths. "You are the loveliest thing I have ever seen in my entire life."

My heart pounded because I knew it was the truth. He couldn't lie.

I drew his face to mine and kissed him, my tongue invading his mouth. He gave way, letting me slide my tongue over his. My hands moved down his body. The fabric of his shirt was soft, but it wasn't what I wanted to feel. I needed his skin on mine.

"Take this off," I growled, yanking on the hem. Cethin complied, then mashed his lips to mine. I ran my hands over his chest and felt his muscles tense beneath my touch. His hair hung around us, tickling my cheeks as he hovered over me. I yanked on the ties on his trousers, undoing them and shoving the stiff fabric down.

Cethin kicked his trousers off and laid on me, our cocks brushing. I moaned, desperate. I rocked into him, sliding against one another in perfect, silky friction.

"Shit," I forced out.

He placed whisper-soft kisses on my neck and down my chest. His tongue swirled around one of my nipples, and I swore, biting my lip. He grinned up at me before returning his attention to my nipple, sucking and biting it while his fingers played with my other one.

Pre-cum leaked out of my cock as I tried to muffle my cries with a fist. Cethin continued to suck and bite until I was writhing beneath him. Eventually, he moved away from my nipples and placed kisses along the mark on my chest and arm, licking the thorny vines.

When he reached the inner part of my forearm, he paused on the bud. "When did this arrive?"

"Yesterday," I whispered, breathless.

He pressed a gentle kiss to the bud, running his tongue over it. "Beautiful."

I wanted to question him further, but he pressed firm kisses along my hip bones, tasting the delicate skin there. Nuzzling the thatch of hair, he looked at me. "Aidan."

I brushed a hand through his hair. Cethin smiled, his eyes soft and warm. He kissed the tip of my cock, and my hips lifted. He chuckled at my exuberance. His tongue swirled around the head, and I lost all sense of self, whimpering at the sensation. He prodded my weeping slit with his tongue and lapped up the beads of liquid.

"You're delicious."

The only response I gave was a moan.

Cethin placed open-mouthed kisses along my shaft, then licked my balls.

"Fuck," I cried.

He took one into his mouth and sucked on it, tongue swirling around it; he did the same to the other one. "Do you like that?"

I nodded, biting my fist.

He tugged on my tight balls, and his mouth returned to my cock. He took the head into his mouth, sliding down my shaft. I grunted, arching into his mouth, chasing the wet warmth. Cethin pressed down on my hips, anchoring me in place with his superior strength, and bobbed up and down.

My free hand fisted in the silky strands of Cethin's hair as I moaned into my fist.

His fingers slid from my balls and circled my rim, sending arcs of pleasure up my spine. I'd never felt anything like it. I writhed under him as animalistic cries ripped from my throat, barely muffled.

He slid up and off my cock, leaving it glistening with spit. I moaned in protest. I was close. Cethin kissed my inner thigh and pushed my legs further apart and up. My breath was hard and fast. He kissed the top of my cock before moving down.

When his tongue swiped my ass, I bit out, "Cethin."

He licked my hole, his fingers tugging on my balls. Stroke after stroke, he was stealing all my rational thought until I was an incoherent mess under his tongue.

"Please," I begged, not even sure what I was asking for.

"Soon." Cethin kissed the pucker of my ass, then circled it with the tip of his finger. He licked a stripe up to my balls and took them, one at a time, into his mouth. The pleasure built in the base of my spine and everything tightened. I moaned with every breath, no longer caring who heard me.

Cethin took my cock into his mouth, and I fisted a hand in his hair to keep him there. The head of my cock hit the back of his throat, and he moaned, vibrations traveling up my shaft. A cry ripped from my throat when he swallowed around me before sliding up, sucking. My balls drew up tight. The pleasure wracking my body turned almost painful with my need to come. I reached the edge, threatening to tumble over, and then Cethin swallowed around me again.

"I'm coming," I barely managed to force out.

His mouth slid up my cock, sucking on the head, and one of his hands pumped my length while the fingers of his other stroked my rim. I moaned, eyes closing and head arching back into the pillow as I came. White noise filled my ears as I spurted, calling his name.

Cethin sucked my cock, drinking my release, and stroked my shaft, extending my pleasure. When I finally stopped coming, I sagged on the bed, gasping. "God."

"Hmm, I prefer Cethin, but if you must."

I gave him a breathy chuckle. I trembled with the aftershocks of my release, sweat coating my exposed skin. Cethin kissed my stomach, sliding up my body until he covered me, face buried in my neck. "Aidan."

His cock was hard against my spent one. I ran my hands up his back, tracing the line of his spine. "Thank you."

He laughed. "You really must stop saying that."

"Are you going to take advantage of me?"

"No."

"Then I will keep saying it."

"As you will." Cethin snuggled against me, and I trailed my fingers over him, unable to stop touching him. Feeling brave, I snaked my fingers down to his ass, stroking the firm cheeks. He nuzzled my neck, groaning.

I bit my lip. "I want to make you feel good too."

"You don't have to."

"I know."

Cethin claimed my mouth. His tongue pushed through the seam of my lips and swiped against mine. I moaned, cupping his face. I could taste bitter salt on his tongue—my own release. He grabbed one of my hands and brought it down to his cock, caging my fingers around the length. He kept hold of me, sliding my fingers up and down.

His lips ripped away from mine, his breath hard. Cethin pressed his forehead against mine. I increased the speed, and Cethin snarled. "Aidan."

With my free hand, I traced his skin, touching everywhere I could reach. His hips thrusted to meet my movements as he panted, his forehead pushing into mine. I kept a firm grip around his shaft, pumping him, until Cethin mashed his lips to mine, and warm liquid spurted over my hand and stomach.

He collapsed on me, his release slick between us. I wrapped my arms around him, and Cethin snuggled against my chest, head tucked under my chin.

"What happens now?" I asked.

"What do you mean?"

"With us. What happens with us?"

"I do not understand."

I swallowed, unsure of how to voice my question. Were we courting or was this fucking? What did I want? I kissed his temple, letting the matter lie, and instead, basked in the warmth of this moment.

Cethin nibbled on my neck, fingers tracing my chest. "I am a selfish creature, Aidan."

"What?"

His pure black eyes met my gaze. "I take what I want, and I never let it go."

My breath turned harsh. Was he answering my unasked question? Did he intend on keeping me?

"Do you understand?"

I nodded.

Cethin rested against my shoulder, and I delighted in his presence.

A grin stretched across my face as I wandered around the library. For the whole day, I'd been unable to keep the smile off my lips. Oren had asked what was going on, as had his brothers, but I didn't answer. Cethin had stayed with me until Thomas pounded on my door and told me to get my ass out of bed. He'd left with a passionate kiss, promising to come back that night.

My fingers trailed over the spines of the books, while my mind was far away with Cethin. His mouth on mine. The feel of his smooth, cool skin rubbing against me. The sound he made as he came. His silky voice.

I started, coming to a stop. A fae stood in front of me. She was taller than me and had long brown hair, round cheeks, and impossible brown eyes.

"Excuse me," I said, bowing. I started to walk around her, but she laid a hand on my left arm, and then froze.

"What's this?"

"What?" I asked.

She stared at me, head tilting to the side. "I am Lady Blodwen."

"Ah," I said, nodding. The Byrne brothers had spoken of her beauty, and they'd been correct. She was lovely with her curvy form and perfect features. "I am Aidan Ryan. I am Mr. Oren Byrne's aide." Lord Byrne didn't want me to meet the fae representatives, but I couldn't in good manners ignore her.

"You are the one who was abducted by the dark fae, and said fae rescued the humans for you, killing the trolls," she said, her voice even and calm and her expression perfectly serene.

"Yes."

Her eyes, deep brown flecked with gold and green, ran the length of my body. Blodwen rested a hand on my left arm, and I frowned, pulling away from her touch, but she grabbed my wrist in an iron grip. "What's on your arm?"

"Let me go," I ordered in a deep voice as the window shuddered from a sudden gust of wind.

Blodwen blinked, but she didn't release me. Thomas came around the bookshelf and froze.

"Let me go. Now," I demanded.

Thomas came to my side. "Lady Blodwen, release Aidan."

"I do not take orders from you, Mr. Byrne." Her eyes met mine. "You will show me what's on your arm, boy."

Oren appeared like he'd been summoned by magic; behind him was Lord Abnus like a shadow of the night.

"Lady Blodwen, release Aidan or you shall regret it," Oren said.

Her fingers loosened, and I yanked away, glaring at her.

Oren came to my side, grabbing my hand. "Are you hurt, Aidan?"

"I'm fine."

The dark fae stared at Oren's hand on mine with narrowed eyes. "There is fae magic upon you."

"Yes," Blodwen agreed. "That's what I was trying to ascertain. What is on your left arm?"

Thomas and Oren both stared at me.

My hands curled into a fist. "Why?"

"Show us," Blodwen demanded, her features stretching before shifting back into her usual glamour.

"Aidan," Oren said in a soft voice.

There was no escape. Even Thomas and Oren were curious, so they wouldn't defend me. Some part of me balked at showing the tattoo, and I didn't know why. Still, I rolled my sleeve up enough to show a hint of the black vines on my wrist. The dark fae's eyes widened and his mouth fell open before his expression smoothed into a disinterested look. Blodwen touched my wrist, and I swore the thorny vines writhe under my skin to get away from her burning fingers.

"The dark fae marked you," she said.

"I saved his life. He was bleeding out. It's a debt mark."

Blodwen shook her head. "There is no such thing."

"He was bleeding out?" Lord Abnus asked in a careful voice.

My pulse pounded. "Yes. I dragged him to safety."

"This," Blodwen said, "is to tie fates together. He engaged himself to you, tethering your lives together. If he was injured, he might have done it to survive."

"I beg your pardon?" I asked as a buzzing like angry bees filled my ears. *Marriage? Tethered?*

Lord Abnus said, "You are engaged to the fae who marked you. Once the mark is placed, it cannot be removed. The vines shall take root, deepening the bond. Your lives are intertwined. You cannot live without him, and he cannot live without you. If one of you dies, so shall the other."

My knees shook, and Oren wrapped his arms around my waist, supporting me. Cethin. That was why he was here. He'd bound us together to save his own life. The only reason he was with me this morning was because we were stuck together.

"It's an old custom," Blodwen said. "Most fae do not use the marks anymore, because they are permanent. The magic cannot be undone or tricked. Who is this fae? Did he give you a name?"

Even if I wanted to answer, my strangled throat would not have released a single word. This morning was now tainted. Ruined. Cethin had not lied about the mark, but he certainly hadn't told the truth.

"Aidan needs a moment. Excuse us," Oren said as he tugged me from the room.

Thomas was right behind him. Sevrin and Whit peeled away from the bookshelves. They had appeared sometime during the conversation without me noticing.

The buzzing grew louder and louder. Cethin and I were engaged, as good as married. We were bound together. Our lives tethered. Would he die when I did? Or would my lifespan expand to match his? I had no idea, and Cethin was not here to question.

Most importantly—Cethin did not care about me. He'd used me. My knees trembled, threatening to give out. Oren grunted, taking more of my weight, and dragged me away.

Chapter 12

"When choosing which court to align with, the prospective heir should carefully weigh their options. Most lords have allied to the Day Court, though not I, but do not be fooled by their easy manner or their name, for they are as devious as their moon-blessed cousins." – Lord Ian, Sixth Lord of Sídhetír.

Oren practically carried me to my room as I sagged against him, struggling to do anything but breathe. My thoughts whirled and my chest stung with betrayal. The logical part of my brain thought my reaction was horribly dramatic—Cethin and I barely knew each other—but that didn't stop my spiraling emotions.

Cethin hadn't lied to me nor led me on, but he certainly hadn't told me the truth. This morning had been him making the best of a permanent situation.

My eyes closed as the backs burned and my throat clogged. He should have told me.

When Oren shoved me, I crashed onto my bed. He grabbed my face. "You didn't know."

"I thought this mark was because of the debt."

"Well, it could be perceived that way," Oren said with a tight smile. "You and him are engaged. It is a debt for life, I suppose."

"Are you defending him?"

"You like him, Aidan." Oren sat next to me, making the bed dip.

I flopped backward and covered my face with my arms. I did. I liked Cethin. Why? I couldn't say. A worm of doubt wriggled in my thoughts and made my stomach churn. What if the only reason I was attracted to him was because of the tattoo? Were my feelings even real? Did my interest in his mischievous smile and quick humor actually come from me?

"Thomas will tell Father about this. He'll want to speak to you."

Another thing to dread. Lord Byrne wouldn't be pleased about me revealing myself to the fae representatives, or about the engagement to an unknown fae. I shook my head. I didn't want to speak to him or Lady Hester.

Cethin. I had to talk to him. Make him explain himself.

"I need you to help me," I said.

"With what?"

"I have to leave."

Oren's eyes widened. "You can't."

"I have to speak with him. I have to."

"It will have to wait."

I scrubbed a hand through my hair. "You don't understand."

"I know you care for him, but you cannot leave right now. You must speak with my father, and I don't know how he will take this surprise engagement."

"We had sex," I growled.

His mouth opened. "What?"

The hurt was obvious in his tone. I shared everything, besides Iris, with Oren. But now, I'd kept numerous secrets in a short span of time. "It was this morning. We fucked this morning. He snuck in and..." I trailed off.

"That's why you couldn't stop smiling."

"It was amazing."

He rolled to his side and rested his head in his hand. "I'm jealous."

Laughter spilled from my lips, but it was tainted with hurt. "For my forced engagement? Or that my first time was with a man who didn't bother to tell me about said engagement?"

"Neither," Oren said. "Because you found someone, someone you care about."

"Who betrayed me."

His dopey smile dimmed. "True."

"I need to speak with him, Oren. I have to. I can't wait."

He glanced at the door. "Put the pillows under the blanket, and I will tell everyone you fell asleep. It will only stall Father. I have no idea how we'll get you outside because I'm sure Whit, at least, is in the hall."

Getting to my feet, I said, "That's not a problem." I arranged the pillows and fluffed the blankets until they resembled my sleeping form, then shifted to the window. I opened it and slid out, balancing on the ledge with ease.

Oren gaped at me. "That's how you got out."

"Yes," I said with a slight smile.

I shut the window and rushed along the ledge, not losing my balance. I ignored the other windows in my haste—I didn't care who saw me at the moment. I swung over the stone railing of the balcony, snagged the ivy, and climbed down. A vine was always within reach and my feet easily found support. I landed on the flagstones without incident and raced through the hedge maze to the gate, which swung open with the barest twist of the key.

The second I was free of the estate, I headed north, unsure of where to go. I didn't want to talk in Cethin's home, but I wanted privacy. Without truly contemplating, I turned to the apple orchard. The farmhands shouldn't have begun harvesting the fruit yet, so it would be private enough for this conversation.

My feet moved over the fields while my thoughts circled. What should I say to him? I had no idea, but I had to find the words somehow. When I stepped under the laden trees, I looked up. The sky was darkening with clouds. I frowned. The sky had been clear only a few minutes ago. Perhaps Lord Byrne had learned of what happened and was angry. Normally, he had better control of his emotions.

Closing my eyes, I said, "Cethin."

He'd said he would come if I called for him, but I didn't know how it worked or how much time it would take for him to arrive.

A wind stirred my hair and I turned into the breeze, taking deep breaths in an attempt to calm my pounding heart.

"Aidan," a voice whispered not far from me. Arms came around my waist, and lips trailed along the column of my neck. Anger churned in my gut, but my cock hadn't received the notice—it began to stand at attention.

"You called for me," Cethin said. "I did not think I would see you until tonight, though the surprise doesn't upset me in the slightest."

His lips wandered up my neck to my ear. He nibbled on my earlobe, holding me securely in his embrace. I wanted to lean back and forget everything that had happened, but I could not.

I tried to step out of his hold, but he was much stronger than me and I couldn't break free. I wiggled, and Cethin stopped sucking on my earlobe. "What's wrong?"

"Let me go," I ordered in a stony voice. His arms instantly opened. I turned around to face him.

Cethin stared at me, eyebrows pulled together. He lifted a hand, but when I shied away, it fell to his side. "What's going on?"

I shoved up my sleeve as far as it would go. "What is this?"

"Why are you asking?"

"Tell me. Directly. What. Is. This?"

He swallowed. "Someone told you."

"I want to hear it from your mouth."

Cethin met my stare. "It is a mating mark. I placed my own tattoos on you and bound our souls together. You and I are engaged to be married."

I shook my head, asking, even though I knew the answer, "Is this permanent?"

"Yes."

"Why did you even do it? You didn't know me."

His eyes moved away from mine as his jaw tightened.

"Cethin," I barked. "Why did you do this?" When he didn't respond, I continued, "Lady Blodwen said you did it to save your life."

"Blodwen," he muttered. "Of course she said that. She's young."

"*Young*," I repeated, eyebrows raised.

"Yes."

My finger traced over the thorny vines. "Does this influence my emotions?"

He whipped in my direction. "No," he said, his voice a growl. "It does not do anything besides chain your life to mine. Your feelings are your own." Cethin held my face within his cupped hands. "What you feel for me and this morning are real. It is real for me as well, Aidan."

I slapped his hands away. "And I should believe you why?"

"I cannot lie."

I scoffed and walked further into the orchard, fingers running over rough bark that scraped at my skin and distracted me from my raw heart. He could not utter a single lie, *but* that didn't mean his words were the truth.

No one bent or twisted words like a fae.

Besides, what was the truth? He could spout things he believed to be true but were not. It was subjective. What was true for him did not make it true for me.

Arms snagged me, and Cethin growled in my ear, "I told you this morning: I am selfish. It's my greatest weakness. I will do whatever I must to keep what I want, and I want you, Aidan. I wanted you from the moment I saw you."

"Why?"

"Because you are *mine*. I bound you to me, not to save my life, but to keep you with me."

"You didn't give me a choice," I snapped.

"I did not. I acted on instinct, and I do not regret it."

I yanked his arms away so I could face him. "That's not right, Cethin."

"I never claimed it was, but I will not surrender you," he snarled.

"And I don't have to want to be with you." I walked toward Byrne Manor to face the situation I'd left behind. How would I explain this fiasco to Lord Byrne? I had no idea. Hopefully, something would come to me on the way back.

I made it to the edge of the orchard before Cethin stepped in front of me, blocking my path. "You don't understand."

"What don't I understand?" I practically screamed in his face. I barely knew Cethin, but somehow he'd wormed his way into my heart.

He scrubbed a hand through his snowy hair. "You are mine."

"You said that already, and I say no." I veered around him, and he grabbed my elbow, his hold gentle despite the situation. I swatted him. "Fuck off."

Cethin muttered something. His arms wrapped around my waist and dragged me back. I elbowed him, catching his nose. He swore, releasing me. I took off in a run, my feet pounding on the damp grass. Harsh words came from behind me as Cethin chased me.

Despite the tense situation, I was not afraid, not even a little bit. Deep down, I knew he wouldn't hurt me.

He snatched me again, his arms trapping mine against my sides, and my feet lifted off the ground. I ordered, "Let me go." Thunder rumbled and the ground quaked as I shook.

"No," he said right in my ear. "I want to talk to you. Let me explain."

"I don't have to hear your explanation."

"You don't, but please let me tell you."

My wriggling ceased as my harsh breath began to ease.

Cethin buried his face against my neck. "Please don't leave, Aidan. Let me explain."

"Fine, but let me go. Now."

Cethin released me, and my feet landed on the ground again. I faced him, arms crossed. Prickles started in my stomach at the sight of blood on his lip and the bruises around his eyes and nose from where I'd hit him. I buried the sensation. I'd been defending myself.

"Explain," I demanded.

His hand went through his long hair again, the strands falling over his shoulders. "You are mine."

"God preserve me. You've said that three times now. Are you trying to invoke an incantation or do you have a point?"

Eyes narrowing, he snapped, "I have a point."

"Then get to it, and spare me the dramatics. You chose the course of my life without any input from me, Cethin. I don't even want to look at you, let alone hear this, so hurry the fuck up."

Cethin took a deep breath, his eyebrow twitching. He seemed as angry and frustrated as I did. "I was stabbed with a poison-dipped iron knife."

My blood turned cold. Iron was deadly to fae. No wonder he'd been unconscious when I found him in the woods. Unable to stop myself, I moved closer, reaching for his black shirt. I'd seen him naked this morning, and yet that didn't stop the concern burning through me.

His hand grabbed mine and pressed my palm to his sternum. "I am fine."

"So you were badly injured?"

"Yes," he said. "I woke up and there you were, hovering over me." Cethin tightened his hold as he swallowed, his throat bobbing in a distracting way.

"And?"

"And I knew you were mine."

"What does that mean?" I asked.

He looked away, jaw clenched. I waited patiently for him to answer, but as the silence stretched on for an uncomfortable amount of time, I yanked my hand from his grasp, and Cethin let me go.

"Leave, Cethin. I don't want to see your face right now." I headed back to Byrne Manor to face the problems before me while leaving him and the unspoken issue behind.

Chapter 13

"Preparing the heir for the mantle of Lord of Sídhetír is not an easy task, but it will be the most important one of your life, for your heir shall protect the kingdom and uphold the contract." – Lord Finbar, Fifth Lord of Sídhetír.

I stood in front of the desk in Lord Byrne's bookroom. Oren leaned against the bookshelf behind his father's shoulder, fiddling with the silver fob he wore—the jingling was the sole sound in the deathly quiet room. Lord Byrne steepled his hands on the desk, his eyes never wavering from me.

Thomas had told him of the events in the library with Blodwen and Abnus. Lord Byrne had gone to my room to demand answers, and Oren had tried to deter him for as long as possible, but the lord wouldn't be distracted. My room, of course, had been empty.

I came home as Lord Byrne was questioning Oren about my disappearance and organizing a search for me. I'd returned by the secret gate, so no one knew of my arrival until I stepped inside the manor. If I'd had the energy to laugh at the dropped mouths and wide eyes, I would have.

"Aidan," Lord Byrne said, drawing my focus to the present. "You left the manor against my orders."

I wouldn't lie to him. My mother often told me lying was a pointless venture because the truth could only be waylaid not overwritten. "Yes."

"Why?"

"I wanted to see the dark fae."

"Your fiancé?" he asked.

"Yes."

He rubbed his forehead. For once, he appeared to be his true age, close to sixty. "Do you know how dangerous that could've been? It's the transition, Aidan. A fae is making deals in Elmbury, and we haven't been able to catch or eject them from Sídhetír. You almost died days ago."

I stared into his eyes as I blatantly said, "Do you honestly think he would allow me to die? You know what Blodwen and Abnus said. He will die if I do."

Lord Byrne dragged a hand over his face.

Oren pushed off the wall. "He has a point, Father. And the revelation of the engagement has been a great shock to him. Aidan deserved to speak with his fiancé."

"How did this even happen?"

"I saved a fae," I said. There was no point in telling him what Cethin had said because the dark fae hadn't explained his actions or words.

"Why didn't you run?" Lord Byrne asked. "That's what you're supposed to do, but time and time again, you break the rules that have been established for safety. You go into the woods, leave the manor after dark, and now, fraternize with dark fae."

I also had sex with a fae, but that wasn't worth mentioning either. Instead, I said, "He was a living, breathing person in front of me who needed help. How could I turn my back on him?"

Oren shifted to my side and tucked an arm around my waist. "He's not wrong, Father. You often told us our responsibility was to help those in need. You cannot change your mind now that it's inconvenient for you."

Lord Byrne yanked his coat straight and leaned back in his chair. "I suppose there's some truth in that. But what are we to do?"

"Nothing," Oren said, his voice firmer than I'd ever heard before. "It's permanent, according to Lady Blodwen."

"And my fiancé," I added. I still wouldn't tell them his name, and I wasn't sure why.

"I want to meet him," Lord Byrne said.

"No."

"Excuse me?"

Words stuck in my throat, unable to come out. I was of two minds. I didn't want to see Cethin after everything I'd learned, and yet, I wanted him to meet the people who'd helped raise me after my mother died. Still, I was so angry and hurt.

"I need to know exactly who this fae is and what danger he presents," Lord Byrne said.

"I don't want to see him at the moment," I bit out.

"I can understand that. I truly can, but I have to meet him."

Lord Byrne was charged with the safety of Sídhetír and all of its people, and Cethin could be a danger. Hell, he probably was. He'd killed those light fae with ease once I and the other humans were out of danger.

Cethin. Why hadn't he told me the reason he'd tied us together? Forgiving him would be easier if he had.

"How am I supposed to make him appear?" I asked.

"I assume you know where he's staying, or have some way to contact him," Lord Byrne said.

Both true. My brain whirled as I tried to think of another way around the predicament. "We fought, and I told him to leave."

"Aidan," Oren groaned.

"What was I supposed to do?"

"Make the best of a permanent situation," Oren answered.

I frowned. I, and the rest of the Byrne brothers, had said different renditions of those exact words to him over the years regarding his inescapable fate as the future lord.

"He'll be back," Lord Byrne said, voice tired. "Of that, I have no doubt."

"Would you like me to notify you when or if he returns?" I asked, crossing my arms. There was little to no chance of that happening. I had no intention of telling Lord Byrne anything, but he didn't need to know that.

"The instant you see him. This is important," he said.

"It is important." I met his eyes with a blank expression. Oren raised his eyebrows. He wasn't fooled, nor did I expect him to be—he knew me better than any other person in this world. Oren tilted his head to the side, gesturing to the door. If I followed him, I would have to continue this conversation with someone who would see through my obfuscation.

"I apologize, Oren," I said. "You must be busy with the representatives, and I am taking time from your responsibilities."

Oren glared at me, but Lord Byrne stood, the chair scraping on the wood floor. "He is correct. You should see to your duties. I will join you presently."

When Oren passed by me, he gripped my forearm. "This is not over."

I didn't reply.

After the door closed, Lord Byrne ordered, "Do not leave again. I don't even know how you're getting out. One of my sons has been outside your door, and none of the servants have seen you leave."

My eyes moved to the window, staring at the brilliant orange and red leaves cluttering the trees.

Lord Byrne sighed. The soles of his shoes smacked on the floor as he moved to stand directly in front of me. "Stay inside."

"I want to help. Keeping me locked in here will not help this matter. We cannot break the engagement, and both of the fae representatives know of my existence, so what's the point of keeping me locked away? I will not follow Oren around. Besides, he seems more comfortable with them."

He grabbed the lapels of my coat, shaking me. "I am trying to keep you safe."

"And I'm an adult. I can protect myself."

Lord Byrne cupped my cheek. "Promise me not to leave the manor alone."

I would make no such promise, but I smiled as if I agreed and that seemed to be enough for Lord Byrne.

The following day, I decided to behave. Oren was busy with the fae, but Nevan and Neil were hanging around me, even though Lord Byrne had called them off, believing I had promised him not to leave alone, which made me feel guilty. I should be a man of my word, trustworthy, and yet I had swiveled around the promise with ease, letting Lord Byrne believe something that wasn't true.

Nevan leaned back in a chair, its front legs in the air, and Neil read. The twins, though identical in features, differed in interests. Nevan was chatty and active. Neil was quiet and reserved. The twins preferred to be in each other's company, so they made concessions.

They lived in Lord Byrne's townhouse. Neither was employed in the traditional sense. They preferred balls, dancing, and speculating their funds over actual work. Lord Byrne allowed their dallying because Neil was a genius for financial scheming while Nevan's ease with people hooked investors, and they made more than they spent.

I walked around the library, keeping the south-facing windows in my sights. Part of me longed to see a flash of white hair and gray-purple skin. I was furious with Cethin, and yet I was desperate to see him. The thorny vines dug beneath my skin, writhing and burying deeper into me.

"Mr. Ryan," a cool voice said from behind me.

Lord Abnus was tall and rail thin in a fashionable jacket, waistcoat, and trousers. The top half of his chin-length, black hair was tied back, barring a few strands that framed his face. The hairstyle made his sharp features appear harsher and his ears longer than they actually were. His purple eyes ran down the length of my body before returning to my face.

"Hello, Lord Abnus."

He bowed low, lower than protocol demanded. In fact, I should be bowing deeper than him, but I didn't think I'd manage it in my tight jacket. I settled for a normal bow, but when I straightened, he was still bent over. What the hell was he going on about?

"It's nice to officially meet you, Lord Abnus. What can I do for you? Oren is not here."

"I'm aware." His voice had a rumbling quality to it that was oddly soothing. "I was looking for you."

"Yes?" I pressed. He seemed to only speak in short bursts. He bowed once again, and I swallowed. "There's no need for that. Please."

"I must apologize for my kin who put such a mark on you without permission."

"Ah." I motioned to the table against the window, taking a seat with my back facing the wall. The warmth of the sun brushed along my skin. I glanced down at the sprawling gardens, but there was no one within sight.

When Abnus sat down across from me, I said, "It wasn't your fault."

"That may be true, but still, I feel guilty. Perhaps I can offer you more information?"

"That would be welcome."

"Might I see it?"

Heat rushed to my cheeks as I recalled Cethin asking to see it. The possessive gleam in his black eyes. The way he'd kissed every inch, warm tongue flicking my skin. I cleared my throat. The tattoo felt oddly private, and I didn't want anyone else to see it. "The mark travels up my arm to my chest."

"I am aware of how mating marks look."

I swallowed, mouth open to speak more when the words caught in my throat. Cethin had called it a mate mark, but Blodwen had called it an engagement mark. "Mating mark? I thought it was an engagement mark?"

"It is called such in more modern translations, but traditionally, it is known as a mating mark."

"What does that mean?"

Abnus did not answer and instead asked, "May I see the base of your mark?"

Something inside of me resisted showing it to anyone besides Cethin. "It's private."

"It is," Abnus said. "Most noble fae do not reveal their tattoos to many, hiding it beneath clothes or with their glamour, but I need to see part of it if you want me to assist you."

I forced the uneasy feeling aside. I rolled up my sleeve, but I was careful not to let Abnus see the blue bud on my forearm. Cethin had shown an interest in it, and I didn't want to play my hand if it was important. Abnus touched the thorny vines, and they twisted out of reach. He covered his mouth. Hiding a smile, I guessed.

"Your intended is left-handed."

My eyebrows rose. "You can tell that from my mark?"

"It's on your left arm. When humans and fae mate with marks, it always appears on the same arm as the fae's dominant hand."

"Interesting."

"May I ask what mark is on your chest?" Abnus asked, not meeting my gaze as his hands fisted.

"Why?" My eyes roved over him. Abnus seemed invested in the answer—or he was an excellent actor, which was possible. It was impossible to gauge his age. He could be ancient for all I knew.

His jaw worked side to side, and his eyes remained on the window. It seemed he was deciding whether or not to tell me. I crossed my arms and leaned back, waiting for some convoluted story to twist my thoughts around, or for him to not answer the question.

"It is the crest of the one who claimed you," Abnus said directly.

"It's their mark," I whispered. Cethin had the same crescent moon and seven-pointed red star on his chest.

"May I know what it is?"

I did not answer. "What does the mark mean?"

Abnus's fingers tapped along the wood table. "You and he are bound together. You will live as long as him, but if you or he dies, the other will as well. You, as a human, can choose to live your life without him, but he won't be able to live without you. He will long to remain by your side."

I closed my eyes. "Why did he even do it?"

"Did he tell you?"

My lips flattened.

"I understand."

Eyebrows raised, I asked, "You do?"

"You're his mate."

"What?"

"Dark fae," Abnus started, "have a unique talent."

"You have many."

"True," he said, "but this may be more interesting than some of our others. When we lay eyes on our mate for the first time, we know. The instant we see them, we know."

Cethin's words rang in my head. *You are mine.* He saw me and bound the two of us together. "Why didn't he talk to me?"

Abnus chuckled, but there was a tinge of sadness in his tone. "It is almost impossible to resist, and you said he was injured. He would've wanted to claim you before anyone took you from him."

"He warned me he was selfish."

"An adequate description, though not complete."

Abnus had to know Cethin. "Who is he exactly?"

"Who?"

"My betrothed. You know who he is, don't you?"

He got to his feet. "Cethin will not leave you alone for long, Aidan. You are too important."

Chapter 14

"Whom the heir marries must be carefully chosen, for the heir must sire seven sons to continue the contract."
– Lord Rhett, First Lord of Sídhetír.

I rode beside Sevrin through the streets of Elmbury. The fae we'd heard about had been making rounds within the village proper. Fae deals—they were a double-edged blade. On one hand, they could help, and on the other, they had a tendency to hurt those who took them.

Lord Byrne wanted them found, which fell to us, or more accurately, his sons. I decided to join Sevrin when he planned to search the village. Lord Byrne hadn't been pleased, but he allowed me to go because I was not going alone—as he'd thought I'd promised.

Lord Byrne could not keep the fae out of Sídhetír during the transition, and Oren had yet to receive his mantle. But if we found the fae, Lord Byrne might convince them to leave, though he couldn't cast them out if they would not be persuaded. He could appeal to the fae representatives to assist him in forcing the fae to leave.

A crisp fall wind rattled the leaves and stirred my hair, making me look at the pristine blue sky. I closed my eyes as one of my hands stretched, palm to the ground. The clomp of the horse hooves. The scent of flowers. The feel of the sunlight.

For some reason, I had a desperate urge to see my mother's grave. Perhaps it was the flowers reminding me of her. I had no reason for the bone-deep longing that rose up, making me shift on the hard saddle, but I had to go to the church.

I swallowed. The feeling might have nothing to do with my mother, and all to do with someone else.

Cethin slithered into my thoughts.

A week had passed since I'd spoken to Abnus, and even longer since I'd seen Cethin. I saw Abnus daily, because he made a point to greet me, but he wouldn't answer questions or speak about Cethin. Abnus and Blodwen had continued to court Oren, and he still refused to make a decision. Lord Byrne was growing increasingly agitated at his lack of direction, for it prolonged the transition and left people at risk.

"Do you see anything?" I asked Sevrin as we passed by the flower shop, my eyes running over the blooms.

"No."

We'd spoken to several villagers, and while people would admit to seeing a fae, no one would admit to making a deal. They did give us a general description. Tall. Not much help there. Golden hair. Probably light fae. Tan. Broad. Attractive.

I pulled my horse to a stop, and Sevrin looked at me in askance.

"I want to visit my mother," I announced.

"Now?" he asked, a divot forming between his squished eyebrows.

"Yes." The urge to see the church was growing by the second, sending ants scurrying beneath my skin. I slipped off my horse's back and stepped inside the flower shop, a bell announcing my arrival.

Conor looked up from behind the counter. His brow creased and he shoved his glasses up his nose when Sevrin came inside. "Aidan, are you getting your usual?" he asked, but his gaze remained on Sevrin.

"Yes. Thank you."

Conor began to assemble a bouquet with practiced motions. I took a deep inhale of the mixed floral scents. Normally, the fragrance calmed me because it signified I was about to see my mother, but this time, the tension in my muscles continued to grow.

My stomach curled as my legs tensed like I was about to start running. I had to go. Now. The graveyard with its mossy grave markers, broken stone wall, and towering elm tree appeared in my mind's eye.

Something was waiting. Cethin? Possibly.

I bounced on my toes and glanced over my shoulder at the windows. Familiar faces of villagers passed by as they went about their lives, but I didn't catch a glimpse of a fae, or anything out of the usual.

"Do you come here often?" Sevrin asked, making me jolt.

I'd almost forgotten he was with me. "I get flowers for my mother when I visit her."

Sevrin's brown eyes locked on mine as the corners of his lips turned down. "You never told me that you visited your mother's grave this often."

"What's there to tell?" I shrugged, burying my hands in my pockets. "My mother rests close to here. Why wouldn't I visit her?"

"One of us would've come with you. We could have paid our respect to our own mothers."

"Contrary to recent events, I *can* take care of myself."

"I know that. We all know that, but we do like to take care of you."

"Something of which I am well aware," I said dryly, and Sevrin laughed, bumping his shoulder against mine.

Conor laid the flower bouquet on the counter. I slapped a coin down and grabbed the paper-wrapped flowers.

"Thank you," I said. He nodded, turning back to assemble another bouquet.

On our horses again, Sevrin and I went straight to the isolated church. I saw its sharp spire before I caught sight of the building in its entirety. The low stone wall surrounded the graveyard, but its mossy green stones, crumbling with age, did not hold my attention. The man who sat on the wall did. His golden blonde hair fell around his round face. His tapered ears and elegant beauty marked him for the fae he was.

He tossed a pebble in the air and snatched it, whistling a jaunty tune. The fae glanced in our direction and nodded in welcome.

"How did you know?" Sevrin asked.

I shrugged. I truly hadn't known the fae would be here. The sudden urge to see my mother had more to do with the scent of flowers and being in Elmbury. Or Cethin perhaps, though I didn't see him anywhere.

"Good morning, lads," the fae called out, hopping to the ground and shoving his hands in his pockets. "What can I do for you?"

I slipped off my horse's back, ignoring Sevrin's hushed whisper, and dropped the fragrant flowers to the ground. We were not supposed to confront the fae. At most, we were supposed to ask them to leave. The best course of action was to fetch Lord Byrne.

My hand closed around the iron key in my pocket. Like a fool, I hadn't grabbed my iron dagger when we left this morning. Sevrin would have his pistols on him, which shot iron rounds, but I had nothing but a key to protect myself with.

"Why do you think we want something?" I asked, approaching.

He smiled, but it held no warmth. His brown eyes scoured me from my red hair to the tip of my shiny boots. "Such a fine gentleman as yourself would only have one reason to seek me out. You want a deal, and I might be inclined to grant you one—for a favor."

"What favor?" I stood in front of him, subtly slipping the key from my pocket.

With a smirk, he stepped closer. "I'm not sure yet, but I'd be willing to grant you a deal, possibly, without closing your end. I would return one day for what you owe me."

"People are agreeing to this?" Sevrin asked, eyebrows high on his face. I quite agreed. Making an open-ended deal was idiotic. The fae could return years, even decades, later for whatever they wanted, and the human would have no recourse.

"Ah, sorry, lads, speaking about my other deals is off limits. People have a right to privacy."

"I do have something I want from you." Pressure began to build in my chest. I wanted this fae to leave. I wanted him gone from Sídhetír. He was harming the people who lived here. How many open-ended contracts had he made? What would he collect from people in the years to come?

His grin turned predatory. "Of course you do. Everyone does. What can I do for you?"

"Aidan," Sevrin warned.

The fae's eyebrows lifted. "Aidan? Beautiful name that suits you well." He shifted closer until barely any space separated us. His breath stirred my hair as he asked in a low voice, "What do you desire?"

"I won't make a deal for it," I said, which made his aspect harden. "By authority of Lord Byrne, we want you to leave Sídhetír. Now."

"A couple of Lord Byrne's sons," he bit out. The fae's appearance began to morph as his glamour dimmed. His features hardened and his skin took on the texture of stone. Small horns jutted out of the top of his head while a spiked tail slid to the ground.

"You need to leave."

"I have every right to be here, and you two have no power over me."

Sevrin pulled out his pistol. "If I put an iron round in your skull, that would stop you."

"If you can hit me." The fae slammed his hand into my sternum, and I went down, smacking into the ground. My chest ached and the breath left my lungs. The roots of the tree in the graveyard began to shift and tremble, lifting out of the ground and shooting toward me. They encased me, scraping my skin raw.

A shot rang out, and the fae yelped. I jerked up and saw Sevrin holding a smoking pistol in his hand. The fae clutched his shoulder, growling. He waved a hand, and the ground beneath Sevrin rumbled. The horses whinnied. Sevrin's reared, and he tumbled off with a shout. Both of the horses ran off. More roots appeared and rushed in Sevrin's direction, moving to spear him.

"Sevrin," I screamed. The roots caging me fell to the ground, and I was on my feet before I even had a chance to think about what I was doing. I rammed into the fae, pressing the iron key against his face. He shrieked as a burning smell filled my nostrils and awakened my nausea. His skin turned bright red from the contact of iron. The fae backhanded me, and I crashed into the ground, cheek throbbing and blood tinging my mouth.

I whipped toward the fae. Sevrin struggled to his feet, pulling out an iron knife. He'd come prepared, which shouldn't surprise me.

The fae snarled, revealing his sharp teeth. "You will not stop me. I will lay enough hooks until I can traverse the realms at will."

I tackled him again. I shoved him into the ground and stabbed him with the key, ripping it out and moving to stab him again. The fae punched me, fist connecting with my jaw, and I groaned as lights flashed in my eyes. He held a hand to the dirt road and it lifted, throwing me into the air. I slammed into the ground, and the fae did it again and again and again.

Lungs burning and head pounding, I fought to stay conscious. Sevrin rushed toward the fae and attacked, his movements light and steady. Roots shot out of the ground and grabbed Sevrin, dragging him to his knees.

"You, lads, have not been hospitable hosts." The fae pressed a hand to his shoulder. Blood leaked from in between his fingers. A massive key-shaped burn decorated the side of his face, and a jagged stab wound on his stomach bled profusely. He stumbled. The blood loss was getting to him, as was the iron poisoning from said wounds and the bullet embedded in his skin.

"But I think killing you and leaving your bodies for your father will be a good message. Too long the nobles have controlled access to this world. I have every right to be here, and if you humans are stupid enough to make deals with me, that is not my problem."

The fae stalked in my direction, and the ground rumbled beneath my palms as the wind picked up. I lifted my head; strength that I didn't understand began to flood my veins. Moments ago, I'd been fighting to stay conscious, and suddenly, the pain was dulling. I would not allow the fae to harm Sevrin or anyone else. I shifted to my knees, and the world tilted.

"Leave," I ordered. "While you still have a chance."

He seized my chin in a bruising grasp. "The arrogance of humans. You are about to die."

"No. He is not," a voice said, sending shivers down my spine. "You are."

A black cloud of magic encased the fae, yanking him away from me. Blue flowers with long yellow stamens bloomed within the darkness and the cloud morphed into thorny vines. Cethin stepped forward, and Sevrin glanced at me, but I didn't bother to answer his unasked question. Cethin wasn't supposed to be here any longer, but Lord Byrne had known he'd come back, as had Abnus.

He stepped in front of me, crouching, and his hair brushed my cheeks. Cethin gently held my chin, his thumb moving over the split in my lip and the bruise along my cheek and jaw. "Why didn't you call for me?"

"I had it handled."

"If this is how you handle things, we need to have a discussion."

An unwilling smile pulled at the corner of my lips. By God, I'd missed him, even though I was still furious. Cethin pressed a kiss to my forehead.

"I will call you next time," I said.

Cethin frowned. "There should be no next time."

"We'll see."

Chapter 15

"As the mantle shifts, be prepared for changes in the weather, plants, and even the land itself. Sídhetír is adjusting to the heir and the heir is adjusting to Sídhetír."
– Lord Quincy, Seventh Lord of Sídhetír.

Cethin completely ignored the struggling, swearing light fae and the unusually silent Sevrin as he traced the injuries to my face. His fingers moved down to my chest, and I took a sharp breath. My ribs ached something fierce from the pounding I'd taken. He brushed the iron key and jerked back with a slight hiss.

"That was your only weapon?" he asked.

I shrugged.

"If you're hunting fae, you should carry iron daggers. I am happy to supply you with a pair or more. As many as you need to be safe."

"I have one."

"Then why are you unarmed?"

I didn't bother to answer. Truthfully, I hadn't thought about it. My dagger lay uselessly on my nightstand. "I'm not good with a pistol."

"I did not ask about that," he whispered in my ear, kissing it.

"It's the truth."

With a slight chuckle, he brushed my cheek. "Of that, I have no doubt."

The trapped light fae wriggled within the vines, snarling, but Cethin paid him no mind. Instead, he continued to stroke my injuries as his eyes roved my face. He seemed completely oblivious to the light fae's presence.

Sevrin nodded at the light fae in a clear question. I had no answer. What would Cethin do with the trapped fae?

Cethin's thumb traced my bottom lip. "Aidan, I'm sorry I hurt you."

"But you're not sorry you bound us."

"No," he answered. His lips caressed my ear as he whispered, "I will never regret what keeps you beside me."

"Let me go," the trapped fae snapped. "You have no reason to stop me."

"You touched what is mine," Cethin growled, his hand clasping my chin.

"Yours, eh? Interesting," the light fae said.

Cethin's black eyes narrowed and he peered over his shoulder at the fae. The light fae's tan skin turned ashen, and he swallowed convulsively. He wriggled in the tight hold as his eyes darted every which way. "I didn't know," the fae said. "I had no idea. I swear by the sun's light."

"Cethin," I said, drawing his focus.

He pressed a kiss to my forehead. "You're safe."

"I'm not worried about that."

"Then what is disturbing you?"

"What about all the deals he made?"

"Deals?" Cethin asked, glancing back at the light fae.

"Open-ended deals," Sevrin said. "When we were fighting, he mentioned something about hooks."

"That's your game." He prowled toward the fae. "You want enough contracts in place that you can be drawn to this world without the gate."

"T-that's not possible," I said, looking at Sevrin. He had the same wide-eyed expression that I did.

The light fae scoffed. "The things you humans think you know." He fell silent at Cethin's glare.

"There are many paths into this world. The gate is merely the most convenient and by far the safest one." Cethin circled the fae as he spoke.

The light fae tracked his movements as much as he was able. Sweat covered his forehead and his breathing was sharp and audible to even my ears.

"We have a problem," Cethin said.

"Do we? Why would we have a problem?" the light fae asked.

"You know of my Aidan."

"Why would that matter?" he asked.

"Do not play the fool," Cethin said. "If I allow you to live, you could come back and harm him."

My eyes widened. I don't know why I was surprised at the thought of him killing the light fae. Cethin had destroyed the trolls with little thought. Sevrin struggled to his feet and shifted to my side.

"If you kill me, all those good things I did will die with me," the captured fae said.

"Cethin," I called, unsure of what I wanted.

He glanced at me. "I have no choice. He could hurt you."

"What if I promise not to?" the fae said with a broad grin that rang false.

Cethin snorted. "You would tell another, who could harm my Aidan."

"Cethin," I said again as images of Mr. Hillridge began to bubble up. I did not want to watch another person be killed. Sevrin gripped my shoulders and tugged me against his solid chest.

"Turn away, Aidan," Cethin ordered.

"No."

Sevrin started to force me in the other direction. "He has to do this, but you don't have to watch."

"Turn away, Aidan," Cethin repeated. The fae began to scream obscenities as he thrashed in the bindings in an attempt to free himself. The last thing I saw before Sevrin forced me to look away was Cethin approaching the fae, the claws obvious at the end of his outstretched hand.

Sevrin kept his arms tight around me. "It's all fine. I promise, it's alright."

I shook my head, my muscles tense. The fae continued to scream until the sound was cut off by a wet rip and gurgling. A slapping sound was directly followed by a thud.

Bile burned my throat as I trembled.

Sevrin held me close, rocking me as he made soothing noises.

"It's over, Aidan," Cethin whispered.

I understood his actions, yet part of me couldn't look at him. All I saw was Mr. Hillridge writhing on the fire. I breathed heavily through my nose as my hands shook. Cethin was protecting me. I might not know who Cethin was, but he was clearly a noble fae, and therefore powerful. If someone abducted me, they could force Cethin to do what they wanted.

Once again that put the question of why into my mind. Why had he done this? Was it what Abnus said? Was I his mate?

My vision was filled with his face. Cethin leaned down until he met my gaze. He lifted his hand, but I yanked back from the blood on his fingers. His hand fell to his side. "Are you well?"

I didn't know how to answer that question. My stomach churned and cold sweat bathed me. I could not say with any accuracy if it would have been worse to have witnessed this death or not. The ripping sounds. The wet thunking of the fae's head. His frightened screams.

None of it would leave me.

Cethin shifted closer and pressed a kiss to my temple. "I had to protect you. I will allow no one to harm you."

This was something I knew. He'd said and proved it. But that knowledge didn't dampen the nausea curling inside of me. Cethin would protect me, killing every and any threat. I didn't want people around me to die, even the bad ones.

A weed of doubt wiggled in my thoughts. Was Cethin protecting me because he cared, or because he didn't want to die? I didn't know if he truly cared about me, or if everything was simply him making the best of the situation we'd found ourselves in.

Sevrin's arms remained tight around me, squeezing me, but his warm hold didn't soothe the trembles. I felt so weak. Cethin and Sevrin were both fine, and yet, here I was shaking like a leaf in the wind. I urged my body to calm and my heart to return to normal, but it didn't heed my commands.

Slowly, Sevrin removed his arms from around me and pushed me into Cethin, who immediately drew me close. I pressed against him, burying my face in his neck. His deep floral scent tickled my nostrils and made me snuggle even closer. I hooked my arms around his back, gripping his shirt.

His bloodied hands stroked my hair and back, heedless of the gore he was spreading. "Your care of Aidan is much appreciated."

At first, I thought he was speaking to me, even though he'd said my name, but Sevrin replied, "He's like a brother to me. There is no question of me not caring for him."

"Nonetheless." Cethin wouldn't directly thank Sevrin, because to do so would acknowledge a debt existed between them, and he would never admit such a thing. He held me tight against him. "Let me take care of you."

"We have a physician at the manor," Sevrin said as his feet crunched on the loose rocks.

Cethin, with me in his embrace, drew back. "I will care for Aidan."

"He needs to come home."

"I will allow nothing to happen to him and ensure that he arrives back at Byrne Manor tomorrow, but you are not taking him from me," Cethin said, his voice cold and resonating with power.

I squeezed him. I didn't want anything to happen to Sevrin. He was trying to protect me as much as Cethin was.

"Fine," Sevrin said, reluctance laced through the single word. "I will have to notify my father about your return. Aidan said he sent you away."

"I never left."

"Aidan, did you lie?" The happiness in his tone made me start and forced me to glance at him. Sevrin was staring at me with a broad smile. Why he would be happy I'd lied was beyond me.

"No," I answered, returning to my earlier position against Cethin's neck. "I insinuated Cethin was gone. I *had* asked him to leave."

Cethin chuckled. "Very clever."

"Ah," was all Sevrin said.

The moment dragged on, but as Cethin held me and whispered in my ear, my trembles began to calm and my pulse returned to normal. I'd all but forgotten Sevrin was there until he said, "Please bring Aidan back to the manor tomorrow or we will come looking for him."

"I will bring him back if he wants to come; otherwise, he will remain with me." Cethin started to direct me to the trees. "Burn the fae body. You humans have a nasty gift of bringing back the dead."

"There hasn't been a necromancer in I don't even know how long."

"Nevertheless," Cethin said, heading straight to the forest, "burn the corpse to ash."

When the tree boughs covered us, the rest of the tension leaked out of my body and left me tired. I sagged against Cethin's side, his arm propping me up. A few birds chirped from their nests and the damp smell of molding leaves hung in the air. My feet smashed the twigs and underbrush littered on the ground, while Cethin was perfectly silent, passing through the woods with nary a noise.

He wound in a nonsensical pattern I didn't bother to pay any mind to. Cethin wouldn't lead me into any danger. Instead, my eyes followed the pattern of light the interstices in the tree branches created. The light danced as the trees shivered in the wind and squirrels leaped from branch to branch. Soon the rushing sound of water joined the symphony of the forest.

The cottage Cethin claimed appeared. A fish broke through the surface of the clear creek and landed with a loud splash, making me start. The cottage appeared the same with its wood siding and stone chimney, completely surrounded by grass. There was one change, though. A simple log bridge spanned the creek.

"You built a bridge."

"Yes," he replied stiffly.

I turned around, and his eyes wouldn't meet mine. From his tightened shoulders and flattened lips, I could assume he was angry, but I doubted that. In my eyes, he seemed embarrassed.

Without allowing myself even a single thought, I cupped his cheeks and drew him to my lips. The closer Cethin got, the faster he moved until we crashed into one another. I was still angry. I was still scared. And I was still worried about where this relationship would lead, but I couldn't deny these feelings.

Chapter 16

"Pain and love often go hand in hand." – Lord Keegan, Fourth Lord of Sídhetír.

Cethin carefully dried my hair, his movements gentle and slow, as if he was afraid he would damage me. I'd had to bathe to get rid of the dirt and blood from my earlier encounter. The warm water Cethin had heated for me helped ease the pain in my ribs and the tightness of my muscles.

The cottage was unchanged from my earlier visit, except for the fire burning in the fireplace, bringing warmth to the chilly autumn night, and the two new things gracing the mantle. First was the tin I'd given Cethin for the burns on his hands. Second was the apple I'd offered him, though it glimmered with magic. Both rested in the center like treasured objects.

Once satisfied, he tossed the towel aside and snagged a blanket from the bed, wrapping the soft fabric around me. I wished for a cup of Iris's tea or, better yet, to see her, but somehow, I didn't think

Cethin would be amenable to that suggestion. Also, I truly didn't want to move. I felt safe right here.

"Let me clean myself up," Cethin whispered, then moved to the metal tub. I didn't bother to avert my gaze. I'd seen him naked already, and fair was fair—Cethin had closely watched me as I bathed.

He stepped into the same water I'd used and began to wipe the ichor off his skin with brusque movements. My eyes feasted on him, and I couldn't even muster up a feeling of shame or embarrassment for the act.

His long legs were toned, as were his arms. His abs were well defined, much more so than mine. Tattoos wound up his limbs and covered his back. The thorns kissed the edge of his jaw. The mark on his sternum, the crescent moon with the seven-pointed star, glowed in the low light. The center of his stomach was bare, though. It, plus his face, were the only unmarked parts of his skin—even his firm ass had thorny swirls.

"Enjoying what you see?" Cethin asked, scrubbing his long hair.

"Yes." I had no reason to lie. Besides, it was obvious I was. Cethin was gorgeous, and he was mine. My cock started to harden at the thought. Cethin *was* mine. I would never have to part with him. He would give me a place to belong. Someone to belong to, and with. If Lord Abnus was to be believed, Cethin was my mate.

Cethin stepped out of the tub and dried himself with far less care than he had me. Water continued to drip off the white strands of his hair, splattering the floor. He donned a clean set of clothes before sitting behind me, his legs bracketing mine while his arms loosely wrapped around my waist. He buried his face in my neck, inhaling deeply.

My cock leaped again, forcing me to think of innocuous things. The smell of grass. Lord Byrne lecturing me. Iris cackling. The way Whit ate with little care, spraying food every which way. Anything. I thought of anything besides Cethin being as close to me as he was or the light scent clinging to his skin.

The anger from earlier had yet to disappear. It had certainly dimmed, probably due to my arousal and Cethin's close proximity, but I wasn't ready to forgive him, or to accept the fact he'd forced me into a marriage without my leave.

He rubbed his face against my neck. "You need to sleep."

I swallowed as memories began to trickle in. The screams. The wet squelching sound of Cethin ripping the light fae's head off. On their tail was the remembrance of Mr. Hillridge on the flames and the two massive fae's heads swinging from Cethin's clawed fingers.

The instant I closed my eyes, those scenes would come back to haunt me like a ghost living in the corridors of my mind. I didn't know how to excise the memories, and deep down, I feared they would never fade, rearing their ugly heads at the worst times.

"Come. I will guard your sleep." Cethin's hands slid to my elbows. With a light pressure, he helped me to my feet and directed me to the bed along the back wall. A blush heated my cheeks. The last, and only, time we were in bed together came flooding back.

My pulse increased, pounding in my ears until it was all I heard. Several moments passed before I realized the *tap tap tap* sound I heard wasn't my heart, but rather rain beginning to beat upon the roof.

Hugging myself, I sank to the edge of the bed. A stabbing ache in my ribs stole my breath, drowning all else out. Cethin draped a blanket over me before joining me on the bed. His arm came to rest on my waist. When I twisted my head to see his face, I saw Cethin staring anywhere but me. His eyebrow twitched and a tic pulled at the corner of his lips.

Was he afraid I would reject him?

I wasn't going to, because I quite liked the weight of his arm upon me, and I didn't want him to stop touching me. My eyes began to close, but I fought the sensation of sleep, blinking hard. Cethin tightened his arm, not enough to cause me pain but enough to reassure me of his presence. I forced the circling sleep away because we needed to talk.

"Are we mates?" I asked, staring at the ceiling.

"In what sense?"

"In the fae way. Is that why you put your mark on me?"

"Yes."

Abnus had been right.

"I want to not be angry at you."

He pressed his forehead into my shoulder, holding me tight like he was afraid I was going to run. "But you are."

I was and I wasn't at the same time. I cared about Cethin, which made it hard for me to stay angry at him. After speaking with Abnus, I understood more why Cethin had done what he had. He'd been dying, and I was there—his mate. Of course, he'd claimed me.

"My feelings are real, Aidan. Everything I have done is not because of the bond between us, but because of my feelings for you."

"I wish I could believe that."

"I cannot lie. I care about you. I want to know you. Yes, you are my mate, but I would have been intrigued by you regardless."

I turned to look at him. In the low light from the fire, I couldn't see his expression clearly, but what I saw was earnest.

He gently touched my cheek. "I love you, Aidan, and I'm not saying this so you'll forgive me. I truly love you. Deeply."

Wincing in pain, I rolled over with his help. I held his face between my hands and stared at him as tears started to gather in my eyes. I was grateful the low light hid them, or at least I thought it did. I wasn't sure how well Cethin could see in the dark.

"You love me?" I asked.

"I do. Desperately. The polite thing to do was to ask you for your hand. Woo you." He smirked. "But I took what I wanted—you, and I'm not sorry I did. You are the best thing in my life."

I tugged his face closer to rest my forehead against his. He continued to hold me as we simply breathed each other in. His words had softened my anger, dampened my fear, and soothed my worries. I didn't want to be without him. He was mine.

My breath began to deepen as sleep started to take me away. I shook it off, not ready to surrender yet. I wanted to keep talking to Cethin. There was so much to learn, and I had so many questions left. What would happen in the future? How were we going to work as a married couple?

"Sleep," Cethin said when I shook my head again to ward off sleep. "I will allow nothing and no one to harm you."

My hand found his, our fingers intertwining. "Don't leave."

"Where would I go? You are everything."

Heat brushed my cheeks, but I couldn't open my eyes nor force my lips to form a response.

"As I have said, but will remind you again, you are an idiot," Iris commented as she placed a steaming cup of tea in front of me.

Wafts of a bitter medicinal flavor made my lip curl. She raised an eyebrow, staring pointedly at the cup. Nose wrinkling, I took a sip and grimaced. The taste was far worse than I anticipated. The liquid somehow possessed the essence of dirty grass and bitter greens at the same time. It was foul. I wouldn't have even forced it upon my worst enemy, though I might have given it to Oren in a lark to watch his eyes bulge.

I swallowed convulsively in an attempt to rid my tongue of the horrid flavor. It didn't want to dissipate. Instead, the putrid flavor lingered on the back of my palate, making a home there.

Iris ambled over to the kitchenette and pulled a jar painted with roses off a shelf. She placed several biscuits on a plate and set the offering in front of me. "It would serve you right to have the horrid taste of medicine in your mouth for hours to come, but I like you. Have a biscuit."

Crunching on the treat, I gave Iris a full-cheeked smile, which she returned.

When I awoke this morning, Cethin had been curled around me, his breath warm against my neck. It had taken every ounce of control I possessed not to squeeze him tight and trail my lips over his smooth skin, but I didn't move so I could linger in his hold.

Cethin had remained amiable until I'd informed him of my decision to see Iris. My ribs ached something fierce, to the point each breath was short and sharp. My skin was decorated in bruises. All this didn't even come close to the dreams that plagued my sleep. I'd known they were coming, and yet, they stole my breath and sent prickles to the backs of my eyes.

He'd scowled as he hovered over me, attempting to keep me in bed. He'd repeated, several times, that he was capable of caring for me. It wasn't until I placed a quick kiss on his lips and told him I knew he could, but I wanted to see my friend that he'd been mollified. He'd walked me to the glen with Iris's cabin, though he'd refused to approach or enter the clearing. Instead, he remained under the trees, glaring daggers at the harmless-looking building.

Iris cleared her throat, drawing me to the present. "So you confronted a light fae with nothing but an iron key. Idiotic."

"Cethin killed the light fae."

"I'm sure he did." She shuddered. "Noble fae are terrifying."

I frowned. "What?"

"What?" she repeated, taking a drink of tea.

Letting it go, I gripped my left arm. "Did you know what this mark meant?"

"The death curse?" she asked.

I rolled my eyes. "It's not a death curse. It's... an engagement mark."

Her eyebrows raised. "You're engaged to a dark fae. I'm sure you were surprised."

"To put it mildly."

"I knew he had 'fuck your life' aura written all over his inhumanely gorgeous face."

She had indeed said that. It was one of the reasons she wouldn't even touch him when Cethin had been lying injured on the floor of her cottage. In many ways, he had fucked my life, and in others, not so much.

A sly grin tugged on her lips. "I'm sure he will *fuck* you within an inch of your life."

Heat slammed my face.

"Maybe he already has." Iris laughed, her amber eyes twinkling.

My mouth opened, but the only sound that came out was strangled and possessed no logical meaning.

Humor fading, she rested a hand on mine. "How are you handling the change?"

"As well as can be expected." I took another sip of the tea and fought a gag. The brew was truly disgusting, but Iris had promised it would help the pain and promote healing. None of her previous concoctions had failed, and I had no reason to doubt this one, even if it possessed the foul taste of hell.

Iris cocked an eyebrow. "Truly?"

I shrugged.

"Hmm." She pursed her lips. "Should I curse him?"

"Excuse me?"

"I know a good one." Iris rubbed her hands together as a wide smile stretched over her face. "It will turn his penis spotted before making it fall off."

I choked. "I beg your pardon?"

"I've never had an excuse to use it, but I will. For you."

I truly had no words in response, though from the way Iris was staring at me with gleaming eyes, I had to find one, quickly, or Cethin would suffer an unexpected consequence.

"A generous offer to be sure," I said. "But I'd rather you didn't."

She nodded, leaning back. "I see. You enjoy his penis."

Heat swamped my cheeks as I coughed again.

"No shame in it." Iris patted my hand, rising from her seat to totter over to a shelf full of tins and jarred herbs. She tossed me a metal tin without any embellishments on it. "Here."

"And this is?"

"Lubrication."

My mouth fell open and my eyes widened. "W-what?"

"Lubrication. I sell some to couples of all types. Everyone needs some." She waved my question off while she settled back in her abandoned chair.

If I'd thought my cheeks were warm, I did not have a true understanding of heat. Embarrassment gathered in my stomach, making me shift on the chair.

Iris shook her head. "I'll never understand why people get embarrassed about such a basic need. Of course you enjoy sex with him, but you need proper lubrication, no matter who's on top. If you are bottoming, make sure you are well prepared, so it doesn't hurt. Do you need me to explain the process?"

Mouth agape, I shook my head rapidly. Dear God, I truly hoped Iris would be silent. I did *not* want to have this conversation with her or anyone. Shit. The Byrne brothers would want to speak with me about it. There would be no escape from the awkward conversations. They all had good intentions, but damn them, it was embarrassing.

"Let me know when you're out," Iris said. "If you are using it faster than you can call on me, I will give you two next time."

"Iris," I started in a strangled voice.

"Yes?"

"You know I appreciate..." I trailed off and waved at the innocent tin on the tabletop. "But can you stop?"

Laughter spilled out of her. "Oh, Aidan, I do love you."

At her words, a smile forced itself to my face and banished the curling embarrassment. "I love you too."

"Of course you do. I'm amazing. Who wouldn't love me?"

I chuckled and finished my foul tea.

Cethin was right where I'd left him, against the tree outside of Iris's glen. His arms were crossed, but the left side of his lips quirked up as his eyes tracked my every move. As I reached his side, he lifted a hand, pausing. When I didn't shy away, he cupped my cheek, thumb brushing my cheekbone. The arc of his thumb sent tingles down my spine.

"Is all well?"

I nodded.

"Do you want to stay at my cottage?" he asked, stilling.

"I should go back."

His eyes flickered. "I see." After a second, he slid closer until a hair separated our bodies. "Can I visit you tonight?"

"Yes." My hand curled around the tin in my pocket Iris had insisted I take. We would in no way need it tonight, but I wanted to spend time with Cethin. I wanted to fall asleep next to him and wake up next to him. I was fairly certain I was going to desire him staying by my side for as long as I lived.

Chapter 17

"Be careful, dear heir. For where your heart leans, your mind will follow, and where your mind goes, Sídhetír listens and responds." – Lord Louis, Third Lord of Sídhetír.

When I arrived at the manor, I was besieged by people. Oren was in the front of the assault, his eyes wet and his hands hesitant, like he truly feared he would do further injury to me. I appeared far worse than I actually was. My bottom lip was split and a massive bruise decorated the side of my face, and those were the only visible injuries, but it was enough.

The brothers swarmed around me like bees, buzzing in a cloud of worry mixed with anger. The anger was directed at me, but the root of it nestled in fear, so their pinched expressions and tight voices didn't stab deep.

I was hurt and had stayed out overnight with a dark fae; of course they were upset.

I stifled a laugh. If Cethin and I hadn't already been engaged, Lord Byrne could've demanded he marry me because he'd "ruined" me when he took me away without a chaperone. I was over twenty, so an adult, but I hadn't reached my majority of thirty. I required a chaperone, though my low birth helped shield me from scrutiny. Not that it mattered. Cethin was already tied to me.

Oren led the charge, insisting I get seen by the physician, Ilene Maher. I politely declined, but the Byrnes wouldn't hear of it, even when I told them my fiancé had taken care of me. After a quick examination, where she tutted at me as much as Iris had and asked multiple questions about the deceased fae, I was planted in Lord Byrne's bookroom.

This time Lord Byrne and I were not alone. Lady Hester and Oren hovered behind his shoulders while the rest of the brothers filled the space, making the air warm and stagnant. I wished this conversation had been held outside in the garden, but that wouldn't have been private. Though the fae representatives could overhear us through the oak door, if they chose to eavesdrop.

A vision of the two austere fae pressed against the solid door in an attempt to catch the slightest word bloomed inside my mind's eye. I stifled a chuckle, sensing my amusement wouldn't be appreciated in the tense environment and would result in an even more severe scolding than I was about to receive.

Lord Byrne steepled his hands. His even breaths and the tightness of his shoulders spoke to the worry, if not anger, raging within him. During the thirteen years living in his household as a ward, then Oren's aide, I could count on one hand—and have leftover fingers—the times I'd seen such an expression directed at me. Yet in the last two weeks, I'd seen it multiple times.

I'd never caused trouble before, though I didn't regret my actions.

Something rumbled pleasantly deep within me. I didn't know whence it came, but it was there all the same. An awareness of something with no words or thoughts was rooted within me, burrowing deep. My eyes flicked to my left arm as my thoughts turned to the bloom growing on my forearm. Cethin, maybe?

"Aidan," Lord Byrne said in a stern voice tinged with betrayal, "did you lie to me about your fiancé still being here?"

"No," I said, for I truly hadn't, and yet I had omitted the fact he probably was. "I told you I had asked him to leave, which I did."

"Did you know he was here?"

"I knew it was a possibility."

His frown deepened. He opened his mouth to speak, but Lady Hester rested a hand on his shoulder. "Why didn't you tell us?" she asked. "Did you fear our disapproval?"

My feelings at that moment had been complicated. I hadn't wanted to see Cethin, but I had at the same time. Not to mention the unnamed urge to protect him. I parsed through what to say, but I couldn't find the right words. I shrugged in response.

"Do you care for him?" she asked.

"Yes." I would not deny my feelings for Cethin.

Lady Hester came around the desk to hold my face between her petite hands. "While I don't approve of this rushed engagement, he saved your and Sevrin's life. He has earned my thanks, even if I won't tell him."

"I want to meet him," Lord Byrne said before I could reply to Lady Hester. His demand was echoed by each of the Byrne brothers. There would be no escape, and if he was to be my husband, he did need to meet the people who had raised me after my mother died.

"I will ask him."

With that, the tension in the room began to dim, but still an undercurrent thrummed. Thomas and Whitaker shared a look, then glanced at their father, who, in return, met their gazes. Even Lady Hester was tense, gripping Lord Byrne's shoulder. The others seemed calm, but something was setting the aforementioned people on edge.

"Sevrin told me what occurred with the light fae," Lord Byrne said after a few moments of silence. "While I applaud the initiative, it wasn't wise to approach a fae, especially when only one of you was armed."

Whit glared at me, and my shoulders slumped. We'd all been taught how to defend ourselves. I had an iron dagger—several in fact—but I'd left the manor without one each time, even when Sevrin and I intended to search for the fae.

"Next time, if you see a fae, please get help before confronting them," he finished.

It was a reasonable request, and my aching ribs were a testament to my desire not to run into another random fae.

Sevrin slung an arm over my shoulders. "You haven't met Cethin yet, but trust me, he would never allow anything to hurt Aidan."

"Cethin? Is that his name?" Lord Byrne asked, hand lifting to grab Hester's.

I had kept his name to myself for reasons I didn't understand, but Sevrin had heard me call Cethin by his name when he rescued us. "Yes."

The creases in Lord Byrne's forehead deepened as he glanced at his wife. "That name is familiar."

"It is," she replied, placing a hand on her chin. "But I cannot recall from where."

"Have you met him before?" Lord Byrne asked.

"No."

"Hmm. I will have to keep thinking on it," he said. "I expect to meet him. Tomorrow, perhaps?"

"I will ask, but I cannot make Cethin do anything."

"I want to meet him." Lord Byrne's voice hardened.

Thomas stepped forward. "We all do, Aidan. Bring him home."

"I will try."

A sharp rap invaded my consciousness. I groaned, rolling over. My room was dark, except for a low fire warding off the chill from the autumn night. Wind rustled outside, and something rumbled deep within me, soothing me. Waves of sleep washed over me, and I sighed.

The tapping came a second time, and I snarled something unintelligible as I searched for the source.

It had been a long day of people fussing over me, which had been one part lovely, because it made me feel cared for, and one part annoying, because I wasn't allowed to stir without someone saying something.

Oren had been the only one absent for most of the day. When I did finally see him, he'd been speaking with Lord Abnus again, buried in the corner of the library, drinking tea. A huge smile had graced Oren's face; that and his relaxed posture spoke to his ease with the dark fae.

Blodwen had gained no ground, but where she failed, Abnus triumphed. It seemed Sídhetír would align with the Night Court. Oren had made no decisions, even when Lord Byrne pressed. He simply said he didn't feel compelled to do so, though his hesitation was extending the transition.

The sharp noise came yet again, drawing me to the present. I threw off the blankets and scoured the room for the offender. When I shifted to the window, I paused before racing across the room, arm around my ribs. I threw the window open, and Cethin climbed in, wings vanishing.

"Aidan."

"You came."

"I said I would."

"Why didn't you come in like last time?"

His expression tightened. "I didn't know if you would accept me."

I took his hand, and Cethin didn't resist. We settled beneath the covers, and his black eyes ran over my face, glinting in the flickering firelight. His fingertips trailed over the bruise on my face, his touch so light it caused no pain.

"Lord Byrne wants to meet you, as do all of his sons."

"All his sons, you say?"

"Yes."

"Hmm," Cethin commented, his fingers continuing their exploration.

"Will you meet with them?"

"If you want me to."

I wouldn't say want was the correct word. "I think you should."

"Then I shall. When?"

"Tomorrow."

"I will accompany you to breakfast," he announced in a bland voice.

"Excuse me?"

"I'm spending the night. Breakfast seems the most convenient time to meet them. Unless you would like to stay in bed? I would not be opposed to that."

Cethin had no way of knowing the impropriety of such a statement. While it wasn't uncommon for people to conduct sexual relationships prior to marriage, social conventions and the church demanded such relationships were not right until *after* marriage. Most simply kept them secret. Bringing him to breakfast was the same as announcing he had spent the night in my room, even if almost everyone already assumed we'd fucked.

"That may present problems," I said carefully.

"Why?"

"It will not be a private setting, and the fae representatives will be there courting Oren's favor. Do you wish to meet with them?"

"No," he replied.

"Then you will have to wait until later in the afternoon, but you can stay in my room."

He glanced around. "I don't mind that."

With the problem settled, I closed my eyes in an attempt to go back to sleep, but I couldn't. My pulse skittered from the light scent wafting off Cethin. The thorns on my arms throbbed. Cethin rested an arm on my waist as he moved closer, and my stomach swooped. My cock had begun to stiffen from his close proximity. It took literally nothing for Cethin to stir my desire.

Cethin's hand started to slide down my chest. "May I touch you?"

"Only if I can touch you."

"You may touch me whenever you like." His fingers grabbed the base of my nightshirt and pulled it over my head, and I winced.

With quick movements, Cethin tugged off his clothes, leaving him bare to my wandering fingers. The thorny vines moved under my touch, glowing. An invisible wind rushed over the flowers, making the petals move and silver pollen drift over his skin.

I placed his hand on the growing bud on my forearm. "What does it mean?"

Cethin kissed it, tongue tracing the petal. My cock hardened painfully. I easily recalled that skilled tongue on me.

"Our bond is deepening." His mouth slid up my arm, pressing kiss after kiss on my skin until he paused on my collarbone. "There's another bud here."

In the darkness, I couldn't see it, but I trusted his word. "How many will I get?"

"Five."

His lips brushed the newest flower while his fingers curled around my cock and pumped, stroking from base to tip. I groaned, hips arching to follow the movement. My breath sharpened when my ribs screamed.

Cethin growled. "Do not harm yourself, Aidan."

"Don't stop," I ordered as I ran my fingers over his side, feeling the muscles contract. I tried to kiss him, but Cethin drew away. My mouth opened to complain, but he drew me into a seated position. "What?"

"Come here." Cethin settled me on his lap so our cocks touched. The tip of his cock glistened in the firelight as yet another bead of pre-cum slipped out. His breathing was as uneven as my own. His long fingers slid over my slit, making me moan, then swiped the pre-cum off his own cock before wrapping around both of us, pressing us together. Caged between his fingers, he slid up and down, and I groaned at the slippery friction, head falling back.

I gripped his shoulders, biting my lip. "Fuck, Cethin."

He chuckled. "You may if you like, but you are too injured at the moment."

Heat welled in my stomach as my cock stiffened even further. Did he mean that? I'd assumed I would be on the receiving end.

He picked up speed and stole all thought. I pressed my mouth to his, kissing him frantically as I shoved my tongue inside to taste him. Cethin groaned against my lips, his fingers moving even faster.

My balls drew up tight against the base of my shaft as pleasure began to build with each stroke. When I thought I would explode, Cethin stopped. I released a guttural noise and bit his lip. He chuckled, but his fingers did not return to their earlier pumping. Instead, he circled the head of my cock.

Eyes closed, I moaned. "Shit."

He kissed my neck, sucking and biting me. His whisper-soft touches along my cock lit a fire in me until I was writhing on his lap, trying to rub on his stomach in an attempt to seek friction of any kind. I was so close and desperate for release.

I reached down, pinning our cocks together, and began pumping. The touch felt so amazing, it was almost painful. My ass clenched as my balls tightened further. My mouth attacked Cethin's. I sucked on his tongue and nibbled his lips. I knew when he was getting close because he growled my name and panted against my mouth.

With one last stroke, we both erupted. Thick ropes of white cum splattered our chests. I tried to keep stroking us as we came, but I couldn't, lost in the sweeping pleasure that drew a shout from my lips. Cethin's hand wrapped around mine, and he milked our cocks for every last drop.

When we finished, I panted, sagging against Cethin. He kissed me gently, both of us spent and sated. Slowly, he helped me lay back until I rested against the sheets. He hovered over me, kissing me slowly. I traced my fingers over the vines on his ribs, unable to stop touching him.

After a moment, he pulled back and I reached for him. "Where are you going?"

"To get a cloth to clean you up." He grabbed a towel next to the washing bowl on my dresser. He wiped my release off my stomach and cleaned my limp cock, making me blush, before doing the same for himself. Cethin snuggled against me, holding me close.

I kissed the hollow of his throat. "Can I ask you a question?"

"Yes."

"Are you mad that I'm your mate?"

"No," he instantly replied. "You are the best thing in my life, Aidan."

"Then why didn't you tell me?"

"Words are difficult for me, and I feared you would leave. That our bond would scare you. Mates are not a human concept, and all you know is humanity."

"But I needed you to tell me, Cethin. I need you to tell me the words. Not knowing makes it worse."

"I will try. Please be patient with me. I have been alone for a very long time."

Chewing on my lip, I asked, "How old are you?"

"Such a question is impossible to answer. Time moves differently in the fae realm than in yours, and we noble fae are unconcerned with our age once we reach adulthood. But I am very old."

I pushed the thought away. I refused to allow his far greater age to rob the happiness of this moment. "You're mine, right?"

"I am only yours."

Arms hooked around his waist, I pressed my face against his chest, inhaling his scent. Fair was fair. Besides, it was the truth. "And I am only yours."

Chapter 18

"A lie is not the absence of truth, but rather the absence of courage." – Lord Finbar, Fifth Lord of Sídhetír.

I woke once again to a knock, but this was more of a pounding. Cethin stiffened beneath me. I was sprawled on top of him, the blanket askew. My eyes were blurry as I glanced around my empty room.

Cethin's arm tightened around me, a snarl sounding in the back of his throat. "What is going on?"

I patted his chest. "I don't know, but I'm sure it's fine."

Suddenly, my door burst open. Thomas stood in the doorway, and he wasn't alone—Oren and Sevrin were right behind him.

"Sweet God above," Thomas cursed.

"Thomas," I squeaked, seizing the blanket to cover me and Cethin, ribs screaming, while trying to keep him on the bed beneath me. I did not need Cethin attacking the Byrne brothers because they were rude enough to barge into my room unannounced.

Sevrin slung an arm over Thomas's shoulders. "Told you they were close."

Cheeks bright red, Oren moved in front of his brothers and began shoving their much larger frames out of the door.

"Wait," Thomas called. "He's been asleep all morning. We're supposed to bring him to Father's bookroom."

"Let them get dressed," Oren said.

Sevrin laughed. "Now we know why he slept so long."

The last thing I heard before the door slammed closed was their laughter.

Cethin's arm tightened around me as he pressed his face into my hair. "We should stay in the cottage. No one will bother us there."

Somehow, I doubted that was true. The Byrne brothers were nothing if not persistent. If I disappeared for a few days, they would brave the forest to find me, and who knew what trouble they would encounter?

He nuzzled the side of my head, and I pressed close. Normally, his skin was cooler than mine, but since he'd been in bed with me all night, he held the same warmth I did.

"I like awakening to your face," Cethin muttered.

Warmth surged to my cheeks that had nothing to do with the earlier embarrassment. "I do too."

I squawked as Cethin rolled on top of me. My side didn't even twinge from the sudden movement because he was exceedingly gentle.

"You should sleep in the cottage with me tonight, so we are not bothered by overprotective brothers."

"True."

He pressed kisses down my neck. "I will let you fuck me."

I swallowed, remaining firm, and he pressed a kiss to the apple of my throat.

"I will answer more questions. Anything you want to know about me."

My curiosity exploded. Cethin was old. He knew a lot about many things. More than that, I could learn more about him. "We'll see."

"Hmm," he muttered as he continued to trail kisses down my body, stalling on the new bud on my collarbone. He nibbled at the new mark, paying particular attention to it for several long moments. When he dipped even further and my cock twitched, I grabbed his chin to stop his movements.

"We need to get dressed, so you can meet Lord and Lady Byrne and their sons."

"I believe I've already met some of them." Cethin's chin rested on my stomach as his pure black eyes stared at me.

Chuckling, I carded my fingers through his silky hair. "That you did."

He pressed another kiss right above my navel before he sat up. "But I will meet the rest of the horde if I must."

"You must."

I walked down the corridor with Cethin beside me. He wore the same loose black shirt—which was far too revealing—and tight black trousers that he always did, and God, he was lovely.

His fingers slid through my hair, and I leaned into his touch. "Thank you for doing this."

He traced the shell of my ear. "I would do anything for you, Aidan."

"I know." I glanced at him as unease coiled in my stomach. "Please don't keep things from me."

"I am trying to get better with sharing. Tonight, we'll talk again," he said, caressing my cheek. "I shall endeavor to tell you everything you may or may not wish to know."

A secret smile tugged on my lips as I patted the tin in my pocket. I didn't want to forget it. Cethin had offered to let me fuck him, and I wasn't going to turn him down. Talking and fucking, fucking and talking. It sounded like a lovely evening to me.

I rapped on the door to Lord Byrne's bookroom, and not a moment passed before he ordered us to enter. Much like when I'd met with Lord Byrne yesterday, the room was full of the entire family. Hester and Oren flanked Lord Byrne, and the brothers filled the various spaces, leaving the two chairs in front of the desk free.

Cethin smirked at the group and strode forward. Ignoring the chairs, he pulled me in front of him and slung his arms around my waist, resting his chin on my shoulder. "You must be Lord Byrne, though not for much longer. Even now, Sídhetír is slipping from your grasp."

Lord Byrne's jaw clenched, and a tic started in his cheek from the pressure. Lady Hester placed a hand on her husband's shoulder. "You are Cethin?"

"I can be called that, and you are free to do so if you wish."

"You saved both Aidan and Sevrin," Lady Hester said. "Words cannot express how grateful I am for your actions."

I heard the approval in his voice as he said, "You are wise with your words, and I applaud you for the careful choice. Now let me be clear with mine. No force in this or any other realm will take Aidan from me while I breathe."

My cheeks burned. I couldn't see his face, but I knew he was serious. Cethin would protect and keep me. A deep rumble started in my chest again as a sense of rightness flooded me.

"I see," Lord Byrne said while Hester blinked at Cethin's strong words. She was not alone. Most of the brothers stared at him, wide-eyed, though only Nevan gaped like a hooked fish. "You intend to go through with this engagement."

"There is no way to undo the bond between us, and if there were, I would never desire it," he said.

My hand gripped his. "I want to stay with Cethin."

Lord Byrne's face tightened as he stared at the desk. "I do not know if that is wise, or if I can allow it."

"Allow?" Cethin asked, his voice turning frigid as the air in the bookroom dropped. "It is done. As Aidan accepts this bond, why would I abandon him?"

"Aidan is my ward."

"No," I said. "I stopped being your ward last year when I turned twenty. I am twenty-one, and no longer under your care."

"That may be so," Lord Byrne said, standing, "but I cannot allow this."

Cethin growled, his chest vibrating against my back. The room cooled further, allowing me to see my breath.

Thomas and Whit both glanced at their father before nodding at me.

"Break off the engagement," Thomas said. "You don't even know him. This engagement is happening too quickly. He forced you into this, Aidan."

"You'll meet someone else better. A human," Whit said. "Someone you will actually know."

Lady Hester cast me a soft smile, but her eyes would not meet mine.

Why didn't they want me to be with Cethin? None of them loved fae in general, but they weren't biased against them. Humans and fae had married before. Why couldn't I marry Cethin? Something was going on. Something I didn't understand.

Oren stepped forward. "I support you, and I'm to be the Lord of Sídhetír in a matter of days, as soon as I decide."

Phineas and Sevrin moved closer to Oren and pulled him back. His eyebrows lifted in askance, but his brothers didn't respond. Nevan and Neil shifted toward Oren, standing in front of him and forming a wall.

Nevan quietly said, "You don't know him, Aidan. I'm worried you're accepting him because you have no choice and because this engagement is happening too fast."

Neil nodded in agreement.

I looked at Phineas and Sevrin for support and I didn't find any, though Sevrin did give me a sad smile.

My heart began to pound. They were keeping something from me. They all were, with the exception of Oren. Whatever this secret was, it was different from the normal lovers, lies, or harmless scandals.

"I'm staying with Cethin," I said, my voice hard. I would brook no arguments. An answering rumble sounded outside. Thunder, a sure sign Lord Byrne was losing his temper. The ground shifted slightly, but it was enough to make the chandelier sway on its chain.

"Aidan," Lord Byrne said softly.

"If you want me to leave, I will do so posthaste."

"No," Oren shouted from behind the wall of his older brothers. A crack of lightning illuminated the room, followed by the roar of thunder. Perhaps it was Oren, not Lord Byrne, who was upset.

I took a deep breath in a small attempt to calm the hurt boiling inside of me. I wanted them to accept Cethin. Yes, they didn't know him. Yes, I hadn't known him for long. Yes, he'd forced me into a permanent bond. But I cared for him. He and I wanted to be together.

"No, Aidan," Lord Byrne said. "This is your home, and you don't have to go anywhere, but I don't want Cethin here."

"If you make Cethin leave, I will as well."

Cethin squeezed me. "That's unnecessary." He faced Lord Byrne with a hard smile. "I will abandon your manor, Lord Byrne, but Sídhetír is no longer yours and the heir does not desire my absence."

"No, he does not," Lord Byrne replied.

Cethin hugged me tighter and whispered, "I will come for you tonight, dearest. We have much to talk about."

Lord Byrne's expression hardened. "You are not taking Aidan."

"Just for the night. Aidan doesn't wish to leave permanently, I believe."

"No, I don't." I wished I did. I wished I could leave all this behind and stay with Cethin, but I couldn't. I would miss Oren and the rest of the Byrne brothers. Byrne Manor had been my home for over ten years, and to leave would hurt more than words could express.

I led Cethin outside, and we were closely followed by the entire Byrne clan. I paid them no mind. The sun was obscured by thick, gray clouds, and a wind had picked up, rattling the few leaves on the trees and raising gooseflesh on my arms.

Cethin smirked at the people gathered behind us, mischief gleaming in his pitch-black eyes. He pressed his lips against mine as he gripped my ass, drawing me flush against him before attacking my mouth with his tongue. A blush raced to my cheeks from the inappropriate kiss. I didn't pull away, though I did slap his hands away from my backside.

After longer than was seemly, he shifted back. His thumb traced the swell of my bottom lip. "I will see you tonight."

He cast a glance at the people behind me and raised his eyebrows. Whether it was in challenge or an unspoken question, I couldn't say, but Lord Byrne muttered something unintelligible. I gripped Cethin's fingers, unwilling to let him go. Foolish, I knew, for I would see him in a few hours.

My eyes tracked his every movement as he spread his leathery wings and flew over the hedge surrounding the estate. When he became nothing but a speck in the distance, I faced the Byrne family. Oren, red-faced, smiled at me—his romantic heart was clearly pleased with the recent developments—and the rest watched me with wary eyes, as if I would begin spouting questions or accusations about their actions. I held my peace because I wanted to hear what Cethin had to say and gather my thoughts before I demanded they accept my choice.

I held out an arm for Oren, and he leaped forward to tuck his hand in my bent elbow. Arm-in-arm, we started for the gardens. While the air was nippy and the wind fierce, I wanted to stay outside. Both of the fae representatives had met me now, so I had no reason to not spend the day with Oren.

"You know I support you and Cethin," Oren said, ignoring Whit and Sevrin, who followed us.

Patting his hand, I said, "I appreciate it."

"There will be no reason for you to leave."

"So that's your game. Afraid I will leave with Cethin and never return?"

"Yes." Oren wouldn't meet my gaze as he worried his lip.

I yanked him closer. "Never, Oren. If I have my way, we will never part for long. You're my closest friend."

He beamed.

With every passing moment, the wind increased and the temperature dropped. Oren shivered, huddling close to my side, but he never suggested we return to the manor. Maybe he felt as I did; this gut-wrenching need to remain outside among the plants, touching the land.

"Have you decided who you're going to align with?" I asked, though I suspected I knew the answer.

Oren's fair cheeks pinked, and I fought back a smile. "I haven't decided, but I'm leaning a certain way. Father doesn't care in the slightest who I choose. I thought he would have more of an opinion, but since my birthday, he's been pressuring me to sign the contract."

That didn't seem like Lord Byrne. Who Sídhetír aligned with was the most important decision Oren would make as lord.

"Shall I guess where you're leaning?" I asked, keeping my voice light and teasing.

The color returned to Oren's cheeks and spread across the entirety of his face.

"Hmm," I said in mock concentration, placing my free hand on my chin. "Perhaps toward the attractive and attentive Lord Abnus?"

The red deepened, and I chuckled. Oren frowned. "He's offering an excellent trade deal."

"I'm sure he is."

Since the contract's origin, the Lords of Sídhetír had only aligned with the Night Court twice, and the current Lord Byrne's grandfather had been the last one. The Night Court had to be desperate for unfettered access to the doorway between the realms and an increase in their power.

"He is," Oren said, frown deepening, but the red of his cheeks didn't dissipate.

"It does help that he's attractive and easy to talk to."

He glanced at me, divot between his eyebrows. "How did you know that?"

I chuckled. "I've seen you chatting with Lord Abnus on a couple of occasions. You appeared so relaxed, like you were speaking to one of us."

"Ah."

We rounded the corner of the estate near the hedge maze, and Oren pulled out of my grasp to rush forward. Lord Abnus gave him the slightest smile in greeting, his purple eyes locked onto Oren. Lady Blodwen was right next to Abnus, but Oren paid her no heed.

"Lord Abnus," Oren called, stopped right in front of the towering lord. Never had Oren's short stature been so obvious, even compared to me, and I was near the dark fae's height.

Abnus inclined his head. "Mr. Byrne."

"Good afternoon, Mr. Byrne," Blodwen said with a wide smile.

Oren barely glanced in her direction as he said, "Hello, Lady Blodwen."

If she was bothered by his lack of attention, she gave no indication.

I glanced over my shoulder at Whit and Sevrin, grinning.

Sevrin returned it, draping an arm over my shoulder and pulling me down to his height. "He certainly is obvious with his preference."

Whit snorted. "He's obvious with his attraction, even though it will go nowhere."

Unfortunately, Whit was correct. Oren had to marry a human, and one who could bear him sons. He was nearly engaged to Miss Keira Quirke. I and one of Miss Quirke's maids had played chaperone for the couple on more occasions than I could count. Once the contract was finalized, I assumed so would his engagement and subsequent marriage be.

A pit formed in my stomach as Oren chuckled, smiling so brightly at the fae lord, who never looked away. Much like his dream to study at Wellington University, this attraction to Lord Abnus would result in nothing but heartache. Yet again, I wished he could be spared the fate of ruling Sídhetír. I would give anything to free him. But to free him was to damn the rest of us.

If the contract broke, fae would pour from the other realm unchecked. We would have no defense or ability to cast them out. Deals and death would become an everyday occurrence. The atrocities I'd witnessed would become normal, though I supposed other fae would come as well. Peaceful ones who wanted to live in harmony.

Blodwen watched the scene with an apathetic expression, which made me frown. Why wouldn't she care about the two of them connecting since it could end the Day Court's hold on the sole safe passage into the human realm? Perhaps she felt success was guaranteed because Lord Byrne and his father Quincy had chosen the Day Court.

She gave me a congenial smile that instantly set my teeth on edge. I watched her approach with my hands curled into my fists. Her head cocked as she studied me with her deep brown eyes. The flecks of green and gold within their depths began to glow with power.

Sevrin's arm tightened around my shoulders as he attempted to draw me away from the approaching fae, but I didn't allow myself to be moved. Like my feet had grown roots, I became an immovable force, which Sevrin couldn't shift no matter how hard he tugged.

"Mr. Ryan," Blodwen said with a slight incline of her head.

"Lady Blodwen. How are you finding this fall day?"

"Perfectly pleasant, though I much prefer spring and summer, as it aligns with the Day Court."

I nodded in concession. "I find I like all seasons in Sídhetír."

"Do you?"

"Yes." It didn't matter the time of year or the weather, I loved it all. Sídhetír held an air that soothed me. I had never left its bounds and I couldn't imagine doing so. "Have you no interest in speaking with Oren?"

"I am *far* more curious about something else."

My eyebrows raised, and Sevrin's hands were joined by Whit's, both attempting to yank me away from the fae, but I was made of iron. "Are you?"

She smiled again, taking a step closer, so she was a handbreadth away from me. "Indeed."

I gasped when a sharp pain nicked my stomach. Blodwen stepped back and lifted a thin silver needle with blood dripping down its length. My hand covered the offending injury and pulled away. My fingers held the barest tinge of red. My clothes had absorbed most of the blood since the wound was but a pinprick.

"What the hell did you do?" I snapped as thunder roared and the clouds thickened.

"I'm testing a theory. Why are the Byrnes trying to hide you? Why do my senses tingle around you? It makes no sense, and therefore, I must find the answers I seek." Blodwen lifted the needle until the point was straight. I expected the blood to fall, but it didn't. Instead, my blood circled the silver needle in a perfect spiral, not a single drop landing on the ground.

My mouth fell open, but no words came forth. Oren tried to move toward me, but Lord Abnus snagged his wrist, keeping him in place.

"What's this?" Lord Byrne asked when he entered the garden surrounding the hedge maze with the rest of his sons and wife at his side.

"She stabbed Aidan," Oren said, not trying to escape Abnus's hold.

Lord Byrne's brow creased as a deep frown marred his aspect. "You did what, Lady Blodwen?"

"I stabbed him with an enchanted silver needle," she answered in a bland voice, like she was commenting on the weather or an attractive table setting.

"Why?" Lord Byrne demanded, coming closer to me.

"Because I wanted to know what you're hiding, and now I do."

"What are you talking about?" I asked, stepping closer to her. The noise in my head had gotten louder to the point I had a hard time hearing anything else.

"You. He was hiding you. You are a half-fae. Why he felt the need, I have no notion. We care little about who raises mongrels."

I could not possibly be half-fae. "My mother was human."

She chuckled. "It does take two to form a child. Your father must have been a fae, a light one at that, though I doubt he was a noble fae from your aspect. It's why you stirred my senses."

Unwittingly, my gaze turned to the Byrne family, and none would meet my eye, except for Oren. His mouth hung agape and his eyes bulged in obvious surprise. He clearly had no knowledge of my parentage. But the rest of the Byrne family stood next to each other, all finding somewhere else to look.

Bells clanged in my head, drowning out all thought.

"I know you can touch iron, so you must not be able to lie."

"What?" I asked. What was happening?

"Mongrels always have one or the other, or both, weaknesses of the fae. Lie," she said. "Lie about something inconsequential. The color of the sky perhaps."

I opened my mouth to prove her assertion wrong, but my throat constricted and no words came forth. I swallowed and tried again. Nothing. I couldn't say something as simple as the sky was green... because it was not. My breath quickened as I shook my head. This was simply not possible. I was not a half-fae.

Blodwen grinned. "I thought as much. You're a half-fae, though I see no reason for Lord Byrne to hide you from me or Lord Abnus. Half-fae are common enough occurrences."

"My mother was not a..." I trailed off because I didn't know if that was the truth anymore. Had she been a fae? "She died. If she'd been a fae, she wouldn't have died."

With a sad smile, Blodwen wrapped her warm fingers around my wrist. "Oh, little halfling, not all fae are immortal. Some don't even possess any greater healing ability than humans. She could've been a fae and died."

"Let go of Aidan," Lord Byrne ordered, coming closer.

Her eyes flicked in his direction, then up at the gathering clouds. A flake of snow drifted down and landed on her nose. It was far too early in the season for snow, and yet here it was.

My breath came out in short gasps. This was not possible. I tried to force a lie out of my lips, but the untruthful words would not come forth, strangling me. The more I tried, the harder the snow fell and the faster the wind blew until it gusted around us. The ground trembled, making everyone besides me stagger.

"Perhaps it was not Aidan's fae blood you were hiding, Lord Byrne," Blodwen said.

"What?" Sevrin asked.

Blodwen began to whisper, holding the silver needle with my blood on it close. The only word I caught and understood was "athair." Father. My blood leaped off the needle and splattered across Lord Byrne's pure-white cravat.

"So that's what you hid," Blodwen said. "You care not for the fae blood of his mother, but rather, the human blood, your blood, that runs through his veins."

I shook my head. Lord Byrne could not be my father because that would mean... My eyes flicked to Oren. Hope burned on his face as the same thought occurred to him. I looked at Lord Byrne, and he stared at the ground, shoulders slumped. Lady Hester took his hand while Thomas and Whitaker moved to his sides. Phineas, Sevrin, Nevan, and Neil all stared at their father, our father, with wide eyes and mouths. They hadn't known.

Lord Byrne met my gaze. "I sired you, Aidan."

Chapter 19

"Magic can be tricked for a short time, but its vengeance will be threefold." – Lord Quincy, Seventh Lord of Sídhetír.

It felt like the earth dropped from beneath me. I didn't know which way was up. The voices surrounding me became nothing but blurs of noise with no meaning. Lord Byrne was lying. I was not his. How could I be his? It wasn't possible.

My mother would've told me. Wouldn't she? She wouldn't have kept such a thing from me. I swallowed. Vis Ryan had been against lying, but she hadn't told me who my father was. All she'd said was he was as good as dead to me.

She was correct. Lord Byrne could never have been my father. He might as well be dead.

Hands fisted, I tried to slow my breathing, but I couldn't. The bells ringing in my head grew louder and louder like I was in the belltower of the church.

Cethin, I thought. God, I wanted him to take me away from this. To hold me. To banish all thoughts.

"How old are you?" Blodwen snarled, shaking me. Her face had stretched, taking on a sharper, more feral appearance. Small conical horns protruded from her forehead.

I had no idea if she'd asked me this multiple times or if this was the first time. Oren was yelling, but Lord Abnus held him back. Lord Byrne and the rest of the Byrne brothers—my brothers—were shouting. Tears burned the backs of my eyes. I could have had a family. When my mother died, I could've been a part of this family, but Lord Byrne hadn't acknowledged my existence as more than a pitiful ward he'd taken in.

"Why?" I asked him, but if he heard me over the chaos, he didn't react.

Blodwen shook me again. "Are you older than Oren?"

Acid burned my throat. Lord Byrne had hidden his bastard, half-fae child because of when I was born. I was Oren's elder brother. I was the seventh son of Lord Byrne. The ground rumbled as the first tears slid down my cheeks. Oren was freed from his shackles, and I was chained by ones that had always been there.

She shook me again, her fingers digging into my wrists.

"You will let go of him, Blodwen, if you wish to retain your hands."

Cethin's voice washed over me, and some of the all-consuming panic dimmed.

Blodwen hissed, releasing me like I'd burned her.

I turned toward Cethin. His white hair was pulled into a high tail, leaving his long ears exposed. More tears slipped from my eyes, and faster than I could track, Cethin stood before me. He wiped the tears away with the pad of his thumb.

"What's wrong, my Aidan?"

I didn't answer, for the words wouldn't come. How could I iterate the fear, the anger, and the betrayal coursing through me? My language didn't have the words, and if it did, I didn't know them.

"Prince Cethin," Blodwen said, voice low and dark.

My eyes widened. *Prince?* He was a prince. Cethin's eyes didn't leave mine and his thumb continued to move in a smooth arc.

"I was going to tell you. Tonight."

No emotions bled through the wall of shock. His revelation was not even close to the most shocking of the afternoon. The snow continued to float down at increasingly fast intervals, and the wind had turned dangerous.

"Breathe, Aidan," Cethin whispered against my ear, so he could be heard over the gale. "You must calm yourself."

"You are the one who placed the mark on him?" Blodwen asked, but it sounded more like an accusation. "Do you deny it?"

"Why would I deny the obvious, Blodwen? Aidan is my mate," Cethin answered, his hands sliding down my back and hauling me against him.

She snarled, teeth sharp and pointed. "You are not allowed to become involved with the heir. It was an agreement between the two courts after the signing of the contract."

"It wasn't a formal promise, and I didn't know he was the heir until after the mark was struck. There is no unraveling the magic."

"It's an unfair advantage," she yelled.

Abnus said, "It hardly matters, Blodwen. Aidan is only half human. Can the contract even continue?"

"True," she said, facing Lord Byrne, who kept trying to catch my eye, but I couldn't look at him or any of the other Byrnes. *My family*. They were my family. "You attempted to trick us," she continued. "To bind your eighth son to us while holding back your true seventh son."

"Oren is my legitimate seventh son. I was never married to Aidan's mother," Lord Byrne said.

I scoffed. I was his bastard, half-fae son. How nice of him to proclaim it and the fact he didn't consider me his.

"You think magic cares about human nonsense?" she spat. "Aidan is the one to inherit Sídhetír. Even now, the land responds to his call."

"Oren is my seventh son," Lord Byrne repeated like he wanted to believe the words himself.

This time Lord Abnus chuckled without a trace of humor. "Repeating what you wish to be true does not make it so, your lordship."

Lord Byrne looked away, and Lady Hester took his hand. That action hurt my heart for some reason. They both had known who and what I was, and yet they had concealed it from me. They knew of Oren's desire to be free, and yet they'd forced him onto a path he didn't need to follow.

How could they?

The ground quaked, and the manor groaned, windows shattering under the strain.

How could they?

The wind danced across the garden as the snow fell so quickly the world turned white. It was quickly becoming a snowstorm, far too early in the autumn.

How could they?

"Aidan," Cethin said, holding me closer. "Breathe."

I couldn't do as he asked. My lungs refused to inflate, and black spots bounced in my vision.

Blodwen pointed at me. "You would deny who he is, Lord Byrne, when the very forces of nature are responding to him? Aidan is the heir, and you attempted to deceive us. That is an act of war."

"That seems a tad premature," Lord Abnus said.

She waved a hand at him. "I speak for my queen."

Abnus glanced at me and Cethin, not talking, but his look was enough. He couldn't speak for the Night Court when its prince was here. Cethin didn't bother to respond to Blodwen's declaration of war as he rocked me back and forth, making shushing noises.

Once again, Oren tried to move to my side, and once again, Abnus stopped him. I was grateful for his protection of Oren because I felt as if I was unraveling like frayed cloth. I didn't think I would harm Oren, but if something happened, I would never forgive myself.

Blodwen snarled and her glamour completely dropped, allowing me to see the true breadth of her shoulders, the strength of her muscles, and the green wings like a dragonfly's on her back.

"War will sweep you away," Blodwen said. "You hid your blood."

"This is unnecessary," Lord Byrne said. "A new contract can be struck."

Blodwen laughed. "Do you even remember the cost of the contract? Are you willing to bleed your sons dry, except for Aidan and possibly Oren?"

My head shot up, and I was not alone. All of the Byrne brothers turned to their—our father. There was one volume of the Sídhetír Memoirs that we weren't allowed to read, the one detailing the contract. The cost and how it was struck was carefully hidden to all, except for the Lord of Sídhetír himself.

"No," Lord Byrne said. "I am not Rhett. I will not give up my children to save others, but a war is unnecessary. Aidan can sign the contract."

"Can he?" she asked. "Are you positive? And why should we light fae accept it when he will be biased against us because of his bond with Prince Cethin?"

I buried my face against Cethin's neck. I didn't want to hear this. I wanted to vanish, but the land wouldn't absorb me, and I feared that even if it did, Cethin would not react well.

Lord Byrne and Blodwen kept arguing. None of my brothers joined the verbal battle. Around and around, Blodwen and Lord Byrne went, trading verbal blows. Lord Abnus jumped in every once in a while, demanding people calm down—no one heeded him.

"I don't want to be here," I whimpered.

Cethin's hands stalled on my back before returning to their previous motions. "I can take you away. Away from everything."

I didn't care where we went or about the consequences of fleeing. I merely wanted to disappear, to vanish from this fight. I needed to think without the clanging in my ears and the rumble of the ground, which I now recognized as Sídhetír.

"Place your arms about my shoulders and hold on tight," he ordered. I followed his directions, and Cethin's arms slid around my waist, securing me against him. Leathery wings spread out behind him, catching the wind and dragging us back without any effort.

"What are you doing?" Blodwen screeched.

"Cethin," Lord Abnus called.

Cethin's wings flapped, lifting us from the ground. "Taking my Aidan far away."

I felt a flash, as if the earth was warning me, and tree limbs moved in my direction, forming a wall that exploded moments later. Blodwen growled, hands dropping.

"Sídhetír belongs to my mate, Blodwen. No magic you use will touch us. If I die, so does he. It will never allow you to harm me." Cethin rose higher, and the temperature dropped even further, making me shiver.

The world whirled around me. All I could think about was Lord Byrne telling me I was his son. I was his son, and yet, he'd left me alone and Oren to suffer for a fate he didn't want. I was his. I was Sídhetír's. For so long, I'd been left to believe I belonged to no one and didn't have a place in this world. But I did. I had a family—one I already cared about.

I finally glanced around. We weren't close to Cethin's cottage, which I'd assumed was our destination. Instead, he was flying directly north.

"Where are we going?" I asked above the wind, but he didn't respond. I had no idea if Cethin's lack of response was due to him not hearing me or him not wishing to answer.

After several minutes, Cethin dove, and my stomach lodged in my throat. I squeezed my eyes shut, holding him as tight as possible. He landed on the ground, right outside of the treeline, with nary a bump. Cethin snagged my hand, stepping under the boughs without hesitation.

He led me through the trees as if he knew where he was going. I followed without a word, exhaustion dragging down my limbs and making my eyelids heavy. I wanted to lie down and sleep. Cethin walked on and on, steering me around fallen logs, underbrush, and holes with no trouble.

When he finally stopped, my breath was harsh and my bruised ribs ached. Hugging my waist with my free arm, I looked around and froze. My mouth turned bone dry as my heart thundered in my ears.

"Is that what I think it is?" I asked, my voice strained.

"Yes."

The gate to the realms stood before me.

Swirling strands of silver forged the gate, appearing like vines. In the center of the arch was a red seven-pointed star with a full moon on one side, and on the other, a glowing sun. Darkness gathered in the center with pinpricks of light. The hair on my arms raised as magic drifted from the gate in waves. Whispers came from nowhere and everywhere all at once. The voices begged me to walk through, to cross the barrier into the fae realm.

I balked, shaking my head. I couldn't go in there. I couldn't leave Sídhetír. I didn't want to leave Sídhetír. Roots curled around my feet, securing me to the land. No matter what was happening with the Byrnes, Sídhetír was my home.

Cethin tightened his hold on my fingers. "You can enter the gate."

I swallowed. He was right. I could safely step through the gate, but did I want to?

"Trust me."

I did, without question. I nodded, and Cethin stepped forward, leading me into the darkness.

Chapter 20

"The fae realm is as lovely as it is dangerous. Never step across the threshold for fear that you will become lost to its charms." – Lord Rhett, First Lord of Sídhetír.

I could not breathe. I could not see. I could not perceive anything but a crushing pressure squeezing me within an inch of my life. As fast as the pressure appeared, it vanished. The gate spat me out, and I took my first stumbling step into the fae realm—my mother's realm.

It was unlike anything I'd ever seen. A great scar stretched in front of me, jagged and rough with harsh mountains in the distance. On each side was barren, gray land without even a hint of life. The air was stagnant and cool, yet warm at the same time. The sky was twilight, neither bright nor dark.

To the right of the gate, the sun shone bright and unending. To the left hung the moon and the stars glimmering in the sky. The world had been perfectly split in half. The sun side was full of life and heat, and the night half had snow on the ground in places and brown leaves and dying grass in others. The seasons all existed at the same time.

Neverending night and day ruled each half of the fae realm.

Cethin tugged me into the night. "Come. I have a home not far from here."

"What is this place?"

"The seam. Where night and day meet."

He placed my arms around his neck, enfolding me in his embrace. His wings spread once again to lift us into the air. My eyes wandered the barren stretch that turned into night-kissed land. The grass was silvery in places and brown in others. Trees laden with fruit I'd never seen grew sporadically. Flowers bobbed in the slight wind, which held a touch of autumn warmth, though snow fell from the sky at the same time.

This whole place was impossible.

The flight went on and on, but I didn't speak, because the longer we flew, the more a pit grew within me, clawing at me, carving me out. Sídhetír was gone. I'd never left it before. I had lived in Sídhetír, and I expected to die in Sídhetír. Never had I been without its steady presence. A presence that had grown so slowly over the years, I failed to notice until now—when it was gone.

Eventually, Cethin landed, and I wiggled out of his embrace to gape at my surroundings. Blue flowers with long yellow stamens and deep green stems and leaves covered the entire glen. The wind brushed the petals, and silver pollen twinkled in the air like stars. Rugged mountains framed the horizon while trees with deep orange and red leaves surrounded the clearing, lending an air of privacy.

In the center of the glen stood a castle unlike any I'd ever seen before. It consisted of turrets with arched walks between them and the keep and ample balconies hanging from the sides. What made it truly unique was that the entire structure was crafted from frosted glass.

"Is that your home?"

"Our home, and yes."

Cethin held out a hand, and I slipped mine within it. Our steps were slow as we crossed the field of flowers, which matched the tattoos on our skin. I didn't speak, nor did he. The silence wasn't heavy; instead, it was peaceful. My earlier panic slid to the recesses of my mind, allowing me to exist in the moment.

When we stepped inside, a grand hall with a sweeping staircase and a glass chandelier greeted me. It was surprisingly light inside. Every surface reflected the candlelight and enhanced the bright light of the moon coming through the walls. My gaze blindly wandered over the rugs and fine-carved furniture as we went upstairs to a bedroom—Cethin's, I assumed.

A four-poster bed rested on a dais. The four wooden posts had thin spirals of silver topped with pinecone finials. Sheer curtains hung from the corners, open, which allowed me to see the silky black sheets and deep blue blanket that glimmered like starlight. There was no fireplace, but the room was warm enough with thick rugs covering the glass floor.

He directed me past the bed and to a door that opened into a sprawling washroom. A bath, which more closely resembled a pond, sat against one wall. Stones framed the edge, and a flowing stream spilled into the bath. Steam came off the water and filled the air with moisture, fogging the glass walls and the full-length mirror.

With gentle hands, Cethin began to divest me of clothes. "You're shivering."

Was I? I hadn't noticed. I didn't assist him as he undressed me. When the tin fell out of my pocket, he lifted an eyebrow, but I didn't remark on it. I lacked the energy to do so. He set it and my iron key to the side, using my shirt to hold it.

The warm water lapped at my calves, drawing a groan from my lips. I clambered the rest of the way in and sat on one of the many ledges inside. The water was so deep in the center that I could stand and still have my shoulders covered, and it was long enough that I could swim back and forth should I desire to.

Cethin settled next to me and grabbed a towel from the side of the pool. Methodically, he began to scrub me from head to toe, and I allowed him to, not moving. I felt as if I hovered above myself, not truly existing inside of my body. Even his touch seemed distant.

He grabbed a glass bottle glinting with gems and poured some of the liquid into his cupped palm. The floral scent I associated with Cethin tickled my nose. His fingers gently worked the oil through my hair, scrubbing my scalp in circular motions.

Carefully, Cethin pushed me off the ledge and forced me to lean back as he washed the oil from my hair. When he was done, he touched the closest glass wall, and it turned transparent, allowing me to see the sprawling field of flowers. This time, when he settled beside me, he hauled me onto his lap.

"Do you want to discuss what happened?"

"No," I answered in a barely audible voice. I didn't want to talk. If I did, I feared the same anger and panic would rip through me, though, thankfully, here my emotions didn't hold the same power as they did in Sídhetír.

Cethin held me in his embrace as the warm water stole every ounce of tension in my body. I leaned against his shoulder, turning my face into his neck. He kissed my forehead.

An immeasurable amount of time passed. I couldn't even guess, for the sun never rose. It seemed night always reigned in the land of the dark fae.

"Come," he said, helping me to my feet. "You need to sleep."

I offered no resistance. With a towel Cethin gave me, I dabbed my skin and tousled my hair. He tossed it aside when we were done and pulled me into the bedroom. I climbed onto the bed, laying on my stomach, head on one of the many feather pillows.

Cethin flopped down beside me. "What can I do?"

"Nothing."

"You need to talk, Aidan, and I want to listen."

He was right. I needed to, but I didn't want to. How could I articulate the emotions crashing through me? They changed so rapidly that I couldn't even get a grasp on them. A pendulum swung in my mind. On one arc I was angry, another I understood Lord Byrne's reasoning, and then I was furious at my brothers while being grateful they were mine. Also, I was numb—utterly numb. How the hell did I explain that I felt everything and nothing?

What I wanted was something real. Something I knew to be true.

"Can you grab the tin you pulled from my clothes?" I asked.

He lifted an eyebrow, but he slipped back into the washroom. When Cethin returned, I rolled to my back and held out my hand. He deposited the tin into my waiting palm.

"What is it, my Aidan?"

Heat rushed to my cheeks. I opened the container, and he peered inside.

"Ah. I understand." Cethin pursed his lips. "You are emotional right now. This may not be the best time."

I pressed close to him, burying my face against his chest. "I need this, Cethin. I need you."

"I don't want to take advantage of you."

"You're not," I said. "I need something true. I need to quiet my thoughts. And most of all, I need you, Cethin. If you don't want to, I understand, but *I* want this."

He pressed a kiss to my forehead. "Do you wish to fuck me?"

I nodded.

A slight smile tugged on the corner of his lips before he captured my mouth. The pressure was soft and undemanding. I set the tin down to grip his sides. Cethin straddled my hips as his tongue swiped the seam of my lips. I opened my mouth in response, allowing him inside. The gentle brushes of his tongue made me moan and demanded a response.

As my tongue met his movement for movement, I started to rock beneath him. He cupped my cheeks, thumbs sliding over my skin. "Cethin," I groaned against his lips. One of his hands slid into my hair, fisting.

My cock steadily filled until it pressed against him. The tip wept with pre-cum, covering my stomach. Cethin wasn't far behind me. His hips began to rut into mine, making our cocks slide against one another.

"Fuck," I said as my balls tightened.

Cethin opened the tin and scooped up a generous amount, then reached behind him. He released a sharp breath.

I tightened my hold on his sides. "What's wrong?"

"Nothing, dearest." His hand moved faster and his breathing increased. I trailed kisses over his neck. "I'm preparing myself for you, don't worry."

"You seem to be enjoying yourself," I muttered between kisses.

He chuckled. "I am."

My hands continued to trace his skin as Cethin slid his fingers in and out of his hole. I ran my fingers up his stomach and swirled around his nipple. He growled, hips bucking. I pinched the nub, and Cethin released a guttural groan. I pinched and teased one nipple before moving to the other, and all the while, he swore above me.

I slid down his stomach and grasped his cock, sliding my hand lazily over his shaft. The slit of his cockhead glistened with pre-cum. I swiped the bead away with the pad of my thumb and placed the digit in my mouth. The liquid had a bitter tang, but I liked it.

"Fucking hell," Cethin growled.

I drew his mouth to mine and shoved my tongue in between his lips so he could taste himself, making him groan. His warm hand, slick with lubricate, pumped my cock several times before he broke away from my insistent lips.

Cethin went up on his knees and grabbed my cock, angling it toward him. Slowly, he lowered onto me. I moaned as the head of my cock slid inside him. I'd never felt anything like it. The tight, warm pressure of his ass was so perfect, I feared I would come instantly. I clamped down on the growing pleasure. I was not ready for this to end.

He lowered and lifted off my cock, taking more of me each time until the backs of his thighs rested on me. His ass squeezed me tight, dragging an animalistic cry from my throat. I'd never experienced anything even close to this before. I held his hips tightly, trying not to dig in, but I couldn't help it.

"Cethin," I moaned.

He began to move, riding my cock with steady movements. I grunted. Cethin's head tilted back, his long hair tickling the sensitive skin on the inside of my thighs. "Moon above, Aidan. I'm so full."

All I managed was a strangled, "Fuck."

Cethin began to pick up speed. I planted my feet wider to thrust up to meet each one of his downward movements, so I plunged deeper inside of him. He swore. He pounded down against me and I arched up into him, as we found our rhythm. My skin slapped against his with the force of our fucking.

My mouth hung open as uneven breaths intermixed with swears and cries slipped out. My balls hugged the base of my shaft, and pleasure charged down my spine with every passing moment, gathering. My cock was so hard it hurt. I wanted to hold on, to make it last longer, but I couldn't.

"Cethin," I ground out, trying to warn him.

"Hold on, dearest." His hands splayed on my chest as he rode me even faster and harder. I pumped him in time with my thrusts, loving the feel of his silky skin against my palm. Cethin moaned. His eyes slammed closed and his hole squeezed me impossibly tight. Ropes of cum burst from his cock, splattering my stomach. I thrust into his tight ass to prolong his pleasure until I could hold onto mine no longer. I came with a loud shout, tendons in my neck straining, as I ground into Cethin, gripping his hips.

He collapsed onto me, and my spent cock slipped out of him. His cum was wet between us, and yet I didn't feel the need to move. I ran my hands through his damp hair and pressed my lips to his temple. Cethin groaned, lifting his head and meeting my mouth for a lazy kiss.

His black eyes found mine, and I held his face in my hands as I said, "Thank you."

"I should be telling you that."

"I meant when you came to Byrne Manor for me. You came when I needed you."

Cethin kissed me again. "I promised you I would."

"Still."

"I love you, my Aidan. I will always come for you."

My heart thrashed against my ribs. "I love you too."

Cethin grinned, crushing his mouth to mine.

Chapter 21

"Sídhetír is an amazing burden, which can turn deadly. As the mantle switches from lord to heir, the heir cannot live without Sídhetír. The time in which one can be away from the land is short. If the one ruling stays away for an extended time, he will sicken, possibly to the point of death." – Lord Edmund, Second Lord of Sídhetír.

Cethin lay beside me, stroking my spine. The walls and ceiling in the bedroom were clear, allowing me to see the full moon and the stars twinkling in the inky sky. The moon would crest the horizon for a bit before waning or waxing and rising once again. The night might never leave, but the moon followed the same phases as in the human realm.

"Tell me a story."

"Hmm," he muttered. "What do you wish to hear?"

"Anything."

"Anything," Cethin repeated. "What about the star-crossed lovers who made the seam?"

Rubbing my face against his chest, I said, "Sounds good."

"The worlds used to be arranged differently. The fae world used to be two separate realms: the Realm of Night and the Realm of Day. The only way to reach the other was through the human realm. Our realms mirrored the human one. We brought the seasons and changed the time from day to night."

"What happened?"

"A young princess of the night realm journeyed to the human world. There she came across another fae. The light fae was a man with brown hair the color of soil and eyes the color of a fern. He looked much different than her own pale white hair, and gray skin. He was the loveliest thing she'd ever seen, and the instant she laid eyes upon him, she knew he was her mate."

"She knew like you did with me."

"Yes," he answered. "We simply know. Her mark had hinted the light fae was her mate, for she bore a small sun next to her moon."

My fingers found the seven-pointed star. "This is me?"

"It is." Cethin kissed my forehead. "The light fae do not sense their mates as we do, though they also have marks like ours. The light fae prince didn't know she was his mate, but he fell in love with her at first sight. They courted in the human realm, but whenever they returned to their respective homes, they longed for the other. One day, the prince proposed a plan to leave their realms for the human one. Neither was the heir, so they could."

"What happened?"

"They were stopped. The queens of the fae realms barred the young prince and princess from leaving, separating them forever. We weren't always the allies we are today. The night princess concocted a plan from her prison of glass and magic. She reached for the moonlight above her and stretched to the human realm to find him.

"It's said the human world experienced a day and a night at the same time, for that same day the prince reached through the sun to search for her. When her magic brushed his, he held on. They tried to drag themselves to each other, neither letting go, but the realms began to shift with the pull of their magic and the strength of their love.

"The prince and princess were ordered to stop, but they refused in their desperation for each other. The queens tried to stop them, but the prince and princess' love was too great. Nothing would tear them asunder.

"The Realm of Night collided with the Realm of Day, causing a fracture. Magic seeped out of the wound, polluting both fae words and the human one. Magic ran rampant, ripping the worlds apart. The only way to heal the wound and stem the tide was to fuse the fae realms together, creating the seam."

"And the prince and princess?" I asked.

"They died."

"What?"

"They used too much magic, depleting their very lives until they vanished."

My eyes moistened. "They died for their love."

"They did, but it brought our realms together."

I touched the star on his chest. "This is me."

His fingers rested over mine. "I knew once the contract was struck and the Byrne family mark became the seven-pointed star, that one of the Byrne family was my mate."

"You knew I was a Byrne?"

"I did, though I didn't guess you were the heir until later. There are quite a few Byrnes—cousins and whatnot."

"How did you find me? Why were you even in Sídhetír?"

"Every time the mantle passed from father to son, I went to Sídhetír to search for my mate." Cethin gently brushed my hair. "I have waited my entire life for you, Aidan."

I swallowed, fingers sliding over his tattoos. "When did you receive these?"

"When we reach maturity, both light and dark fae go through a ritual to receive our marks."

"You've been searching for me since you became an adult?"

"Yes, dearest."

My hand slid lower to palm his bare stomach. "Who stabbed you?"

"I don't know. I was walking through the woods when a figure darted out of the shadows and stabbed me with a poisoned iron blade," he replied. "While I don't know who stabbed me, I'm grateful to them."

"You are?"

"They brought me to you."

That was the truth, but I couldn't be happy he'd been injured. If he hadn't been, though, I wouldn't have met Cethin. The very thought was horrifying. I couldn't imagine dealing with everything without him. More than that, I couldn't imagine my life without him.

At the thought of the current situation, my mind raced back to all of the secrets I'd learned. So many had slipped from Lord Byrne because of Blodwen's interference. I doubted the light fae had wanted this outcome, and yet, the truth had come free as it always did. I was the future Lord of Sídhetír. I was engaged to a fae prince.

My eyes turned to Cethin. He held my gaze as his fingers slid through my hair. I rested my chin on his chest. The secrets revealed hung around us like a fog we both ignored, but needed to address.

"We should go for a walk." I shifted off him, sliding across the silky sheets, and stood. My knees trembled and my stomach roiled. I swallowed the sudden nausea as pain bloomed in my ribs and spine.

Cethin hooked an arm around my waist. "Are you well?"

"You like to worry, don't you?" I teased as I shook off his hold and headed to the washroom, but my clothes were nowhere to be seen. "Where are my clothes?"

"They're being washed."

"So you do have servants."

He chuckled, snagging me close, and pressed a kiss to my bare shoulder. "Yes, I do."

"So am I to wander around naked?"

"I have no problem with that." He grabbed my ass, squeezing. "You are lovely."

I frowned at him, and Cethin laughed, rocking me in his embrace. The slight movement made my bruised ribs throb worse than before. Not only that, my stomach rose, burning the back of my throat.

What the hell?

"You can borrow some of my clothes. We're nearly the same size."

"Thank you."

"Think nothing of it. I relish the thought of you in my clothes."

The trousers were too long and tight because he was taller and slimmer than I; the shirt hung oddly, exposing more of my chest than was strictly appropriate, but all in all, the clothes fit.

He took my hand and led me through the corridors of the castle. This time, I paid more attention to my surroundings, clocking that Cethin's room was in a tower. Rugs lined the opaque floors; paintings of people, battles, and scenery hung on the walls. Delicately carved furniture was perfectly placed and topped with expensive-looking baubles.

We stepped outside the double doors and the flowers greeted me. They bobbed in the slight breeze, which bore a chill that raised gooseflesh on my arms. In the distance, clouds hovered and snow drifted down, an odd contrast to the golden browns and reds of the fall leaves.

With no destination in mind, I walked around the clearing with Cethin at my side. I bowed to touch one of the many flowers, the petals smooth as silk beneath my fingertips. The silver glimmers of pollen came off the yellow stamen and drifted on the wind like miniature stars. My bare feet dragged through the thick grass, not finding any rocks or sticks. The dew clung to the leaves and grass, flicking onto my trousers.

Cethin remained beside me as I wandered aimlessly. When I approached the treeline, I settled on the ground, ignoring the dampness.

Cethin lay down next to me. I drew his hand onto my chest, right above the mark. "Are you a prince?"

"I had planned to tell you before Blodwen announced it."

"Are you going to inherit the throne?" Already, I was inheriting the mantle of Sídhetír—a burden I wasn't prepared for but couldn't refuse. I couldn't handle Cethin being the next in line to the throne as well.

"No, dearest. The throne will eventually pass to my younger sister. The fae courts are always ruled by women."

A long breath rushed out of my lips. I had known that, but in the moment, the fact had quite escaped me.

"Were you going to tell me about being the Heir of Sídhetír?"

"I planned to tell you when you came to the cottage. I meant what I said. I will keep nothing from you."

"When did you figure out I was half-fae?"

His fingers tightened around mine. "The first time your blood spilled. When we rescued the humans from the trolls, I could smell the magic. Until then, I assumed what tingled my senses was the mark binding us together."

"And that I was the heir?"

"When you were attacked by the light fae. He should have killed you, or at minimum damaged you further, but you survived. Something I am extremely grateful for. But when that happened, I thought back to the way the weather changed in accordance with your emotions. It simply made sense. It also made sense why Jonathan hid you."

I rolled onto my side and took a sharp breath from the sudden stabbing in my ribs. Cethin's eyes flickered as his brow creased. I didn't comment, ignoring the ache. "What's going to happen to us?"

"What do you mean?"

"I'm going to be Lord of Sídhetír."

"So?"

"Do I have to pick the Night Court to align with? Can you even stay in Sídhetír? What are we going to do?" I asked rapidly.

His fingers began to tug my shirt off, and I frowned, shoving his hands away. "What are you doing?"

Cethin laughed. "I'm not trying to romance you. I simply need to see your mark."

Shaking my head, I pulled the black shirt off with his help, and Cethin ran his fingers over the mark, lingering on the blooms. The flower on my forearm was fully grown, while the bud on my collarbone had been joined by a second smaller one.

"When five flowers bloom, our marriage and bond will be solidified. That is one thing we have to wait for. As for your other concerns." Cethin shrugged. "I will stay in Sídhetír with you. I care not what my mother, father, or sister say. You are my reason for breath. You can align with whomever you like. I have no opinion on the matter. We will have to see if the contract can be made with your mixed blood first."

"You would give up your realm for me?"

He cupped my cheek. "I would give up everything for you, Aidan. You are my everything."

Chapter 22

"The contract was forged in blood, and by blood, it must be maintained." – Lord Louis, Third Lord of Sídhetír.

A spread of food covered the table from roasted meat to vegetables to bread to sweets. The savory and sweet aromas tickled my nose, which should've elicited a growl from my empty stomach, but my stomach curled in on itself as bile climbed my throat. I swallowed convulsively to keep it where it belonged.

Cethin pushed a full plate at me. Not wanting to appear rude, I nibbled on the edge of a piece of crusty bread.

"Are you alright, dearest?"

I couldn't lie. A laugh bubbled in my throat, but I kept my lips closed since I didn't want to have to explain the inappropriate response. Prior to learning of my heritage, I'd assumed I was a truthful person due to my mother's words about lying being pointless. My inability to lie had indeed come from my mother, but by blood, not by word.

He didn't look away from me, waiting for a response as his hand snaked over mine. I flipped my hand to wrap my fingers around his. "My stomach is a bit upset. The last few days have been stressful." My fork scraped on the plate as I pushed the food from one side to the other. "Will Blodwen actually call for war?"

Cethin took a sip of a deep blue wine before responding. "It depends."

"On?"

"The Day Queen's mood."

"I beg your pardon."

"Fae are like any other creature, Aidan. We suffer from boredom, but as our lives are significantly longer, our boredom is proportional. I doubt Queen Laoise would wage war against my mother, for we noble fae get along fabulously, besides the occasional pranks. Our world is too small to do anything but get along. Humans? She might. It depends on how slighted she feels by your father's lies."

Lord Byrne being my father was difficult for me to comprehend. It didn't seem real. But my heritage couldn't be contradicted, so I didn't bother to remark on it.

"How do we keep a war from starting?" I asked, dropping my fork with a clang and with it, any pretense of eating.

"I can speak with my mother. She will assist, for a price."

"She'll want the gate placed within her lands," I surmised.

"Most likely."

"Won't Queen Laoise want the same?"

"Most likely."

I sighed, scrubbing a hand through my hair.

Cethin brought my hand to his lips, kissing my palm. "I shall be beside you the entire time."

Warmth rushed to my cheeks. "How do we go about speaking with your mother?"

"I will send her a short missive. I don't think it would be wise for me to bring you uninvited to her home, even if you are my mate."

A different kind of heat flushed my face as needles of unease poked down my spine and settled in my gut. Meeting Cethin's mother and father. I'd never thought much about my marriage, and yet, now I was meeting my future in-laws. Would they like me? Or would they be upset that Cethin's future husband was a human? No. I wasn't human. I was half-fae. A mongrel, Blodwen had called me.

A loud squeak of wood scraping glass broke the tension moments before Cethin jerked my chair away from the table and crouched in front of me. His hands rested on my knees as he stared into my eyes. "The only reason I cannot bring you home uninvited is because you are the Heir of Sídhetír. There is no other reason."

"Were my thoughts that obvious?"

He straightened to kiss my cheek. "Yes."

I stood, ignoring the food. Nothing was going to settle anyway. "Can I explore your house?"

"Our house, and yes. Let me write to my mother, then I shall join you."

Cethin lay at my back, his arm under my neck. I played with his fingers as I stared at the blooming flowers, which never seemed to fade, through our bedroom wall. Most of the day—if you could call it that—had been spent wandering around the castle, exploring the nooks and crannies. I'd lingered in the library for far longer than I normally would because guilt at abandoning Oren burned through me.

The nausea hadn't abated, and as the day progressed, it increased until I was almost constantly swallowing bile. My bruises and ribs ached more than they had before I left Sídhetír. I had no explanation, and I didn't mention my discomfort to Cethin.

He'd written to his mother, but there had been no response. I had no idea how long it took letters to traverse the Night Realm, so I couldn't guess if this was normal or if she was slighting my presence. We would remain at Cethin's home until she responded. I might not want the mantle of Sídhetír, but I couldn't abandon it or my... brothers to war.

Warm breath on the back of my neck drew me to the present. I leaned back against Cethin as I stared at our intertwined fingers on the silky sheets. It seemed incomprehensible that we were mates. That the fates had aligned in such a way to bring the two of us together. Cethin had been alive so much longer than I, and yet, I was his.

"Are you sure you don't know your own age?" I asked.

His face rubbed against the nape of my neck as he took a deep inhale. "As I said, the fae realm moves in a different rhythm than the human one. I'm old. That is the most I can say."

"Ah."

"Does my age bother you?"

"No," I answered. "It merely saddens me that you had to wait so long to find your mate."

"Every day of waiting was worth it, Aidan. I cannot put into words the feeling that came over me the first time I saw you. All my previous years were for naught because they were but a bridge leading to you."

I closed my eyes against the sudden sting. "Thank you."

He pressed a firm kiss against my neck. "There is no need."

"Still, thank you."

Tightening his arm about my waist, Cethin snuggled close.

My eyes remained on the expansive flower field. A steady wind caressed the flowers while snow drifted from the sky and golden brown leaves littered the ground. "Is it always like this?"

"What?" he asked. "Us? I assume all mates are similar enough."

"No," I replied with a slight chuckle. "The weather. It's like fall and winter exist at the same time."

"It is said that before the seam our seasons transitioned, but when the two fae realms collided, so did the seasons."

"Interesting." Part of me didn't understand how this realm worked, with the mixed weather and no day or night to mark the hours, but it did. Magic, I supposed, was the answer. Magic made the realm turn, but magic also made it nonsensical.

"You need to sleep," Cethin whispered.

"It's always night. I can sleep later."

"True, but the moon has set."

He was right. The moon was nowhere to be seen. "What does the moon setting signify?"

"It is the same as the sun setting in your world. While our realms rotate differently, our lives revolve around the rising and setting of the moon. Moonrise to moonset, businesses are open, though our nights lengthen and shorten at random."

"That sounds inconvenient."

He shrugged against my back. "It has been that way for as long as I can remember."

"And you're old, so most fae wouldn't remember a time before."

"There are noble fae alive who remember the time before the seam, but they are few in number. Not even my mother is that old."

I rolled over to face him. "Do you remember the contract?"

"I do. My mother was the night queen who signed it."

That was an interesting thought, and by interesting, I truly meant overwhelming, but I refused to allow it to distract me. "Blodwen mentioned something about Lord Byrne sacrificing his sons, besides me, if he wanted to reforge the contract."

Cethin slid a hand through my hair, stroking the back of my head in soothing motions. "Fae and humans have not always had the relative peace we have now. Noble fae for the most part were uninterested in humanity. Humans are so short lived and boring."

"Boring?" I raised my eyebrows.

He chuckled. “Not you, dearest.” When I didn’t say anything more, he continued, “Common fae would journey to the human realm through the many paths and wreak havoc. Humans killed fae; fae killed humans. The slaughter was indescribable. Death and deals were daily occurrences.”

“Lord Rhett?” I asked.

“Six of his seven sons died by fae hands in the same battle. When Lord Rhett walked the battlefield and found his dead children, madness stole his mind. He took each of his sons' bodies and consulted a necromancer.”

Necromancy was a purely human magic. Fae couldn’t raise or use the blood of the dead, but we could, making soldiers that were nigh impossible to destroy. However, the magic corrupted the humans beyond recognition, according to the stories.

“With her help and the blood of his dead and living sons, he forced most of the paths between the realms into one gateway in Sídhetír, Lord Rhett’s province, though it had a different name at the time. His thinking being that it would be easier to defend one entry instead of innumerable amounts.”

My stomach churned as I shook my head.

“There were unintended side effects.”

“Such as the land needing to be passed to the seventh son?”

“That is one. Another small one is the inability of the Heir or Lord of Sídhetír to sire a daughter. There were two main side effects Rhett did not plan for were: firstly, being tied to the land. He never thought he would be bound to the very ground of his home, though he gained the power to sense and cast out every fae within his lands.

The second was the sentience of Sídhetír. Rhett breathed unexpected life into the land when he tethered the magic of realms to one place."

"Sídhetír wasn't always sentient?" I asked.

"No."

"When did the Day and Night courts get involved?"

"After. We noble fae didn't care about the human realm, but when we were all restricted from it, the common fae fought our control. We were all locked in a very small space. Suddenly, the human realm seemed much more appealing and we wanted access, but we were trapped. No full-blood fae could walk through the gate.

"My mother, Eilidh, and the Day Queen, Laoise, sent a half-fae representative through with letters. He was killed, as were the following three. Eventually, Rhett let one live and a contract began to form.

"Noble fae had to restrict access on their side, controlling how many fae could escape. Rhett wanted to keep animal fae from coming through, but it extended to all fae, and we nobles had to hunt the fae who were still in your country.

"To this day, we are charged to hunt the fae who come into the human realm to cause trouble. Mostly that happens when the transition takes place and the gate moves to the seam. But nobles are sent each reign to the human realm to purge the fae who do not belong. We tend not to bother those who leave humans alone."

"What do you do to these fae?" I asked, fearing I knew the answer.

His cold look sent a shiver down my spine. Fae were brutal.

"It took time, but a contract was struck, and blood fueled the magic, so the same has to continue. Every seventh son signs the contract in blood, keeping the magic alive."

My mouth went dry as I asked, "If the contract has to be remade, do you think my brothers will have to die?"

"I don't know. I truly don't. The contract states that the Lord of Sídhetír's seventh son must sign. It's assumed the heir must be human, so no fae can interfere or the Lord of Sídhetír could not live forever."

"What's going to happen?"

Cethin kissed my forehead. "I do not know, but I shall remain by your side to the end."

The void in my mind was growing with each passing moment, but so was my dread. If I couldn't sign the contract, would war come to Sídhetír and the entire country? Or would my brothers have to die to reforge what my birth had broken?

Chapter 23

"Fae can be charming, helpful, and humorous, but remember, dear heir, they always have a plan." – Lord Finbar, Fifth Lord of Sídhetír.

Flowers surrounded me, releasing their silver glimmers and light scent, and my eyes remained on the trees, the leaves ranging from golden brown to pure red. Cethin had received a missive a few moments ago, and he'd left to respond to what I assumed was his mother's letter, which left my back cold. I rubbed my arms to ward off a chill as snow drifted from the sky and clung to me.

Cethin hadn't related the contents of the letter before walking to his—our home. I hadn't asked what his mother wrote, because I worried she wouldn't speak to me or was upset about Cethin and I being together.

My own family had an issue with us.

I scoffed and flopped back onto the flowers, crushing them. The main reason they had a problem with Cethin was because of the secrets they'd kept. All of them besides Oren had known of my fae blood, though it appeared only Thomas, Whitaker, and Lord and Lady Byrne had known I was Jonathan's son.

A soft thump came from my side moments before arms drew me into a solid embrace. I hissed at the sudden stabbing in my ribs, and Cethin frowned, hands smoothing the tension from my face.

"Did I hurt you?"

"I should be fine." The pain had quickly dulled to a throbbing ache.

He stroked the back of my head. "I didn't mean to injure you."

"It's not your fault," I said, for it truly wasn't. My injuries from the fight with the scheming light fae hadn't healed yet, and they seemed to be worsening. "What did your mother say?"

"She wants to meet you."

"That's good." When Cethin didn't say anything, I asked, "Isn't it?"

"Yes and no."

"How can it be both?"

"I'm not sure, and yet it is," Cethin said. "We need to meet with her, so you can discuss Sídhetír as well as the potential war, but..."

"Yes?" Worry prickled my gut, making the nausea worse. Would his mother hate me? I wasn't a fae—or solely fae, I should say. Perhaps she desired Cethin to wed someone of prestige and of his own species. He *was* a prince of the Night Court.

"Her phrasing was odd when she requested to meet you."

"How so?"

Cethin shook his head, his black eyes never straying from mine. "It was as if she was expecting you."

"Did you tell her of me?" We hadn't known each other long, and I knew little of how communication between the realms worked. Was it possible for a letter to reach her within such a short amount of time?

"No. I did not."

Unexpected hurt poked my heart, and I scolded myself. Cethin was in a different realm than his parents, so it wasn't unreasonable for him not to share my existence with them. I hadn't shared our relationship with any of the Byrnes until I had no other option.

My face must have displayed my emotions because Cethin's arms tightened and he trailed soft kisses up the column of my neck, nibbling on the tight tendons. He bit my earlobe sharply, and my cock twitched.

"I never would deny or hide my affection for you, Aidan, especially not from my parents. The distance and my utter distraction of finding you are the only reasons for their lack of knowledge."

"I'm not trying to doubt you."

"I know, dearest." Cethin kissed the sensitive skin behind my ear. "Much has changed in a short span. Such upheaval is not easy. And you are not as old as I am. I'm used to change."

I laughed. "I'm not ancient like you."

He nipped at the tip of my nose. "No, you are not."

My smile dimmed as the intrusive thoughts returned. "Will your parents like me?"

"Yes."

"Will they care that I'm half-human?"

"I don't believe so."

That was not a no. "Will they be upset that I'm the future Lord of Sídhetír?"

Cethin shook his head as he smoothed a thumb over my cheekbone. "I do not know."

"If," I started, swallowing the sudden tightness strangling my throat. "If they will not accept me, what will happen to us?"

"Nothing."

I blinked.

He rolled me onto my back and hovered above me, placing his weight on his elbows to keep from hurting me. "Nothing will separate us. No realm. No person. No magic. No distance. You and I are bound to one another, and I will allow nothing to rip us apart."

My heart thrashed against my ribs as if it tried to escape the confines of my chest. Cethin. This thing between us was something I'd desired my whole life. My soul must have been searching for him among the chaos of life, needing him when I didn't even know his name. Now that I had him, I would fight to keep him as hard as he would fight to keep me.

I straightened the black tunic I'd borrowed from Cethin. My clothes had completely disappeared, and when Cethin investigated, he found one of his servants had disposed of them—stating they stunk of humans.

While Cethin and I were close in size, he was taller than me and I was broader than him, which left his clothes fitting oddly on my frame. He'd used magic to alter the clothes, and yet they hung off me, not quite perfect. He wasn't a magical tailor, much to his annoyance to admit, and he lacked the touch to make the clothes perfect.

He grabbed my hand and tugged me against his side. "Calm yourself, dearest. You look as lovely as ever." Cethin kissed my neck, then whispered in my ear, "Besides, I quite like the look of you in my clothes."

Heat went straight to my cheeks.

Cethin smirked, looking particularly smug as he brushed the redness. "I'm excited to divest you of them."

If possible, I turned even redder, excited for the same thing. Thoughts of him slowly stripping off the black clothes invaded my mind and made my body react, though, from the amount of pain I was in, I doubted we would do much. And now wasn't the time, with his parents impending arrival, and yet I had a hard time forcing the desire away.

His grin widened, and a gleam entered his eyes. "I shall suck and lick you until you're screaming from pleasure."

"Cethin," I groaned. "This is not an appropriate time for such words."

"Probably not, and yet, I find myself enjoying your arousal."

"Your parents are arriving shortly," I said between clenched teeth, taking jagged breaths and rearranging my semi-hard cock. Cethin stroked the back of my neck, which made it difficult for me to concentrate on anything other than him.

With a sigh, he drew away. "Yes, they are."

"Don't you want to see them?"

"I do, but at the moment, I would much rather whisk you away and explore you."

I swallowed and forced my gaze away from him. I wanted that as well, but I wasn't sure I was up to it. With every passing moment, I was feeling worse. I hadn't told Cethin about how much pain I was in, though.

"Shall I?" Cethin pressed his lips against my ear, stealing my breath.

A flapping sound interrupted us, and my eyes darted to the sky. My mouth dropped open. A sizable carriage formed of the same opaque glass as the castle appeared. Wings the same color as starlight fluttered on the sides, keeping the carriage aloft, as did the four pure gold pegasi with white feather wings.

The carriage landed on the grove of flowers with nary a sound. The driver, a type of dark fae I'd never seen before, leaped from the box. The fae appeared male to my eyes. He had a long black beard that was neatly braided and a bulbous nose. Two ram's horns curled on the side of his head, and his skin was gray as ash and his eyes glowed red as fire. His stout form filled his black breeches and smart coat.

He lowered a step, then opened the door with a low bow. A man stepped out first, and I had no doubt of who he was, since he resembled Cethin. His long black hair hung to his trim waist. His features were as sharp and feral as all noble dark fae, though they held the delicate quality Cethin's did. His eyes, though, were a deep green.

Cethin's father held out a hand, and slim fingers slid within his grasp. The second the woman alighted from the carriage, I flinched. I'd never sensed magic like this before, but the Night Court Queen exuded power. Her silvery-white hair, the same shade as Cethin's, hung to her chin in soft waves.

Deep black eyes ran from the top of my head to the tip of my toes before settling on Cethin's hand wrapped around mine. Her thin body, with the barest hint of feminine curves, was clad in a white dress that appeared almost ghostly in the moonlight. The gauzy fabric hid most of the dark purple tattoos covering her body, but I caught a glimpse of what looked like sprawling branches of a tree with silver leaves. Cethin's father also bore marks, but his were swirling black curls from what I could see.

"Mother. Father. May I introduce my mate, Aidan Byrne, future Lord of Sídhetír?"

A frown tugged at my lips at the surname. I had been a Ryan for as long as I remembered.

"Dearest," Cethin said, holding my hand to his heart, "This is Queen Eilidh of the Night Court and Consort Keefe."

"Charmed," I said, bowing, which made my ribs throb. Neither of his parents reacted; they both stared impassively at me. Sweat began to gather on my temples and nausea churned in my gut. God, I did not want to be here. My knees trembled. A wave of weakness crashed over me, making me wobble.

Cethin's arm wrapped around my waist. His eyebrows drew together, forming a deep divot. "Aidan?"

Queen Eilidh approached, hand stretched toward me. Cethin yanked me away, forcing a groan from my lips as my ribs screamed from the sudden movement. He growled at his mother, and she lifted her eyebrows while his father said in clear warning, "Cethin."

"I mean your mate no harm, my son." She slid past the tense wall he formed and wrapped her long fingers around my wrist. Her skin was as cool as her son's, but unlike his touch, it made me shudder and brought forth images of a full moon over snow-capped mountains.

Her fathomless eyes ran over my face. She pressed her fingers to my forehead and wiped the sweat from my temple. "How long have you been separated from Sídhetír, mate of my son?"

"I don't know."

She looked at Cethin, and he said, "A few nights. Why?"

"You haven't forgotten the contract, have you? You were there at its creation."

"Of course not," he snapped.

Keefe said, "Calm, Cethin. We are not a threat."

Cethin took a deep breath and his shoulders relaxed, but he snagged me around the waist and drew me to his chest. "Why?"

Her fingers stroked my cheeks as she stared at me without even a hint of emotion to soften her icy features. "Aidan is dying."

Chapter 24

"Sídhetír is a jealous lover who will never release their hooks. Once the heir has been born, his fate is sealed." – Lord Ian, Sixth Lord of Sídhetír.

Cethin's arms became a prison around me. My ribs complained and my voice followed suit, but he didn't loosen his hold until I patted his trembling arm.

"No, he's fine," Cethin protested.

"He is not." Her eyes remained on my face. Keefe moved past her and tried to reach out to Cethin, but his son pulled away, dragging me further from them.

"My Aidan is fine."

"No, he is dying," Queen Eilidh said blandly, seemingly unbothered by my coming demise and with mine, her son's. "You're feeling sick, are you not? Having a hard time keeping food down? Weak?"

I nodded.

"You are quite bruised."

"I did not harm him," Cethin said, and his father shifted toward him again. I didn't believe he meant to harm Cethin or me, but Cethin spurned his touch.

"I am aware, my son. I know you. You would never injure your mate," she replied in an even voice, her ice-like expression never changing.

Cethin's breathing had not calmed, so I grabbed his hand and kissed his palm. Some of the tension drained from his muscles, and he finally allowed Consort Keefe to grab his shoulder.

I understood what the queen was saying. I'd read most of the Sídhetír Memoirs throughout my childhood, inexplicitly curious for some reason. Once the mantle shifted, the Lord of Sídhetír couldn't leave Sídhetír for long without falling sick. The heir had the same problem during the transition. Sídhetír and its lord were inextricably linked. I should've realized when I was feeling sick, but being the heir was new to me. For my entire life, it had always been Oren, and now it wasn't.

His face pressed into my neck, and I squeezed his fingers. "I will be fine. I must return to Sídhetír. Soon."

"Are you sure?"

"Yes."

He took a shaky breath. "I will take you home. Now."

"No," I said, turning in his grasp. "War still threatens Sídhetír."

Cethin frowned, and I easily read his thoughts. He didn't care in the slightest about the war. He wanted me to go home, so I was in no danger of dying. But I cared. If a war could be avoided, I had to do it.

"Lady Blodwen threatened war," I said.

"Why?" Queen Eilidh asked.

I figured she knew the answer to the question, but she wanted to hear it from my own lips. I told her the truth, every sordid detail that I'd found out. Eilidh didn't look shocked in the slightest, though I wondered if she could be surprised. If Cethin was ancient, his mother must be incomprehensibly old.

"War is always possible, but Lord Byrne shouldn't fear the wrath of the fae. Magic will exact its revenge for the trickery."

"Maybe it already has."

"What do you mean, mate of my son?"

"I'm a half-fae. Can I even sign the contract?"

"I do not know. But your conception was prior to your father's scheme, and yet magic knows no concept of time. Or perhaps its revenge was more ingenious."

"What do you mean?"

She touched my cheek. "How can you love a father who abandoned you? His trickery cost him you as his son. A far worse fate, but one of his own making."

My heart oddly throbbed as the backs of my eyes burned. I cleared my throat and asked, "Will you help?"

The queen's head cocked to the side as she stared at me. "Walk with me." When Cethin stepped forward, she said, "You stay with your father."

He glared at her, and she returned his look impassively.

Keefe shifted to his side. "She will not harm Aidan. To harm him is to harm you. Calm yourself, Cethin. You are acting a fool."

I gave Cethin a warm smile, but his expression didn't calm, though he remained by his father.

Queen Eilidh slid an arm through mine and led me further into the clearing, past the golden pegasi. My eyes remained latched on the beasts as they pawed the ground. "Are those pegasi?"

"Indeed. They used to be as black as night, but Queen Laoise changed their color with magic."

"You didn't change them back?"

"No," she said. "I cast a haze of shadow over her bedroom in revenge, which blocks the ever-present light."

"You must not like her," I commented, sweat dripping down my temple. My muscles strained to turn around and look at Cethin because Queen Eilidh made me nervous.

She chuckled, the sound empty and flat. "I grew up with her. Long ago, after the seam was formed, fae royalty began to send their heirs between the two courts to build trust. Laoise and I spent our youth together."

"That doesn't mean you care about her."

"You are correct, but I do. Laoise is a dear friend. Such pranks as the horses or the clouds are how we relive our youths. My own children engage in such folly now to keep boredom away."

"Will you help me?" I asked, directing the conversation back to the matter at hand.

Eilidh didn't answer me and instead said, "I have been waiting for you."

"Me?" The thorny vines dug into my arm, but I didn't glance at Cethin and his father.

"Yes," she answered. "I have been." The queen's fingers went to the dip in the collar of my shirt and dragged it down, making me blush. I wanted to shove her hand away, keeping the tattoo private between Cethin and I, but I refrained. She touched the mark that matched Cethin's. "When he reached adulthood, my son underwent the trial for his mark and a hint about his mate."

"He told me."

"This," she said, touching the star, "confused me."

"Why?"

"No noble house bore this mark. Cethin searched, but no mate presented himself."

"But then you saw the mark for Lord Rhett Byrne."

"Yes." She finally removed her fingers from my chest. "I knew he or one of his children would be Cethin's mate. When Cethin did not claim any of them, I waited. The whole while, I guessed the Heir of Sídhetír would one day claim my son."

"Why?" I asked, even Cethin hadn't thought the heir was his mate.

"Magic in balance. The paths between the realms were not meant to be tethered to one juncture. Rhett twisted most of the paths into one gate with the blood of his children. Magic cannot allow the unnatural connection to continue. So Cethin and the heir. No children. No continuation."

"You knew to wait for me."

"Not you specifically, but when the transition continued and Cethin did not return, I wondered. I would not have predicted you would be half-fae."

"I love him," I blurted. For some reason, I wanted the queen to know this was more than a chance of fate to me.

The first emotion to break the icy exterior was a slight quirk of her lips, so similar to Cethin's smirk. "I guessed from your and his actions. My Cethin, or your Cethin I should say, is very attached to you."

"Will you help me? I can't allow war to touch Sídhetír."

"You care about it, even though your family lied to you?"

"Yes."

"I will not call for war and will send a message to Laoise to grant you my support. She probably will not accept it, for the obvious conflict of interest. She most likely will assume that if you can sign the contract, you will give the door to the Night Court."

"Is that what you want?"

"That is not what I'm asking in exchange for my assistance."

"Then what?" I asked.

"Balance. I want you to remember, magic demands balance. And what are you, Aidan, if not balance?"

"I don't understand."

"You will, mate of my son. Do watch out for Cethin, please. He tends to run away with his emotions. That will cause you trouble, no doubt, but he will never leave you guessing about his affection, though said affection may stifle you."

"I love him," I repeated, unsure why I did, as if it explained everything. Maybe it did.

"Of that I am aware." Eilidh nodded, and I bowed.

I tracked her movement across the glen to Cethin. He crossed his arms. She ignored his stance and drew him into her embrace, smoothing his long hair with her fingers.

Keefe headed in my direction, and I bowed. "Lord Consort."

He smiled, a reflection of Cethin's. "Lord Aidan."

I flushed. "I'm not a lord."

"Not yet, though at the same time you are." Glancing at his son, who watched us, Keefe grinned. Cethin tried to move in our direction, but his mother laid a hand on his arm. "He dislikes being away from you."

"I don't like being away from him."

"You are well matched," Keefe said. "His worry is heightened due to your injury and the threat of your demise. He will calm down when you return home."

Cethin once again tried to walk toward me, but his mother stopped him. "Why is he upset about us talking?"

"I think he fears our disapproval or that we will chase you away from his side. Both are foolish, but Cethin loves you, and it makes him irrational."

"And I him," I said with a blush.

He pulled me into a hug, and I stiffened. "Come and visit. I know Sídhetír will not allow you to leave for a long time, but I would like to get to know my son's mate. I would like to get to know *you*, Aidan. We have waited a very long time for you."

"I would like that."

"We are family."

My heart throbbed. Days ago I'd had no family, and now I had two.

I stumbled as a wave of exhaustion crashed over me, and Keefe caught my elbows, stabilizing me. "I should go before Cethin storms over here and makes a fool of himself."

"Too late," I muttered. Cethin slipped out of his mother's hold and raced across the flowered glen, the stomped blooms releasing silver pollen. When he approached, I stepped back from Keefe and held my arms open.

Cethin crashed into me, holding me tight. "Are you well?"

"Yes." I rolled my eyes, and Keefe laughed. He slapped Cethin's shoulder and strode to his wife. "You are being ridiculous."

He didn't respond, carding his fingers through my hair. Cethin held my cheeks and captured my lips. I shifted back after the barest moment.

"What?" he asked.

"Your parents are watching."

"So?"

"It makes me uncomfortable."

He pressed his nose against my cheek. "I'm sorry."

"You didn't know."

"The kiss was not what I referred to, though I am sorry about that as well. No, I am referring to being anxious about my parents meeting you."

"Why?" I slung my arms around his waist. "Do you not get along?"

"We get along well, especially me and my father."

"Then why?"

His body radiated tension as he pressed flush against me. I tried not to look at his parents over his shoulder, but I couldn't help it. Both of them stared at us with blank expressions. My cheeks turned red, and I forced my eyes away.

"Cethin," I pressed.

"I fear you will drift from my reach. I cannot live without you, but as half-fae, you can live without me. What if they convinced you away from my side?"

I tightened my hold and firmly kissed his neck. "That will never happen. I'm going to remain right here within your arms."

"Do you promise?"

"I do." I kissed him again. "Now let's say goodbye to your parents. I probably won't see them for some time."

He looked at me.

"Your father *did* invite me to visit."

Cethin frowned, which made me laugh. I darted forward and molded my lips to his. In time, Cethin would grow assured of my love, and I would make sure he knew every day how much I cared for him.

"I thought you were going to thoroughly explore me," I remarked as I lay on the bed. Cethin hovered over me, but he didn't initiate anything. I ran my hands through his long hair. He'd wanted to go to the Day Court instantly, but we had to wait for Queen Laoise to respond to our letter. We, or I specifically, could not simply appear in her realm.

"I want to take you to Sídhetír for a few days before we visit Queen Laoise," Cethin said again. We'd had this argument already.

"No."

"Aidan."

I rested my fingers against his lips. "I know."

"Aidan."

"I cannot allow the war to garner any more traction than it already has. I need to end the threat before it begins."

"And I need you to not be in pain."

"I will survive. It will be a quick trip. I promise."

Cethin frowned. I pulled him close, hooking my legs around his waist. I ignored the twinge in my side and rocked against him. If he was careful, we could at least stroke each other.

His frown deepened. "Do not try to distract me with sex."

I dropped my legs, hurt. "I wasn't. I want to be with you."

His expression softened. "I'm scared, Aidan."

"I would never endanger you, Cethin."

A war took place in his eyes. The battle waged for some time as he stared at me until, finally, he said, "A quick trip. No more than a rotation of their realm, then back to Sídhetír, even if we simply stay at the cottage."

"Deal." I kissed him, brushing my tongue against the seam of his lips. While my body ached and my stomach roiled, I wanted Cethin.

He pulled back. “No.”

“What?”

“When you heal, we shall fuck again,” he said. Now it was my turn to frown. Cethin nuzzled me. “Soon, dearest.”

“If you insist.”

“I do.”

Chapter 25

"The sun and the moon both shine in the fae realm. Light is the source of the fae power. Without the lights in the sky, the fae would wither like plants on the ground." – Lord Rhett, First Lord of Sídhetír.

The carriage lurched, and I leaned against Cethin. His arm was wrapped firmly about my waist, holding me against his side. Since I'd woken up, I'd felt worse—even worse than yesterday. I couldn't keep any food down, and I barely drank any water. My vision wobbled and my knees refused to hold my weight. Still, I refused to go to Sídhetír without meeting with Queen Laoise.

When Queen Laoise extended an invitation, Cethin had asked his mother to borrow her carriage, and she lent it without question. The carriage rocked beneath me, and I closed my eyes, taking a deep breath. Cethin's light scent tickled my nostrils and eased some of the pain.

"Don't think you're getting out of what you said," I whispered.

"What?"

"To divest me of your clothes and explore me thoroughly."

I expected him to chuckle, but he didn't. The divot didn't disappear from between his eyebrows either. I rested my head against his shoulder, and he pressed a kiss to my temple. "Recover and I will do whatever you want."

"Cethin, you're being dramatic. I will be fine."

"And you are taking unnecessary risks."

I snorted, and he didn't speak further.

We continued our journey out of the Night Court, over the seam, and to the Day Court. A shudder went through me, and I straightened, feeling miniscully better. For a moment, I thought Cethin had ignored my wishes and taken me home, but this felt different.

I was intimately familiar with Sídhetír, and this sensation wasn't that. Warmth rushed up my spine, and I sighed. I almost felt like I was coming home, though not quite.

"Aidan?"

"Where are we?" I asked, touching the side of the carriage, which turned transparent. Bright sunlight filtered in, and Cethin pulled back. Green trees greeted me. The air was fresh with the dew of spring. Flowers bloomed and fruit hung from the trees. Everything was alive.

"The Day Court."

My eyes closed of their own volition. "I like it."

"Of course you do. You're half light fae. This is your other home."

His voice bore a hint of bitterness that forced my eyes to open. Jaw clenched, he turned away from me and the blinding sun. I climbed onto his lap, and his hands settled on my hips. I captured his mouth and slid my tongue against his.

Cethin started beneath me from my aggressive kiss, but he returned it with equal fervor. When I broke away, his breath was ragged. "I don't want anyone else. It doesn't matter if I'm part light fae or not. Only you, Cethin."

He looked down, but not before I caught sight of the pleased smile on his lips.

We were not meeting Queen Laoise at her castle, since Cethin refused to travel any distance into the Day Court, and the queen didn't want me close to her castle either. Cethin, she had no problems with, but me? She refused to have me deep in her realm, for I was an unknown entity.

Cethin hopped out of the carriage first, then helped me down. My steps were unsteady, and my knees shook. Being in the Day Court helped ease some of the pain, but it didn't take away the bottomless need for Sídhetír.

We were right on the border of the seam and the Day Court. Sprawling land with gentle green hills, alive with flowers, greeted me. The clean air rushed into my lungs with every inhale, soothing me. I relaxed against Cethin, and he supported my weight with his arms about my waist.

A woman with deep brown hair like that of the richest soil stood in front of me. Her skin was golden-brown and practically glowed. Her curvy frame, strong muscles, and round features spoke to the light fae she was, but the power that came off her in waves told me *exactly* who she was. Queen Laoise was not alone, though the two other light fae dressed in green armor didn't hold my gaze.

She smiled broadly with a friendly air as she bounced on her toes. "Lord Aidan, an interesting pleasure to meet you."

"I'm not a lord. Yet."

"Yet," she agreed. "And yet you are. Both you and Lord Jonathan Byrne are the Lords of Sídhetír at this moment. The mantle is shifting from father to son."

Fatigue weighed me down and made my thoughts stagnant. Maybe Cethin had been right? Maybe I should've gone to Sídhetír first, even for a few hours, to sleep or recover before attempting to deal with the Day Court queen. Unlike Eilidh, Laoise was not my friend or vested in keeping me alive.

Not wanting to prolong this moment, I said, "I won't allow war to come to Sídhetír."

"Won't allow. What strong words you have."

"Sídhetír is mine, and I will keep any unwanted fae from the premises."

"Yes, but there are other, more desperate ways in, and you are young. Your grasp on Sídhetír will take time to deepen. It will be easy to end the threat."

"I will protect him, Queen Laoise," Cethin growled.

With a broad grin that contained no humor, she said, "I'm sure you will, Cethin, but it does not take much to kill a half-fae, especially a common one at that."

He snarled, but I kept my hand on his arm to waylay him from stepping closer to her. "What do you want?"

"You don't play the game, do you?" she asked with a sigh, bottom lip sticking out. "How boring. I hoped to have fun."

"I have no patience for this."

"Youth. In such a hurry. Or perhaps it's your humanity." Laoise prowled closer, making my back stiffen. "Or perhaps you are ill from being away from Sídhetír for so long."

Cethin hauled me behind him. "I will slay you if you move toward him."

Both of the light fae who stood behind Queen Laoise stepped closer, unsheathing their blades. She lifted a hand, stalling them. "Oh, Cethin, you cannot kill me, but I don't intend to harm him at the moment."

"At the moment," he repeated.

She smiled congenially. "Your demise would upset Eilidh, and that would be unfortunate, Cethin. Unfortunate, yet not unthinkable."

I squeezed Cethin's arm. While I was half-fae, fae were something else separate from humanity. Laoise would slay her friend's child if he got in her way, and I didn't think such actions would bother her.

"But no matter," Queen Laoise said, turning to me. "I don't believe you can sign the contract. I believe the magic will reject you."

"It might," I agreed.

"At least you're honest. Not all half-fae are. Can you touch iron?" she asked.

"Why?"

"Not all half-fae can."

"Hmm," I said, not answering.

Queen Laoise said, "You want me to call off Blodwen, and I want something in return."

"I assumed."

"The gate. If the contract accepts you, I want the gate. You are not going to die anytime soon."

"What makes you say that?"

She smiled. "I am not an idiot, young Aidan. I have been alive for a very long time. Longer than your mortal brain can comprehend. Half-fae live longer than humans, even without noble blood, but you are mated to Cethin. His life is yours." Laoise glanced at Cethin. "Not the wisest action you've made, son of my friend, but not the stupidest either."

"And if I can't sign the contract?"

"Then I shall march through the gate and enjoy humanity until I grow bored."

My veins turned to ice. If the day queen stepped onto Sídhetír, I doubted Lord Byrne or I could banish her. "Will you call Blodwen off?"

"Sign the contract. I'm sure she's having fun."

I moved around Cethin and stepped closer to her. "If Blodwen injures one human, I will kill her regardless of whether I sign the contract or not."

My words did not seem to bother her. In fact, they seemed to delight her. She moved closer and held my cheek. Cethin growled in obvious warning, which she ignored.

"You are more fae than I would've guessed."

"Am I?"

"Beautiful and serene on the outside, yet full of wrath like molten fire on the inside."

I had no words, but I feared what she said was true. Hell, I knew it was the truth, or at least, as she perceived me to be. I was angry, and that anger burned violently within me, searching for an escape. I would destroy anyone within my path.

Cethin's hand grabbed mine. His mouth pressed against my ear. "I know who you are, dearest. Do not allow her to manipulate or enchant you. You are who you've always been."

If the queen heard Cethin, she gave no indication. "Who was your mother?"

The sudden anger vanished, and I sagged. So fae could enchant people, or merely draw forth emotions I would rather not think about. I'd read stories about fae being able to do so, but I hadn't known if it was true or not. Now I did.

"I don't know her fae name," I said. "I only know what she called herself."

"Yes?"

"Why do you care? She wasn't a noble fae."

"Still."

I glanced at Cethin, but he was watching the queen and her lackeys. I saw no harm in it. The name wasn't her true name. "Vis Ryan."

"Never heard of her."

"I would've been surprised if you had."

"Do what I want, young Aidan, and bloodshed need not taint your land."

My lips would not form the word yes, because I didn't intend to give her what she wanted. I didn't know how I would work around her demands. Would Eilidh allow Queen Laoise to march armies through the gate if it rested on her land? I didn't know. And there were others, more precarious entries into the human realm that we couldn't guard against.

As trembles wracked my body and my knees gave out, Cethin caught me. "We must depart. Now."

"You may leave."

Cethin lifted me into his arms, and I had no energy to protest. "If you die, I will chastise you most heartily in the afterlife."

"Will you?"

"Yes, dearest."

When Cethin was about to place me in the carriage, Queen Laoise spoke again. "Should this all work out in my favor, come visit me, young Aidan."

I glanced over Cethin's shoulder. "Why?"

"You are one of my people. And this, in part, is your home."

"That is a kind offer."

"It is. Don't disappoint me."

I didn't bother to reply, and Cethin set me in the carriage before climbing in after me. He pulled me onto his lap, arms locked around my waist. His lips trailed over my neck as he rocked me.

"When we return to Sídhetír, we will go to my cottage. You will bathe in the creek water, though I will heat it first. I may even dab moss and dirt on you."

"Will you?" I croaked.

"Yes," he said, nibbling my ear. "I will rub dirt and moss onto you, then bathe you until you are covered in Sídhetír."

"Will that help?"

"I believe so."

My eyes closed as I settled closer, head on his shoulder. "I love you."

"And I you, so you are not allowed to die," he said. "Next time we visit, I will more closely monitor you and we will not stay as long."

"Hmm," was the only response I gave as waves of sleep dragged me under.

Chapter 26

"Bloodshed was the true reason I forged the gate. War. We were at war. Humans killing fae. Fae killing humans. I wanted to end the bloodshed. I regret the cost of peace was six of my seven sons' lives." – Lord Rhett, First Lord of Sídhetír.

Something dripped on me, then a cool dampness swiped over my forehead. A desperate voice whispered my name over and over again. Groaning, I opened my eyes. Cethin hovered over me with a piece of moss. Rain fell from the sky and the air was frigid. My hands ran over the ground and I sighed.

Sídhetír. I was in Sídhetír.

"Aidan," Cethin said, pressing the moss to my cheek. "Look at me, dearest."

"I'm here."

"You fell unconscious."

"I did?" We were in the woods with the gate right behind Cethin. The looming trees covered the ground in shadows, dimming my sight, but it didn't matter. I could sense everything. The dirt. The trees. The rain. Even the people wandering across the land.

Cethin patted my cheek, and my eyes opened. I hadn't even realized I'd closed them. "Stay with me."

I grabbed his hand and slid it over my heart. "I'm not going anywhere."

He continued to bathe me with the moss and rubbed dirt along my cheeks and in my hair. I had no idea if drenching me in Sídhetír actually helped, but it didn't hurt. To keep my eyes open took more energy than I truly had to spare. I was so tired, but any time my eyelids slid closed, he would pat my cheek and growl at me.

Sídhetír greeted me, magic flooding my body, but behind the coursing river, I sensed anger. Sídhetír didn't like me leaving for so long.

I'm sorry, I whispered to it. *I will never leave like this again.*

I couldn't tell if it was appeased, but I hoped so, because this time I would like to rest before I faced the fae representatives or Lord Byrne.

Other things came to my awareness. Fae. I could feel them. Light fae. Dark fae. They peppered the landscape of Sídhetír like gleaming stars and burning fires. My senses didn't end at the treeline as the Memoirs said. I felt the forest as easily as I did the land. More fae. So many fae.

Everything was blurry like I was looking through a frosted glass. I could perceive the land, but not clearly. Not yet.

Cethin lifted me to a seated position, and the world tilted. He kept an arm firmly around my back, supporting me. I could barely focus on him, though. Sídhetír was too overwhelming. There was too much. Fae. Humans. Plants. Animals. There was far too much. It was raining here over the forest, but it snowed at Byrne Manor. Fire. There was a fire burning near the manor too.

I sensed blood in the dirt. Human blood. Fae were attacking the manor.

I pushed out of Cethin's arms and stumbled to my feet.

"Aidan?"

"We have to go back to Byrne Manor."

"Why?"

"Blodwen is attacking them," I said, not knowing how I knew.

His eyes narrowed, but when I took another stumbling step forward, he drew me to his chest. "You need to rest."

"I have to protect them."

He didn't release me, and I squeezed his arm. His worry was reasonable, but there was no other option. I had to protect Sídhetír and its people.

"I will go with you."

"I expected nothing less."

Cethin pressed a kiss to my dirtied cheek before he swept me into his arms. I squeaked, which he ignored. Wings spread from his back as his horns appeared and his features sharpened. Unable to stop them, my fingers brushed the jagged black horns.

"Don't distract me, dearest," he whispered, lifting off the ground.

"Can you feel them?"

"Dimly, yes."

"You don't have to hide them or your true face."

His gaze flicked down at me as he wove through the trees. "You don't mind?"

"No," I said, gripping them. "I like it."

A grin tugged on his lips, and he repeated, "Don't distract me."

We flew through the grasping tree branches and into the sky. Rain pelted me. Shivers swept up my spine, but despite the cold, every drop made me feel better. The aches in my sides and the bruises on my face began to dim while my exhaustion started to wane. Sídhetír was healing me, and the void inside me slowly filled.

The closer we got to Byrne Manor, the more magic bombarded the area. Cethin's arms stiffened around me; he must have felt it as well. Snow fell from the sky and blanketed the land. It was much too early in the season for weather like this, but Sídhetír had been angry about my absence and continued the snowstorm I'd called forth.

Fire kissed the hedges around the manor, but didn't make it through the green barrier. Fae like of which I'd never seen surrounded the grounds. Tall. Short. Human-appearing. Animalistic. None of the light fae, though, attacked the village; all were focused on the manor.

Right outside the gate were a couple of mages mixed with soldiers fighting the light fae. Lord Abnus was among the soldiers throwing magic at the light fae while he sliced at them with his sword, his expression icy, and his movements impossibly quick. Abnus was doing more damage than either the soldiers or mages. His magic, black and scattered with blood-red petals, kept the light fae at bay, while icicles as sharp as knives plunged into the invaders.

Lord Byrne stood behind the gate. The land rose around him, shoving the fae back, and roots and vines entrapped them. He lifted a hand to the clouded sky, then jerked it toward the fae. Lightning crackled and stuck where he pointed. Fae screamed as they flew through the air, and fire sparked to life on the wet ground.

I'd never seen Lord Byrne wield the might of Sídhetír before, but I knew the magic was immense. Yet with the mantle shifting to me, he couldn't force the fae out of the human realm.

"Cethin, hurry."

His dragon wings flapped even harder as he raced over the gentle hills. "Where should I land?"

Landing behind the hedge would be best, but I didn't want anyone to mistake Cethin for the enemy and injure him. He was too important. But fighting through the horde would be difficult.

As I was about to order Cethin to fly over the hedge, a light fae with golden skin and curled horns spread their white feathery wings and launched at Lord Byrne. A glimmer of green shimmered around the manor grounds, and the fae slammed into an invisible barrier. Shrieking, the fae fell to the snow, flames licking their wings.

Flying over the hedge wasn't possible.

We would have to force our way through the light fae.

"Land behind the horde."

"Are you sure?"

"Yes." There was no other option, unless I wanted to attempt to break the barrier, which was probably not a good idea—or something I could actually do.

"I will protect you."

"And yourself?"

"And myself because your life depends on it."

I rolled my eyes.

When we landed, I grabbed his cheeks and threw his own words back at him. "If you die, I will scold you most heartily in the afterlife."

"I would expect nothing less, dearest." He maneuvered me behind him. "Stay close." He stretched out a hand and a cloud of black magic encased him. Thorny vines and blue flowers with silver glimmers appeared. A sword grew within the magic until it solidified.

"When you get inside, sign the damn contract. I don't care who you choose. Sign it so you can cast them out." Cethin faced the manor, free hand extended. "How do we get in?"

"The same way I snuck out to see you." My hand went to my pocket. The iron key was still there—it had never left me.

Despite the tense situation, he glanced over his shoulder and smirked. "You had to sneak out for me?"

"Focus."

None of the light fae paid attention to us as we crept around the back of the horde to the side of the manor. I didn't know if Cethin was using magic to conceal us from their sights, or if because we weren't causing trouble, they couldn't care less about us.

I spotted the iron gate covered in vines, and I swore the plants moved in welcome. As I took a step forward, Cethin knocked me to the side right before lightning smashed into the ground where I once stood. Dirt rained all around us, clods hitting my face and Cethin's back.

My ribs were not happy about being slammed into the ground, but I would live, which was all that mattered. I pushed him off, then snagged him closer as yet another strike of white-hot lightning crashed not far from us. More clumps of dirt and rocks smacked into us.

"Lord Byrne is not holding back."

"I do not blame your father," Cethin said, hauling me to my feet. "The mantle and control is slipping to you, and he must protect his people while he can."

I bristled at Lord Byrne being called my father, but now was not the time to talk about it. I grabbed Cethin's free hand and headed to the secret gate. His sword glowed in the low light. With every flurry of snow hitting the blade, the light increased.

"I should thank you for the snow, dearest. It increases my power."

"Happy to assist." I crept to the side entry that no one besides myself knew of. The light fae were less numerous on this side, but not non-existent. As we neared the wall, a particularly massive light fae shifted in our direction, his bright eyes landing on me, and he grinned. His jagged teeth and leathery skin were all too familiar and brought images of a fire to my mind. This was the same type of fae as the ones at Hillridge Farm. Trolls, Blodwen had called them.

The troll growled and four more joined the leader, all massive. Their movements were liquid despite their sizes. All of them carried massive cudgels with iron spikes. Cethin had been downed by a single iron knife dipped in poison. I would guess the trolls used similar tactics.

Cethin slipped in front of me. "Keep going."

"I want to help."

He ordered, "Go, Aidan."

My fingers tightened around the iron key. I had no weapons. The magic of Sídhetír might be mine to command, but I had no knowledge of how to use it. I gripped the back of his tunic. "I will see you later."

I ran the moment Cethin launched at the trolls, sword extended. I heard growls and clangs, but I didn't turn around to look. Cethin could take care of himself. He didn't need me to worry over him, even though I really wanted to.

Before I even shoved the key into the lock, the gate sprang open and the vines curled toward me. I patted the leaves. "Thanks."

My feet knew the path through the hedge maze, but I'd never moved so fast in my life. It was like the land lifted to meet my feet and yanked me along. I whipped out of the maze. I needed Lord Byrne. Only he would know where the contract was kept.

I ran to the front of the manor, searching for the lord. I saw lightning strike with some frequency, but I did not catch a glimpse of Lord Byrne. I peered at the hedge; on the other side, somewhere, was Cethin. God, I hoped he was alright.

A solid wall of flesh appeared and arms surrounded me, making me start.

"Aidan," Whit said, squeezing me.

I patted my older brother on the back. Tears pricked the backs of my eyes. He *was* my brother. My actual older brother. I hugged him back, then shoved him away. "Where is Lord Byrne?"

"Why?"

"I need to sign the bloody contract, so I can force all of the fae out."

"All of them?" he asked with an eyebrow raised.

Not even the threat of death was enough to keep Whit or any of the others from teasing me. "Not my... mate, but everyone else."

Whit laughed, drawing my attention to a long scratch stretched on his forehead. I touched it. "Your wife is going to kill me."

"Yep. She likes my handsome face."

"Poor taste."

He shoved my arm. "Not all of us have fae blood to pretty us up."

"We *will* have a conversation about all the lies when we're not about to die."

He swallowed. "I know."

We dashed to where Lord Byrne stood on the front steps. His blonde and gray hair was mussed and his face was drenched in sweat. The magic creating the dome around the manor, plus the multiple lightning strikes, was costing him. If he wasn't careful, it would kill him.

His green eyes landed on me. They were the same shade as mine. I should have seen it sooner. "Son," he said, and I assumed he meant Whitaker. "Aidan."

A roar ripped through the air, and I jerked, glancing up at the dome. Fae bombarded the barrier, burning. Each time the fae hit the dome, it glimmered, growing dimmer by the second. It was weakening. Blodwen stood in the middle of the throng of fae with a feral smile on her face—simply waiting to break through.

"Where's the contract? I need to sign it. Now," I said.

"Can you?" Lord Byrne asked.

"We are about to find out."

Chapter 27

“Balance must be struck. Blood was spilled and so by blood must the contract remain. The gate to the human realm shall be tethered to Sídhetír and its lord. He shall sire seven sons, and the seventh will inherit his title. When the heir reaches his twenty-first year, the contract will be remade anew and the mantle of lordship shall fall to him. His words shall mark the place of the gate within the fae realm. Blood will forge the balance.” – From the contract of Sídhetír

Could I even sign the contract? There was no way to answer that question until I tried to put my blood on the paper. The magic of Sídhetír would either accept or reject me. Despite the consequences, I had to try. Cethin was outside, fighting the light fae, risking his life. The Byrnes and everyone in the estate were in danger. I had to protect them.

Queen Laoise had said she would wage war unless I gave the gate to the Day Court, but I didn’t want to. I wanted to give it to the

Night Court. Cethin was my future husband, and he needed to be able to journey between his realm and mine without trouble.

We stepped into the manor, and Oren skidded to a stop in front of us. His eyes widened as he took in the dirt covering me and the leaves stuck in my hair. "Aidan." He pulled me into a quick hug. "You're back, *and* you're dirty."

I lifted an eyebrow.

Lord Byrne glanced at me. "I was curious about your state as well."

"I passed out on the way back to Sídhetír. I was gone too long."

"It was only two days," Oren said.

My mouth fell open. I had been gone for several days.

"Time passes differently in the fae realm," Lord Byrne said. "And the dirt?"

"Cethin covered me in the land, hoping it would help me recover faster."

"Did it?" Lord Byrne asked.

"I have no idea, but he thought it would."

Lord Byrne led me deeper into the manor—hopefully to where the contract was stored. I had no idea where it was kept, but we needed to reach it before the light fae broke through the dome. Only Lord Byrne's will kept them out, and from his trembling steps and sweat-covered brow, I guessed he wouldn't hold out for much longer.

Oren bumped my shoulder, making me look at him, and I finally realized Whit had left—he'd probably remained outside to protect the estate. I tried to smile at Oren, but I feared it was more of a grimace. Doubts circled my mind and made my heart thrash against my ribs. I didn't know if I could save us, and at this moment, I wished to God I wasn't the heir.

Like Oren read my thoughts, he said, "You're the heir." A long sigh sounded, and he smiled peacefully. "Not me. You're the heir."

At least, Oren seemed pleased with this development, even though now was most definitely not the time. He stared at me with wide, hopeful eyes as he chewed on his bottom lip. I practically saw the request he had. Oren wanted to study in town at Wellington University. It had been his dream, and now he could.

"Let's survive first," I said.

"Sorry."

I squeezed his arm. I was not mad, but his freedom was a reminder of my shackles.

Lord Byrne stopped in front of his bookroom and looked back at me as he pushed open the door. "Are you ready, Aidan?"

"As ready as I'll ever be."

We stepped inside, and Lord Byrne moved to the left. He removed a book, and the shelf slid open to reveal a room I'd never seen. In the center of the perfectly square, windowless room stood a stone pedestal. On it rested a crinkled parchment glowing in the dim light.

My heart thudded in my chest as my eyes locked onto it. With a will of their own, my feet moved to the contract. The glowing grew brighter and brighter as I shifted closer. When Oren tried to follow me, Lord Byrne grabbed his shoulder, stopping him.

I stretched my hand out to the contract. The words were written in deep black ink that had not faded with the years. Near the base were the signatures of the two fae queens and all the lords who came before me.

Night Queen Eilidh's signature was black with silver glimmers like stars. The crest of her moon was right beside her name, appearing like the full moon in the sky. Day Queen Laoise's signature was deep brown with striations like bark, and a sun glowed beside the letters.

Lord Rhett Byrne was right beneath them with a burning-red, seven-pointed star beside his name. All the lords who followed were beneath him, each name signed in blood that still appeared wet to the eye, as if they'd been signed moments ago, not years earlier.

My fingers stretched toward the contract, but before I could touch it, the ground rumbled. I jerked up. Lord Byrne rushed to the window. I moved back to the entry of the secret room, but my feet wouldn't cross the threshold. Sídhetír's hooks were embedded in my skin, drawing me to the contract.

The dome flickered outside of the window, then vanished.

Lord Byrne yelled, "Sign it, Aidan." He grabbed an iron knife off the desk and threw it toward Oren, who snatched it out of the air with ease. "Protect Aidan. I will hold the light fae back for as long as possible." He dashed out of the room without a backward glance.

Oren said, "Sign it, Aidan. Hurry."

I faced the contract, my fingers hovering over the parchment. There was no quill or needle to prick my finger, but I didn't need one. At that moment, I knew when I touched the contract, my blood would come forth, adding my name to the many before me.

What should I do? Queen Laoise pledged war if the gate was not gifted to the Day Court. But I was not human. The contract would last as long as I did. My tie to Cethin would keep me alive for as long as we wanted to live. There would be no children of my blood, let alone seven sons. I was the end.

"Balance, Aidan. For what are you if not balance?" Queen Eilidh's words echoed in my ear as if she stood right behind me, not deep in the fae realm. That was all she wanted me to consider for her help. The word balance. Magic in balance. I was light fae and human. I was mated to the dark fae prince. I was magic and not. I was from the human realm and the fae realm.

I was balance.

I placed my hand on the contract and the world vanished around me.

My eyes opened to an expanse covered in gray fog. A human appeared. They had no true shape, shifting like the clouds in the sky. They approached, and my first instinct was to embrace them.

"Sídhetír," I whispered.

They laughed. "Yes. The fastest anyone has ever recognized me, but you are not anyone, are you? You are Aidan."

"I suppose I am."

Dark words that instilled a chill in my soul began to reverberate around me. I looked around, but no one was speaking. Magic swelled and the specks of lights in the grayish cloud surrounding us turned into a single burning light.

"The forming of the gate," I guessed.

"Yes," Sídhetír replied. "Lord Rhett was driven mad by the deaths of six of his seven sons. To save the last one, he, with the help of a necromancer, used the blood of the dead to force magic to comply and join into a single gate."

The closer I got to the gate, the greater the sense of wrongness grew within me. It was not meant to be like this. "You're not going to allow me to sign the contract."

"Why would you say that?"

My fingers stroked the swirling silver of the gate. "Because it is not in balance, and you are magic. Sídhetír is magic." I finally understood. The sentience the land had received was not new. It was magic, all of magic, human and fae, tethered to one single point. Sídhetír and magic were one and the same.

"How much more you see and understand. Perhaps it is because you stand between the nexus of both realms, but you truly do not belong to either."

Turning from the gate, I faced Sídhetír. "What happens now?"

"What do you want to happen?"

"Balance," I said, thinking of Eilidh. Had she known what would happen? She'd known I was coming, so perhaps she'd guessed this outcome.

The clouds vanished, and I saw the battle waging. Blodwen led the charge. Abnus held her at bay while my brothers and the soldiers fought the light fae. Lord Byrne stood on the step, directing lightning at the invading forces. Lady Hester was at his side, guarding him with a bow as she felled anyone near him. Cethin was in the center of the horde, bleeding, as he fought the light fae.

The images shifted until I saw Oren guarding the door, blood spilling from his cheek as he attacked two winged fae that had breached the manor. All of us, including Oren, had been taught how to fight, so he was holding his own. But two fae against one human? It was only a matter of time until he faltered.

"I have to end this," I said.

"Then what do you want?" Sídhetír asked.

"Is it my decision?"

"If you want it to be."

"What?"

"You can shatter the contract and be free of me. Sídhetír will return to the land it once was and the gate will break into the many openings into the fae realm. Or you can sign the contract and tether it to your life. The choice is yours. It always has been, Aidan, as it was for every seventh son who walked before you."

My eyes darted back to the fight. Lord Byrne was drenched in sweat, his wrinkles and age more pronounced than ever. Lady Hester defended him to the best of her ability. Thomas and Whit stood back to back, fighting. Nevan and Neil felled fae with their pistols. Sevrin and Phineas on horseback fought in tandem with the soldiers. Lord Abnus attacked Blodwen. Oren protected me as I stood lifeless in the secret room.

Finally, my gaze locked on Cethin. Blood dripped from various wounds. He snarled at the light fae, sword in one hand and magic in the other. Our life in many ways would be simpler if I shattered the contract. I would not be the heir. We could live in the fae realm, together. Oren could be free. I could be free.

But what about everyone else? The fae would rip through the human realm like they once did. Humans would fall. Not only them, though. Humans would kill fae. Once again, needless blood would spill.

Perhaps that was balance.

I shook my head. I would never be able to live with myself if I chose that path. Every drop of blood spilled would become a stain on my soul that would never scrub clean. I would never know peace. And yet. If I chose Sídhetír, I would never know peace.

"Fate is an odd thing," I whispered.

Sídhetír smiled. "It is indeed. Your fate was written in blood. It was written in the stars. In the moon. In the sun. Your fate was written long ago, and still I wonder what you will choose. Magic knows no right nor wrong, only balance. And you, Aidan, are balance. What shall you choose?"

"I will choose as all the lords before me have," I said. "I shall give my blood in exchange for everyone else's."

"Once written, it cannot be undone except in death."

"I understand."

With even steps, Sídhetír raised their hand and said, "Then place your name by all your forefathers."

I pressed my palm to Sídhetír's, and agony unlike I'd ever known ripped through every nerve ending, forcing me to my knees.

Chapter 28

"When the heir accepts the mantle, beware, for the earth shall rise with their blood." – Lord Louis, Third Lord of Sídhetír.

The clang of metal meeting metal broke through the agony piercing my mind and flesh. I could not breathe. My senses were too much. I saw too much. I felt too much. I *was* too much. I was Sídhetír and myself, and yet I felt like neither. I was a creature forged of flesh and blood mixed with magic and an ancient awareness.

Fae were everywhere. Blemishes in the human realm, though they were familiar to me. Humans were like flickering candles in the shadows. They belonged, and yet they were strangers.

I was on my feet before I recalled thinking about it. Oren fought two fae, bleeding. He would not give an inch as the fae struggled to reach me. Sídhetír and I were in accordance; we were one. I could not differentiate where I started and they ended. I stepped from the secret room, glass crunching under my boots, and raised a hand. The light fae seized, stopping in place. Oren jerked toward me, though I couldn't pay him any attention.

My hand curled into a fist, and the very air tightened around the two fae's throats. "You are not welcome in my home. You are not welcome in my realm. You are not welcome in Sídhetír."

I thrust them backward with nothing but magic, and they flew out of the window. Screams tore out of their throats as the gate dragged them to the fae realm. Never would they step on Sídhetír land again.

"Aidan," Oren called.

I walked past him without sparing him a glance. My feet led me out of the manor. The clatter of swords, the thunk of arrows, the bang of pistols, the screams of the injured, and the silence of the dead all rang within my ears. I stood on the steps, and Jonathan Byrne faltered. No magic came forth from his hand. He looked at me, then bowed. "Lord of Sídhetír."

Much like Oren, I heeded him not. I walked down the stairs, every stone familiar. The very dirt was known to me. The grass was known. The plants. The animals. The humans. All known to me.

Slowly, the fighting stopped as I impassively moved to Blodwen and Abnus. Blood dotted Abnus from the injuries inflicted by Blodwen and the others, while she bore only minimal scratches, as she'd remained safe in the middle of the horde for most of the battle.

"Lord Abnus, stand by Oren," I ordered.

"Yes, Sídhetír."

My head tilted to the side as I studied Blodwen. Cethin forced his way through the crowd to my side, but I could not focus on him. My eyes landed on the blood that coated her fingers and the dead who called out in silence for revenge.

"I told your queen I would kill you if you but hurt one human."

"And you mean to kill me, Lord Aidan? My queen will rip every human to shreds if you do. War and blood will spill with every breath." Blodwen grinned.

I stepped closer, my hand gripping the front of her gown. "I fear no one. Fae, human, nothing. I am Sídhetír, and you are nothing but meat."

Her smile died. She lifted her hands to attack, but it never came, for a shock went through her and she fell to the ground, dead.

"I am Sídhetír," I said, stepping over her body and toward the light fae. "You are not welcome." I shoved the air in front of me and the ground lurched at the same time, casting the fae into the sky as the gate snagged them. Their screams rang as they sailed out of Sídhetír.

I turned around, and the crowd bowed, except for Cethin. Jonathan placed a fist over his heart. "All hail the new Lord of Sídhetír."

"Aidan," Cethin called, but his voice came from a distance. Sídhetír held me within their grasp, and we were one and the same. "Aidan. Dearest. Let Sídhetír go." His hand grasped mine and his mouth pressed against my ear. "Remember who you are."

Trembling began in my hands as magic swirled beneath my skin. It was too much. I was too much.

"We are safe, Aidan. Let Sídhetír go before you are lost to it."

Sídhetír brushed their fingers across my chin and began to settle. The magic drifted away, leaving me empty but once again myself.

My eyes dropped to Blodwen's lifeless body at my feet, and bile burned my throat. I swallowed, but it didn't help. I fell to the ground, and the meager contents of my stomach emptied onto the grass. Cethin's hands smoothed over my back.

I shook my head. My lungs burned and my eyes wouldn't tear away from Blodwen. I'd killed her. I'd *killed* her.

Another hand joined Cethin's on my back. Jonathan pressed a kiss to the back of my head and whispered, "Sleep, Aidan. Rest. Allow us to protect you."

Like his words contained magic, I slumped against Cethin and gave into oblivion.

Chapter 29

"Love is the greatest gift life can give us, and yet it is the hardest. Nothing hurts as badly as lost love. I wish with every fiber of my being that my heart stopped the same time Margaret's had." – Lord Jonathan, Eight Lord of Sídhetír.

"He's asleep," Cethin said. I fought to open my eyes, but it felt as if a great weight pressed them down.

"Still?" The new voice belonged to Thomas.

"Yes," Cethin answered. That single word was laced with worry. I tried to force myself to move or even make a single noise, but my body didn't respond, frozen in place. Shuffling sounded before Cethin continued, "He has slept longer than I anticipated."

"Father said he would sleep for a while to adjust to Sídhetír."

"It's been four days."

"Aidan expended copious amounts of energy when he first bonded, and he was tightly linked to Sídhetír. It's going to take time."

"I'm aware," Cethin said. "But I want him to wake."

"He will." There was a slapping sound like Thomas hugged Cethin and patted his back, which I didn't imagine my mate enjoying, but no snaps or harsh words followed. Cethin must have tolerated the touch. "Do you know how the Day Queen reacted to Blodwen's death or what exactly Aidan did with the contract?"

"No," Cethin replied. "Aidan is not allowing any fae in or out of Sídhetír in his slumber."

Thomas sighed. "We shall have to wait and see."

"Go," Cethin said, his voice steady. "I will notify you when Aidan wakes." His footsteps were almost silent on the wood floor before the bed dipped with his weight. Fingers brushed along my jaw, then cool lips pressed to my forehead. I wanted to open my eyes and respond, but my body wouldn't cooperate.

Sleep began to drag me away from Cethin, and I clung to awareness. Cethin needed me. But no matter what I wanted, sleep took me.

A beam of sunlight streaked in through the open window and kissed my face. I took a deep breath, eyes closing against the bright light. The warmth of magic slid under my skin in greeting. Sídhetír. They were still there, in the depths of my mind. The sensation of being bonded to the land wasn't as overwhelming as it had been the first time. Perceiving Sídhetír and all who inhabited it was odd, but not painful.

My mind instinctively raced across the face of the land, searching for any issues. I paused on Elmbury. Two full-blooded fae walked through the village, and I recognized them both. One was Fergus, who co-owned the florist shop with his very human husband, Conor. The other was a farmer whose name I didn't immediately remember, but I'd seen around. Neither had I guessed were fae. And they were not the only ones; I sensed a dotting of half-fae as well.

I was not the only half-fae in Sídhetír. Not even close.

Another distant light glimmered from the trees. The trees were not a boundary to my senses. The woods belonged to Sídhetír as much as the rest of the land, but the previous lords had been unable to perceive them because of the magic within the roots. Fae had lived among the trees, their magic saturating the woods. But as a half-fae, I saw what those before me were unable to perceive.

Iris. She was a light fae.

An arrow crashed right through my heart at the realization. I should have known. She never left the woods and had healing abilities. She'd most likely known what I was. Iris, much like everyone else in my life, had lied to me.

Cutting through the sting of betrayal, warm breath tickled my ear. Cethin slept right next to me. His arm was thrown over my waist while one of his legs was slung over mine. His head nestled against my neck and his even breath rushed over my skin. I slid my hand up his arm, fingers tracing the thorny vines encircling his limb. The marks shifted and throbbed under my touch, which sent a smile to my lips.

"Cethin," I whispered. He groaned and rocked into me. I stroked his arm. He must be exhausted. I couldn't see any visible injuries, but I wasn't sure how much time had passed since the battle or how fast his healing abilities worked.

I lifted his hand to my face and kissed his palm. "Cethin."He sighed, awakening. When his fathomless eyes met mine, he stilled, then shifted closer. "Aidan." His lips pressed against mine. "How are you?"

"I believe I am well." I ran a hand up his back, feeling his muscles tighten under my fingertips.

"Truly?"

The image of Blodwen's lifeless body at my feet rose from the depths of my mind, and my stomach churned. I'd killed her. In the moment, taking a life hadn't bothered me in the slightest. Sídhetír demanded recompense for the dead, and my anger had outweighed any other thought.

His hand strayed from my face, down my neck, and rested over my pounding heart. He rubbed my sternum as he whispered, "It's alright."

"I killed her."

"Yes," he said. "But you protected us. All of us."

I swallowed, shaking my head. Cethin settled on top of me, practically squashing me. The cool comfort of his body and the familiarity of his scent calmed my skittering pulse. I relaxed beneath him and hooked my arms around his waist, accepting the gift Cethin was.

After a moment, he leaned up. "What did you do with the contract? I can sense that you signed it and that you are the Lord of Sídhetír, but nothing more."

"Balance. Your mother asked me to consider that word in exchange for her help."

"She did?"

"That's all she wanted. When I was signing the contract, I couldn't help but think about it. So that's what I did."

"What?"

"The door will follow the seasons of the human realm. During the spring and summer, the gate will be tethered to the Day Court, and during the fall and winter, the gate will remain in the Night Court."

His mouth hung agape.

"What am I but balance?" I asked, repeating both Eilidh's and Sídhetír's words. I ran my hands up his back, fisting them in his long hair. "Do you think your mother knew this is what I would choose?"

"I do not see how that is possible, but it does not mean she didn't."

"She knew I was your mate. That the Heir of Sídhetír would be your mate."

"She never told me so," Cethin said with a frown.

I smoothed the crease between his eyebrows. Arching, I kissed him. "We're together now."

"Yes," he said. "I will never let you go."

"How very convenient, for I plan on keeping you right beside me."

Cethin kissed my chest where his mark lay. Warmth flooded my veins as my cock twitched, starting to fill with my burgeoning desire. His lips moved over the crescent moon and star, his tongue occasionally swiping at my skin. He moved up to the two flowers on my collarbone, one larger than the other. My breath quickened as Cethin pressed whisper-soft kisses down my arm.

He rolled me onto my side and kissed the thorns covering my shoulder blade, only to stop on the back of my arm. "Is that another bud?" His voice was so smug, I rolled my eyes. He nipped at the skin. "One more, dearest, and you will be my husband."

My cock stood at attention from his words. "Do you wish to wait until then?"

"What do you mean?" he asked, lips trailing down my side and teeth nibbling on my skin.

"I mean we could get married in the human way. Now."

He forced me onto my back, and his eyes scoured my face. "Is that something you desire?"

"You would be Lord Byrne, then. Well, if you want to take my name in the human realm." Though Byrne as a surname was difficult for me to think about. I had been Aidan Ryan for my entire life, not a Byrne. But that was now the surname I would have to use.

Cethin held my face in a firm grasp. "I would wed you this instant, Aidan. You and I are bound together. A marriage ceremony is but a formality in my mind, but I would if you wanted."

"I want to."

"Then let us do it now. How do we go about it?"

I laughed and arched up, so my hard cock pressed into his stomach. "Maybe not at this moment."

Black eyes glowing, he said, "I concur."

His fingers traced my shaft, then formed a cage and slid up. I groaned, my hips moving to chase the friction of his touch. His hand slid up and down my cock, moving faster. I grabbed the back of his neck and crushed my lips to his. I waited only the barest moment before forcing my tongue into his mouth, desperate for him.

Hands fisted in his hair, I kept him right where I wanted him. As Cethin stroked me, the kiss got wetter and hotter, but I had no desire to stop. I could not believe this was where my life had led. Only weeks ago, I hadn't known of Cethin's existence, and now I couldn't imagine living without him.

Cethin's fingers wandered away from my cock, and I growled in protest.

He kissed my neck, biting me. "I don't want you to come yet." Cethin leaned up, and his aspect changed, growing sharper and his horns appeared.

I brushed his harsh cheekbones before running my fingers along his jagged horns. His expression tensed and his eyes remained on mine. "Fucking hell, you are lovely, Cethin."

Smirking, he replied, "As are you."

When he tugged on my balls, I whimpered. His lips trailed down to my chest, taking one of my nipples into his mouth and sucking on it. I clutched his horns as I panted.

"Fuck," I moaned when he bit my nipple and his fingers alternated between my shaft and balls.

He moved to my other nipple and gave it the same treatment as the first. His fingers slid from my balls and circled my ass. "Aidan," he whispered against my skin. "I want to fuck you."

I nodded, biting my lip. My cock twitched at the thought of Cethin nestled inside of me and more liquid leaked out of my slit.

"I will be gentle."

"I trust you," I said in a harsh voice, breath uneven.

Cethin kissed me. "I love you."

"I love you too."

His lips quickly moved down my stomach as he stood. Cethin disappeared for only the barest moment before he returned with a plain tin I recognized. He settled in between my legs and took the head of my cock into his mouth, tongue lapping at the liquid.

"Moonlight, you taste good," he growled. I grabbed his horns, keeping his face close to me. Cethin didn't seem to mind, because he smiled, then took me fully into his mouth. He bobbed up and down, and I grunted, fingers tightening. The wet, warm heat of his mouth was addictive. I wanted to arch up into him, but I controlled the urge. His tongue lapped and swiped my shaft as he sucked on me, drawing breathless cries from my lips. One of his hands cupped my balls and played with the sensitive skin until I was writhing beneath him.

"Cethin. Fuck."

There was a quiet clank of metal, and a slick finger began to trace the rim of my ass. I tensed. Cethin sucked up and off my cock. "Relax, dearest."

"I'm nervous."

His finger stopped its circular movement. "We don't have to."

I shook my head. "I want you, Cethin."

"And you have me. No matter what."

He didn't understand. "I want you to fuck me."

Cethin kissed the inside of my thigh, and I groaned. His mouth returned to my cock, and his finger gently prodded my ass before sliding inside. He did not move it, allowing me time to adjust to the invasion as he sucked me. After a few moments, his finger slid in and out in time with his mouth. My breath quickened. My hips began to move with his thrusts.

A second finger joined the first, and I gasped when Cethin brushed something deep within me. It was as if he was stroking my cock from the inside.

He kissed the weeping tip of my cock. "I will make you feel good." His fingers returned to that spot, brushing it repeatedly. Stuttering moans came out of my throat as I gripped Cethin's horns tighter.

"You are perfect, my Aidan," Cethin whispered against my thigh.

I couldn't reply, because with each movement of his fingers, the pleasure inside of me grew until I was impaling myself onto his fingers.

"Cethin," I demanded, unable to force more than his name out of my lips. My heart was beating too fast and cries mixed with moans kept leaking from my lips while pre-cum dripped to my stomach. He placed my legs on his shoulders, pressing a kiss to one.

"Cethinathiel."

"W-what?" I asked, panting.

"My true name."

I paused. "You choose to tell me this *now*?"

He chuckled, kissed my calf. "I love you."

I wanted to respond, but his fingers picked up speed, a third joining the other two. An animalistic cry came from my lips and my head went back as Cethin prodded that perfect spot.

"Aidan." He guided his throbbing cock to my ass. The tip pressed against my hole, and I groaned at the tightness. "Bear down and exhale, dearest."

I followed his direction, and the head of his cock slid in, stretching me. I swallowed. Tears pricked the back of my eyes from the burning sensation.

"I can stop."

"No," I said. "Give me a second."

Cethin grabbed my cock and began to pump me, which made my breath quicken. Slowly, he pushed in deeper, then pulled back before thrusting in deeper. Each time, he slid further into me, opening me up, and my body relaxed.

"I'm inside you," he whispered, practically bending me in half to kiss my cheek.

I panted, unable to get any words out. Fuck. I was so full. I'd never felt anything even close to the sensation of him stretching me. Cethin rocked into me, the head of his cock hitting me perfectly. I groaned, gripping the sheets until my knuckles were white. My cock was impossibly hard. I wanted to stroke it, but I didn't want to come yet and end this.

Sweat dripped from Cethin's face as he thrusted into me in long, smooth strokes that left me shaking. He pulled out, and I whimpered. "Don't stop."

"I'm not." He kissed my ankle. "I'm shifting positions." Cethin guided my legs around his hips and pressed back inside of me. I wrapped my arms around his shoulders, and he picked up his pace pounding into me.

Loud moans escaped my lips, and I fought back the urge to come. "Cethin. I'm..."

His lips found mine and he moved even faster, jerking me in time with his thrusts. My head pressed back into the pillow as my mouth opened in a wordless cry and my eyes squeezed closed. Pleasure ripped through me as my cock spurted my release all over my stomach. Cethin squeezed my cock, milking my orgasm for all it was worth as he rode me through my pleasure. With one last ram, Cethin snarled my name and warm liquid spilled inside of me.

Cethin collapsed on top of me, panting. His cock was still inside me, softening, and my legs held him close. Trembles wracked my body from my hard release. I'd never come so hard in my life. He shifted so his cock slid out, but I tightened my arms around his shoulders to keep him on top of me.

I breathed in his scent, trying to calm the pounding of my heart and the tremors in my limbs. He kissed me, lips trailing over my face. "Aidan," he muttered between each kiss. He brushed gentle touches along the line of my jaw before nibbling my ear. His lips found mine, and the kiss was soft and slow.

"Aidan," he whispered again.

My fingers trailed over his back as a tired smile stretched over my face. "Cethin, I love you."

His eyes met mine. "So you will marry me in the human way and make me a lord?"

I laughed. "You are already a prince, but yes. I will marry you."

"Excellent. When your mark solidifies, you shall be a prince too."

"More responsibilities."

He chuckled, pressing his face into my neck. "I shall keep you happy."

"I have no doubt of that."

Chapter 30

"The truth can be hard to say, but once said, you will be free of the lies you have encased yourself in." – Lord Edmund, Second Lord of Sídhetír.

When I awoke for the second time that day, I slid out of bed, and Cethin didn't react. I cleaned up because we'd done a poor job before passing out in each other's arms. I yanked on some clothes, not Cethin's altered ones, though I imagined I would wear more of his clothes in the future since he liked it so much. Dressed in a proper waistcoat, jacket, cravat, and trousers, I stepped into the hall. I needed to speak to Lord Byrne, or Dowager Lord Byrne now.

But Jonathan Byrne was not the one who greeted me.

The hallway was lined with all seven of my brothers. Brothers. I had brothers. They all stood when I stepped out. Oren took a single step in my direction before stopping, chewing on his bottom lip. My eyes ran over each and every one of them. This time, I picked out the similarities between us. Never had I noticed them, but now I did—the strong jaw I shared with most of my brothers, the breadth of our shoulders, the shape of our hands, and the light green eyes Phineas and I shared with Jonathan.

"You all knew."

Oren shook his head. "I didn't."

I waved his comment away. "I know that. But the rest." I swallowed the sudden sting of betrayal. They had all known.

"Only I and Whit knew you were the Heir of Sídhetír," Thomas said, speaking for all of them as he often did. "Everyone else, besides Oren, knew you were a half-fae."

"And you kept it from me," I said, my voice raising. I peeked over my shoulder at the closed door. If I got too loud, Cethin would wake up and he needed to rest. "Come," I ordered. Without a backward glance, I walked down the hall to the family parlor.

Nerves wriggled in my stomach. Technically, I was Lord of Sídhetír, but that meant shit in the reality before me. My brothers didn't have to follow my orders, nor did I know if they actually would. Being lord had never been a future I'd planned for or thought of. Now, it was my truth. One I would have to reconcile myself to.

The room was well-furnished and a large pianoforte sat in the corner. My gaze didn't linger on the familiar furniture or paintings; instead, I looked out the glass doors, which led to the balcony. Days ago, I'd scaled down the columns to sneak out and see Cethin. How different my life was in a short span of time.

Once the last of the Byrne brothers had entered the parlor, Nevan shut the door. They spread around the room, taking various seats, as I focused on the sight of Sídhetír out the window. Oren was the only one who came near me. He lifted a hand to touch me, but it fell to his side.

"Aidan," Thomas started, but I waved off his comment.

I didn't know what words I needed to ease the sting in my soul. No words might be sufficient. Though could I truthfully blame them? Thomas and Whit had had no reason to tell me the truth. I was their brother in blood alone. And the rest? Why should they have felt the need to tell me about my heritage? I hadn't been their brother, only a Byrne family ward.

"Aidan," Thomas said again. His feet padded across the hardwood floor in my direction. He placed a hand on my shoulder and turned me toward him. I stared into a face I'd known my entire life. His hand tightened on my shoulder. "We should have told you, but..."

"We and Father hoped the magic of Sídhetír could be tricked," Whit finished. "For we feared that you couldn't sign the contract."

I had guessed as much. "Tell me."

Thomas glanced at Whit. "This is Father's story."

"Tell me," I demanded. I needed to know, but I didn't want to speak to Jonathan yet.

"Your mother showed up one day," Thomas started without preamble. "She had you with her." He smiled. "You were such a small thing of two. Vis insisted on speaking with Father, and he agreed."

"You two were here, not at school?" I asked, glancing between them. I was fourteen years younger than Thomas.

"Visiting," Whit said. "It was near Oren's birthday, and all of us were here."

"You were sitting outside of Father's bookroom when Oren found you," Thomas continued. "He grabbed your hand, and you followed him outside to play. Me and Whit went with you two. You started to fall at one point, and a vine wrapped around your arm and stabilized you."

I closed my eyes. "You guessed."

"Yes," Thomas said. "I truly studied you. Your green eyes were Father's and you looked like us—as much as a toddler looks like anyone."

"Did you guess I was half-fae?"

Whit shook his head. "No. Father eventually came to the garden with Vis at his side. He didn't even glance at any of us, just walked straight to you. He picked you up and held you close."

"We knew then," Thomas said. "You were our brother. Father simply held you. When he met our eyes, he nodded. Father told us about you being half-fae and the heir. He did not hide it from us. Mainly, I believe, because we suspected and he couldn't conceal it from us. In time, Whit and I told the rest of our brothers of your fae heritage to protect you, but we kept the fact you were heir to ourselves."

Nevan crossed his arms and a deep scowl marred his face. He was not alone. Most of my brothers had a similar expression on their faces—even calm Phineas appeared annoyed. None of them compared to the red-faced Oren.

"None of you bothered to tell me, either," he said.

"You can't keep secrets from Aidan," Sevrin explained, and Oren scoffed.

I shifted from them and stared out the window. What should I do? I wanted to curl against Cethin and ignore the world around me. Unfortunately, that wasn't viable or helpful. Though I imagined Cethin would be perfectly happy with such a scenario.

"Why did Lord Byrne hide me?" I asked, unable to keep the words buried. "Yes, I am a bastard, a half-fae, but I'm his son."

Gentle hands grabbed my arms, and I knew who it was before Oren tugged me into a hug. He had no answers either, but at least he offered me comfort. The others probably would have, but I would've spurned them, which they probably guessed.

I shifted to return the embrace and looked over Oren's shoulder. Each of the Byrne brothers, my brothers, had stood. My anger at them was irrational, for they had had little choice in keeping the secret. Besides, they must have thought keeping everything from me was the best.

And maybe it was. I got to live my life without the burden of being heir or half-fae, and yet, I couldn't accept such an assertion. Oren had spent his life in terror, forced into a position that wasn't meant to be his, and I was shunted to the side—longing for a family that was right there for the taking.

Thomas stepped forward to speak for the Byrne brothers. He looked not only at me but all of us. "Father ordered Whit and I not to tell any of you about who Aidan was. He feared the end of the contract, and what it would mean, not only for Sídhetír but the whole of the country. But we were wrong."

Whit nodded in agreement.

Holding out his hands, Thomas said, "We have always stood together, as we should. No matter what Father wanted, I should have told all of you. Especially you, Aidan."

Oren let go of me and stood at my side. "You should have told us. Aidan deserved to know."

"So did you," I said, bumping his shoulder. "Oren deserved to have a life. A choice."

Oren grabbed my hand.

"You're right," Thomas said.

Whit added, "He did. You both did." He glanced at the rest of his younger brothers. "You all deserved the truth about why we were protecting Aidan."

"We did," Sevrin said. "We truly thought we were shielding you, Aidan. You never presented any magic and could touch iron. Your mother was gone, and you had no one."

"And," Nevan said, draping an arm over Neil's shoulders, "we liked you and didn't want you to leave."

"I wouldn't have wanted to leave either," I said. It was the truth. Sídhetír was my home, and the Byrnes had been my family even before I'd known.

Thomas stepped forward with his arms open, but I shifted back. While I accepted why they had kept the secret, I wasn't ready to forgive them. His smile fell, hurt easily displayed on his face.

"I'm not quite there yet."

"I understand."

The door opened, and I expected to see Cethin striding in, but it wasn't him. Instead, Lord Byrne stepped inside. "Good afternoon, my sons." He smiled at all of us, but his gaze lingered on me. "All of my sons."

My heart hardened into a solid mass. "I am not your son."

Lord Byrne faltered in his step. "You are, Aidan."

"I may share your blood, but you lost any chance you had of being my father when you rejected me and hid my existence. You are not my father, and I am not your son."

"Aidan," he tried again, but I pushed past him and fled down the hallway. I could feel him following me, but I darted to a window. Without a single hesitation, I leaped outside. Ivy vines curled about me and the ground rose to soften the landing. My feet hit the flagstones with a small thud, jarring my aching ribs, but I did not stop. I raced to the hedge maze and out of the iron gate. The key wasn't in my pocket, but it opened for me without a single touch.

The fields of Sídhetír sprawled in front of me. The snow had disappeared, since my magic was no longer fueling the clouds, but the air remained chilly and leaves steadily fell from the branches to the ground. I headed to the trees. Yet another person who I needed to confront remained.

Iris.

Why hadn't she told me she was a fae? Perhaps I should've been able to sense her, or maybe she didn't know that I was half-fae. The answers weren't as important as the reason why she'd concealed herself. Hopefully, she wasn't another person who'd known exactly who I was and had chosen to keep it from me.

When I stepped under the boughs, the trees shifted toward me, their branches leaning to caress me. The forest had never responded to the previous Lords of Sídhetír, but I sensed the woods as easily as I did the rest of the land. The trees were mine.

Even as a child, I'd been drawn to the forest. Was it because of my fae blood? Possibly. It truly didn't matter. I loved the woods, and the trees loved me.

Taking a deep breath, I knocked on Iris's door. Shuffling came from the other side before the door cracked open, and Iris peeked out. She smiled at the sight of me, but as she opened the door, her smile faltered and her eyes narrowed.

"Aidan, what happened to you?"

"The bruises?" I asked, touching my face. "You've seen them."

She shook her head, eyes wide and pupils blown. "You are the Lord of Sídhetír. How is that possible? She would have told me."

My stomach dropped to my feet. "*She*? My mother? You knew my mother?"

Her hand tightened on the door. "It hardly matters in the end, I suppose."

I scoffed. "It does matter. You have to know it matters. You knew my mother?"

"Aidan," Iris said, drawing out my name. "I don't understand how this is possible."

"Iris, answer the bloody question. Did you know my mother?"

She pushed the door open. "Come inside, Aidan. I suppose I must tell you what happened."

I followed her inside, taking a seat at the table. She poured us both a cup of tea, then sank down across from me.

"Your mother, Vis, was my best friend and my first love. She snuck into the human realm when Jonathan Byrne was the heir and the mantle was shifting. She was enamored with humans. I was not."

Those few words told me more about my mother's past than I'd ever heard in my entire life. "How did you come to be here, then?"

Iris ran her fingers over the rim of her cup and her aspect changed. Her brown hair fell free of the braid, all of the gray fading. Her skin became pure gold with the texture of bark, and white horns grew out of her head. Her teeth were jagged and sharp, and her hands lengthened, gaining an extra knuckle and wicked claws. "I snuck in through a less desirable passage. I didn't know if it would lead here or simply back to the fae realm or possibly nowhere at all. I wanted to see Vis again and bring her home."

"And?"

Iris took a drink of her tea. "When I arrived, she was dying and you were entrusted to Lord Byrne. She begged me to care for you, and I agreed."

"You knew I was half-fae."

"Naturally. Your mother was a fae, but she did not tell me who your father was. I would have never guessed Jonathan Byrne, let alone you being the Heir of Sídhetír. Did he tell you how this came about?"

"No," I said. "I ran when I saw him."

"Hmm."

"Why didn't you tell me, Iris?" I asked, hurt stabbing me. "We've been friends for years."

"I was protecting you, Aidan. You didn't know you were fae, and you were Jonathan Byrne's ward. I didn't know how much he could or could not sense. Did he know you were half-fae? Or would me telling you endanger you to banishment? You knew nothing of the fae realm, and I didn't know if you'd survive there. Not many half-fae can without protection."

My hands fisted around the cup. "Everyone keeps trying to protect me by lying."

"I didn't lie. I cannot."

I glared at her. "You may not have uttered a lie, but you certainly did not tell the truth."

She shrugged. "I am fae. And I *was* protecting you."

Pushing the teacup away, I stood. "I do not need you to protect me. I needed the truth. Why didn't one person tell me the damn truth?"

"The truth can be a difficult thing. One person's truth is another person's lie. I was keeping you safe. If no one knew of your fae heritage, no one could hurt you, whether Lord Byrne or fae."

"Hurt me?"

"Fae are not allowed to be here without permission. Half-fae have more leniency. But what if a noble fae found you? You could say you truly didn't know. Ignorance would be your shield. If I'd known you were the Heir of Sídhetír, I might have told you, though I might not have. I cannot say. But you were simply my little Aidan, son of my childhood friend."

I sank onto the chair. "Why didn't she tell me?"

"That I do not know, but Vis loved you more than anything, Aidan. You were the most important thing. She gave up the fae realm for you."

"That she did." I met her gaze. "So did you."

"For now," she said with a gentle smile. "Someday I will return, but for now, I shall remain by your side."

God, I was furious with her. The betrayal of her half-truths and secrets burned me, but I didn't want her to leave. She had been a mother and friend to me when I needed one. I whispered, "Tell me about her."

"Vis wasn't a noble fae like you are used to. She was as average as dirt, but she was breathtaking. Her magic leaned to the trees, much like I believe yours does, slight as it is."

It was a nice thought to be similar to her.

"She loved humans. It was her dream to come here. I didn't understand it. Vis had no healing magic or skills to sell. That plus her common heritage meant she was never going to be allowed to travel through the gate, so she snuck in during the transition, despite the danger. Perhaps fate knew you needed to be born."

"Was it really so dangerous for her? Is it for you?"

"Yes. Nobles will flood through the gate once you allow it, and they will seek any fae who do not have permission to be here. Once the fae makes it past the border of Sídhetír, they are free of your power, and the noble fae are bound by the contract to hunt them down. Your Prince Cethin may even be called to action."

A random thought popped into my mind. "Iris, you didn't..."

She took a long drink of her tea, staring directly at me. "I didn't do what, Aidan?"

The way her expression had frozen when she saw Cethin for the first time bloomed in my mind. Other remembrances crashed through me. The way she hadn't come near him or touched him. She'd wanted him to die, but when I forced her to help me, she'd fed him a potion to cure poison—poison she'd stabbed him with.

My eyes turned glassy. "Iris, tell me you didn't."

"I will always protect myself, Aidan."

"You stabbed him!" I slammed my hands on the table, which was echoed by a deep rumble in my chest. I took a deep breath to calm down. I wasn't used to my emotions affecting everything.

She slowly stood. "You do not understand. You see Cethin and are enamored by him, but noble fae are brutal. They have remained in power for a long time despite their smaller number, and they will kill anyone who threatens them. Fae are not humans. We do not think as you do, so stop attempting to impose your same morals on us.

"I stabbed Cethin and would have gladly seen him dead to keep myself safe. But," she said, cupping my cheek, "I am glad for you that he lives. I am glad he is your mate because you shall live a long and happy life. But you must remember, Aidan, fae are not human and you cannot expect us to act the same."

I slapped her hand away, standing. Cethin had said he wasn't mad at the person who stabbed him, and he truly meant it. He'd killed three fae in front of me during our short acquaintance to protect me. Violence was a way of life for fae. They were different. I'd known that, but it was difficult to remember.

My heart clenched. She was my friend, but Iris had lied to me and stabbed Cethin. Granted, it was prior to her knowing Cethin was my mate, and yet, anger burned in my gut. I wanted to forgive her, but it would take time—like everything else.

"I should go."

Iris gave me a sad smile. "I will be here, Aidan, but I will not apologize."

When I reached the door, I paused. "No one will harm you here, Iris. I will protect you."

"Of course you will. I'm amazing."

I wanted to laugh as I normally did, but I couldn't. I was so angry and hurt about her lying to me.

Iris continued, "I would like to tell you everything about Vis someday."

Prickles burning the backs of my eyes, I didn't answer her and went outside. The first thing I spotted was Cethin leaning against a tree with a slight smirk on his lips. I threw my arms around his neck. Cethin lifted me off the ground and his lips found mine.

"My Aidan," he murmured. "Why did you leave without me?"

"I needed to talk to my brothers and Iris."

"The fae?"

I frowned at him. "You knew?"

"You did not?"

"No."

"I see," Cethin said. "I would have told you if I'd known about your lack of knowledge."

"Would you have?" I played with his long hair.

"Yes." He bit my nose before lowering me to the ground.

Swallowing, I said, "Iris is the one who stabbed you."

He paused, then said, "I see."

I gripped his arm. "Please don't hurt her." As angry as I was, I didn't want anything to happen to her, let alone by Cethin's hand.

"I won't."

"She thought you were here to hunt her."

"Iris snuck into Sídhetír?"

"She hasn't caused any trouble."

"Then she has nothing to worry about," Cethin said.

"But?"

Cethin brushed my cheek. "We nobles hunt and, yes, kill wayward fae when they cause trouble or make excessive deals, but otherwise?" He shrugged. "We truly don't care. We meet the demands of the contract, and nothing more. Your Iris is safe as long as she doesn't cause significant trouble."

I sighed, shoulders sagging in relief, then straightened. "But she stabbed you."

"And I am grateful because she brought me to you."

Going up on my toes, I pressed my lips to his. Cethin deepened the kiss and grabbed my ass, lifting me back into the air. I wrapped my legs around his waist. My tongue battled his while I fisted a hand in his hair.

"Shall we adjourn to our cottage where your brothers cannot find us?"

A groan slipped out of my lips before I could stop it. I bit my lip. Cethin and I spending time beneath the trees, the babbling of the creek soothing every tension, sounded perfect.

He kissed my neck. "I believe that is a yes."

His touch was intoxicating. I tilted my head to the side stupidly to allow him more access. With every brush of his lips, thoughts fell from my mind and my body loosened. My cock twitched. Cethin moaned, nibbling the shell of my ear.

"Come with me."

I wanted to say yes. I wanted to disappear with Cethin for a few days, but I now had responsibilities that I couldn't ignore.

The tip of his nose dragged along my ear. "Aidan."

It took everything I possessed to shift away, feet hitting the ground. Cethin stared at me with hooded eyes. Desire burned in the black depths. An answering desire swelled within me. "I want to."

"Then we shall."

"I can't, Cethin. I have duties now. I cannot run away from them."

Cethin frowned, but he said, "I do understand."

"I know you do, Your Highness."

His frown deepened. "I do not like you calling me that."

I chuckled, dragging my hands through his long hair. "I won't in the future, but I was teasing you."

"I will kidnap you from your responsibilities later."

"I look forward to it."

Chapter 31

"As the lord, you will have to make decisions you don't like. I had to make a choice—a choice for the best of Sídhetír and my son. God forgive me, I hope it is not a mistake, but what else can I do?" – Lord Jonathan, Eighth Lord of Sídhetír.

I stepped into Lord Byrne's bookroom, or rather my bookroom. How truly odd. This room had been the one I associated most with Jonathan Byrne. All throughout my childhood, he'd been there, sitting behind the desk, reading. My fingers ran along the spines of the books on the shelves. The Memoirs of Sídhetír. He would add his last thoughts to his journal, then it would fall to me to continue them. I would be the last Lord of Sídhetír. There would be no others.

"Aidan."

My eyes closed at the sound of Lord Byrne's voice. He was such a distant figure. I hadn't spent much time with him growing up. Now I had to reconcile with the fact he was my father.

"Aidan," he said again, "or I should say, Lord Byrne."

Not even the barest hint of a smile touched my lips.

"I would like to speak with you."

"About what?"

"The truth. You deserve to know what happened, and I would like to tell you if you will allow me."

I gestured for him to continue.

He moved to the window. "My first wife, Margaret, was my heart. I felt as if she was a part of me. I loved her dearly. I knew when I was young that she was the one I would marry. I married her days after my twenty-first birthday. I thought I knew what my life would be. She and I talked of all the sons we would have, and what we would accomplish. Margaret was my everything, and she died giving birth to Whitaker."

This was something I'd known, though he rarely spoke of Margaret.

"I don't know if you can imagine such devastation. Perhaps you can since you care for Prince Cethin."

"I love him," I corrected.

"Indeed."

"Did you consider not continuing the contract?"

"I did," he said. "I truly thought about giving Sídhetír to Thomas and breaking the contract because I could not imagine being with anyone else. Margaret held my heart, and she still does."

"What happened?"

"Briella. She came to me. We were childhood friends. She knew I was heartbroken and wanted no one else, but she also knew I needed to continue the Byrne line. She offered to marry me. There would be no romance between us, but we could have five more children."

The end of this story was not a happy one either.

"A year after Nevan and Neil were born, Briella got sick. No matter how many physicians I consulted, she didn't get better. Death claimed her." Lord Byrne shook his head as his eyes turned glassy. "I could not continue. I could not marry another, even though I needed one more son to carry on the line. I was done.

"My queen did not allow that. She arranged my marriage to Hester, who understood there would be no love between us. For God's sake, she's over ten years younger than I am. I hated the idea of wedding her, but Hester wanted out of her parents' house, and I was a way to do that."

"You married her," I said.

"I didn't want to. God help me, I didn't want to, Aidan. I have never hated being Lord of Sídhetír more than I did at that moment. I hated Sídhetír. I hated everything, including myself. I didn't want to marry again. I didn't want any more children. I didn't want to be myself."

"What happened?"

"We married, and I couldn't bring myself to look at her."

"When did you meet my mother?" I asked, shifting closer to him.

"A few months after Hester and I married, we went to town for a short visit, and I snuck away and ended up in a cheap tavern. I drank. A lot. Vis came in. She was the most beautiful woman I'd ever seen with her deep red hair and bright blue eyes. We started talking. She didn't know who I was, and I didn't know she was a light fae. We spent the night together."

"You strayed?" I should've known that since Oren and I were only seven days apart in age, but somehow, even though I was a bastard, I had assumed Lord Byrne hadn't betrayed Lady Hester.

"I did. When I awoke in the morning, Vis was gone, and I thought I would never see her again. I did what I had to in regards to Hester."

I scoffed at the obfuscation. "You bedded her."

"Yes, if you wish to be direct about it."

"When did you learn about me?" I asked, moving even closer to him until we stood shoulder to shoulder.

"Over two years later. Vis showed up on my doorstep with a young child hiding behind her. She told me you were mine."

I closed my eyes.

"When she got pregnant, Vis had no intention of finding me. I wasn't important. But after you were born, you were exceedingly sick, so she planned to take you to the fae realm. The second she crossed into Sídhetír, you recovered."

"I was the heir."

"Yes," he said. "The first one to be born outside of Sídhetír since the contract."

"Why didn't she seek you immediately?"

"Your mother didn't know who I was, but she soon figured it out, and more importantly, she found out who you were."

"What happened?"

Lord Byrne sighed. "She asked me to change your fate. She didn't want you to be the Lord of Sídhetír for fear of what the fae would do to you, and I feared you would not be able to sign the contract. I already had Oren as my heir, but how could I not acknowledge you?

"I wanted to meet you, and you were in the garden playing with Oren. I picked you up, and you stared at me with eyes so like my own. Only Phineas had eyes like mine. I didn't want to let you go, Aidan, but you could not be the heir, so I did. Though you and Oren refused to part. Always playing and seeking each other out." He laughed before growing quiet. "When your mother died, I made you a ward of the Byrne estate to keep you safe. I forbade Thomas and Whitaker to tell anyone who you were."

"You told Lady Hester?"

"I did," he answered. "She deserved to know, and she agreed to keep the secret. She did tell me I was foolish to try and trick the magic of Sídhetír."

Hester had known I was a child of her cheating husband, and yet she had never treated me badly. Not once. She'd known *I* was the heir, not her own son, and yet she was always kind to me. That level of decency and forgiveness made me cringe at my own anger.

The old Lord of Sídhetír faced me. "You are right, Aidan. I am not your father. I made a choice long ago, and that decision precludes me from ever being your father. I thought if I acted like I was, this would be easier. For the next five years, per tradition, I will be here guiding you, and I thought it would be easier for me to let go of Sídhetír if I acted like you were like Oren, my son.

"I have spent thirty, almost forty, years bound to Sídhetír, and now, it's missing from my mind. I am bereft without it." He placed a hand on my shoulder. "I will guide you as best I can, Aidan, but I will expect no more than that."

My eyes closed as I swallowed. I barely remembered my own mother. I'd longed for a family, and now, I had one. I had seven brothers. A sister in Whit's wife, Frances. A sibling in Thomas's spouse, Georgie. Nieces. An aunt of a sort, if Iris considered herself as such. A step-mother. A father, if I was willing to forgive him.

I grabbed his hand and whispered, "Give me time. I want to be a family, but I cannot just yet."

"I can give you time."

When I reached the door, I turned around. "I plan to marry Cethin. Soon."

He chuckled. "I suspected. Apparently, he's already sleeping here. If you weren't already engaged, I could make him take responsibility for ruining you."

Heat rushed to my cheeks. "You know about that."

"Your brothers like to talk."

"Damn them."

Laughing, Lord Byrne said, "They love you."

"And I them."

Looking around, he said, "This is your bookroom now."

I swallowed. True, but uncomfortable. "One step at a time."

He inclined his head. "We'll start small, but there are decisions you will need to make."

"I want to marry Cethin first."

"Then we shall start there."

I sat in the garden as the chilly air pressed against me. No one bothered me or Cethin, who lay with his head in my lap. I finger-combed his silky white hair as I watched the clouds drift over the sky.

"Were you serious when you said you would marry me?" I asked.

"Yes."

"Do you want to marry me?"

"Yes, Aidan. Now?"

"Well, not at this exact moment, but soon."

Cethin closed his eyes, and I trailed my fingers over his face. His gray-purple skin was impossibly smooth. My heart raced at the mere sight of him. A flush rushed to my cheeks. How long would such feelings last? Hopefully forever.

I bent down and found his lips. His hand fisted in my hair at the nape of my neck. I groaned, deepening the kiss as I pushed my hand under the neckline of his shirt to run my fingers over his chest, tracing one of his nipples.

"Aidan," he whispered.

God, I loved the sound of my name on his lips. My touch turned frantic as I kissed him. He arched up into me, holding me close.

Someone coughed, and I started. Cethin didn't react, continuing to kiss me. I pulled back, and Cethin muttered something dark and glared at the intruder. Oren stood not far from us, red faced.

"We are occupied, brother of my mate," Cethin said in a low voice.

Oren turned an even darker red.

I smacked Cethin. "Be nice."

He glanced at me. "We *are* busy."

Ignoring him, I asked, "Oren, what do you need?"

"Can I talk to you? Alone. Preferably."

Cethin growled, but I clamped a hand over his mouth before he said something inappropriate. I took several deep breaths, trying to get my cock to relax. It had started to harden with Cethin's intoxicating touch, and Oren didn't need to witness the tenting of my trousers.

"Yes," I told him, keeping my hand over Cethin's lips. "Give me a moment. I will meet you by the stables."

When Oren disappeared, Cethin bit my palm. "You want me, Aidan. I can feel it. He can speak to you another time."

"Oren is important, and I haven't had much of a chance to speak with him since everything happened."

He frowned.

"He helped me sneak out to you."

Cethin sighed and swung off my lap. "Fine. Speak with your little brother. I shall devour you tonight."

My hand wrapped around his neck as I tugged him close for a kiss. "I love you, Cethinathiel."

"And I you." He nuzzled my face. "Can you open the gate, so I may speak to my parents and sister about our wedding?"

"You'll come back, right?" I asked, not looking at him.

Cethin growled and kissed me fiercely before biting my bottom lip. "Nothing can keep me from you, Aidan. We are bound together. You are everything."

My erection was not going down, and his words in combination with his addictive touch weren't helping. "I will allow you to leave, but no other fae can come in yet. I need to speak with the different queens first."

"Wise." He pressed his forehead against mine and took a deep breath. "I will come back soon."

After Cethin had been gone for several minutes, I was able to calm down enough to meet Oren at the front of the stable. "I'm sorry," I told him. "I didn't intend anyone to see us."

"Which is why you were kissing your husband-to-be in the middle of the *public* garden?"

"I guess."

Oren pushed his arm through mine. "I'm happy for you."

"About Cethin?"

"I don't think you want to be congratulated on inheriting Sídhetír."

"I don't." I took a deep breath. It wasn't Oren's fault I was a week older than him. It wasn't his fault Lord Byrne had slept with my mother. Oren deserved the best. "But you are free."

He sagged against me. "I can leave. I can go to school." Oren beamed at me. "I'm so happy."

His radiant expression was like a punch to the gut. Bile burned my throat and my heart attempted to escape my ribcage. But I would not allow it to sour our relationship. Oren was my best friend, and I had always considered him my brother, which was now true.

"I'm happy for you."

"I don't suppose…" he trailed off.

"I will arrange for you to go to school. Lord Byrne wants me to begin training as the lord. I'm sure he would be happy to help me."

Oren bit his lip, eyes averted as he led me around the garden. "You should call him something else. You're Lord Byrne now."

There was some truth to his words, but I couldn't bring myself to call him Father, or anything similar. "You might be correct. Should I call him Jonathan?"

He chuckled. "Perhaps."

I tightened my arm around him. Soon Thomas would go back to his spouse, Whit to his wife, Phineas and Sevrin to their ranch, Nevan and Neil to town, and Oren to school. I would be alone with Jonathan and Hester. They wouldn't move to the dower house until I was ready to lead by myself. I didn't want to let Oren go, but he deserved to be free.

"Promise me something."

"Anything," Oren said.

"Be careful saying that to a fae."

"I do not fear you, Aidan. You're my older brother."

Tears pricked the back of my eyes. "I am that."

"What do you want me to promise?"

"Write to me. Frequently. I will miss you."

Oren tugged me into a hug. "I'll miss you too."

I squeezed him. I wanted to keep him here beside me, but he wanted to go. I loosened my hold. "Promise me."

"I promise."

With that said, I started toward the manor. I would have to speak to Lord Byrne. Before I made it, Oren said, "Thank you."

"For what?"

"Giving me my dream."

A wide smile pulled at my lips. "I would do anything for you, little brother."

"Damnation," Oren groaned. "I have seven fucking older brothers."

I laughed. "You do. You gained one, and there's no escaping any of us."

Gentle caresses on my neck woke me. The room was dark with only the fire providing flickering light. Arms held me tight as someone nibbled and sucked on my neck. "Cethin," I said, voice rough with sleep, "you're back."

"I am."

"What did your family say?"

"My mother congratulated you on your ingenuity with the gate."

It had been her idea.

"My father did not understand the need for a wedding, because we are already bound, but they gave their permission, which I do not require."

I chuckled, rolling to face him. "Do they want to come?"

"No, but they will if their presence is required. I wasn't certain, as I haven't attended a human union before."

"They don't have to, but I would like it if they came."

"Then they shall." His fingers brushed my cheek as his eyes darkened with need. "I promised to devour you later. It is later."

My arms snaked around him. "So that was your intention in waking me?"

"One of them, yes." He pressed his nose against my neck and took a deep breath. "I cannot get enough of you, Aidan. It's hard to contain myself from touching you."

I pulled him on top of me and yanked off his shirt. "Stop trying."

He crushed his lips to mine, growling, "You may regret that."

"I will not, because I cannot get enough of you either."

Cethin groaned but said no more as he quickly tugged off my nightshirt.

Chapter 32

"Becoming the Lord of Sídhetír is more overwhelming than I can say, but I will say this: I do not regret it. Sídhetír is me and I am Sídhetír. I have my brothers, my stepmother, and my father behind me. They shall help me every step of the way, and when I falter, my mate Cethin is more than happy to hold me up. While I would not have chosen this fate only a year ago, I choose it now. I choose it every day. And I shall continue to choose it for as long as I live." – Lord Aidan, the Last Lord of Sídhetír.

"This does not make sense," Cethin said, staring at me. "I'm not allowed to spend the night with you because we are getting married tomorrow? Nor can I see you in the morning, *and* we have to attend a sermon and family breakfast before we can fuck?"

I rubbed my temples. I had tried, repeatedly, to explain human weddings to him, and he didn't understand. I thought he was purposefully not comprehending, because last week, the fifth flower had budded on my tattoo, making us married in his culture.

"Repeat what the vicar says, and it will be fine." It was the best I could hope for.

He scowled. "I *am* trying, Aidan, but it makes no sense. We are married. We are mates. We are bound. We fuck almost every night. Why is this night different?"

"It simply is. You will sleep in another room or in the cottage, and we will be married tomorrow."

Cethin pressed against me, arms around my waist. "What if I miss you?"

"Handle it yourself."

"That is not what I mean," he said. "What if I miss *you*? I do not like being apart."

I returned his embrace. "Suffer until our wedding." At his expression, I laughed.

A little over a month had passed since I became Lord of Sídhetír, and much had happened since. My brothers and I had repaired our relationships. Thomas, Whit, Phineas, and Sevrin all had returned home, though they came back for my wedding, but Nevan and Neil had stayed. They'd agreed to wait until spring to return to town. Oren had made the same agreement.

Lord Byrne and I still struggled to relate to each other, but our relationship was slowly improving—though he often compared me to Oren, which I didn't enjoy. Hester had started to act like my mother, and truthfully, I didn't mind. Iris and I had repaired our relationship, and she finally left the woods, on occasion, though she still didn't care for Cethin. I had seen Cethin's parents a couple of times and met his younger sister, Cerridwen.

Cethin and I had spent basically every day together, and my feelings for him had not dampened. Instead, they grew with every passing moment.

Carding my fingers through his hair, I glanced at the door before whispering, "One of my brothers will be guarding my room to keep you out, so sneak in through the window tonight."

He grinned. "I prefer this plan, and it makes more sense. We belong together."

I forced him out of the room to appease my brothers as well as maintain propriety, but Thomas lifted an eyebrow, and I guessed he knew Cethin would not be far from my bed. Each of my brothers slapped him on the back. Nevan even threw an arm over his shoulders and whispered something that made Cethin grin.

Slowly, he was getting to know them, and more shockingly, Cethin was starting to care about them, especially Oren. Much like me, he felt overprotective of Oren, who complained that he was now inheriting *yet* another brother. Whit's wife and Thomas's spouse would often dote on Oren, but they were not as overbearing.

Nevan called over his shoulder, "Never thought you'd be leg-shackled before me, Aidan."

"Careful," I said, "Hester has been giving you all appraising looks. Your own marriages are coming."

Nevan paled—he was not alone—and Cethin smirked at me, dragging Nevan along.

Oren moved to my side as my brothers followed Cethin down the hall. "He's going to fly through the window, isn't he?"

"Yes."

"Of course he is. You two cannot be apart for even a moment."

A blush rushed to my cheeks. Oren had accidentally walked in on us in my bookroom only two days ago. I'd been bent over the desk as Cethin pounded into me. We'd forgotten to bolt the door, but in all fairness, I'd been loud enough that Oren should have known what was happening.

"Sorry about… you know."

"I will always knock now."

More heat rushed to my face.

He glanced away, chewing on his lip. "Are you sending Lord Abnus away?"

"Why?" I asked. Abnus had remained in Sídhetír as the representative while the Day Court sent another fae. They both negotiated for access to Sídhetír, and we had finally come to an agreement, once Queen Laoise stopped threatening war. During his stay, Abnus and Oren had continued to develop a friendship—a first for Oren.

Oren shrugged. "I'm curious."

"Queen Eilidh ordered his return. Abnus has responsibilities there. He is the queen's nephew and Cethin's cousin, not to mention his own property."

He nodded, eyes on the ground.

"You will be at university in the spring."

"True," he said, straightening. "I was merely curious."

"I see." I didn't believe his words for a moment. "If you write to him, I will send your letters to the Night Court."

"You will?"

"Yes."

"Thank you," Oren said with a bright smile. Ducking his head, he walked down the hall. I shook my head. His affection at least had a chance now. An offer of engagement to Miss Quirke wouldn't have to be extended. Though her mother might claim injury because it had been widely assumed Oren would wed her. No matter. I would protect Oren from any threat to his happiness.

Whether Abnus would return Oren's affection remained to be seen. I also didn't know if Oren should be with Abnus. Being with a fae wasn't the easiest, and Abnus had a fated mate somewhere. I didn't want Oren to be hurt.

Time would tell, I supposed.

I turned to go into my room, where I had no doubt Cethin was, when a voice stopped me. "Aidan."

Lord Byrne—Jonathan—came down the hall toward me. Straightening, I paused. "Yes?" I still could not bring myself to call him Father, but he didn't want to be called Lord Byrne any longer, because it confused people, and calling him Dowager Lord Byrne was odd. So I didn't call him anything.

"Cethin's parents have arrived."

"Excellent. I should greet them."

He glanced at my door. "Isn't Cethin waiting for you?"

"Why would you ask that?"

He laughed. "Aidan, you cannot lie, and you and Cethin are nothing if not obvious. He's in your room."

"Yes." A blush returned to my cheeks again. It was lucky we weren't in town or my reputation would be in tatters. Though, I was a half-fae and a bastard; I wasn't sure I *had* a decent reputation.

"I showed them to their room since Consort Keefe said they needed privacy. I do not believe they would care to be bothered."

I cleared my throat. Cethin's parents were very much in love. "I see."

"At least you know Cethin will not tire of you."

Even more heat seeped into my face.

Jonathan laughed. He had been doing that more and more since I'd taken the mantle of Sídhetír. I think when the burden of the lie was lifted, much of his stress disappeared. Also, not being in charge of Sídhetír no doubt helped.

Slowly, he placed a hand on my cheek. "I am very happy for you."

"Thank you."

He patted me. "Go see your husband before he comes looking for you."

"Probably a good idea."

"Bolt the door."

My mouth fell open. "Oren told you about me and Cethin?"

"No," he said with a snicker. "Nevan spotted the two of you in the hedge maze, Neil said you and Cethin were quite busy in the library, and I happened to see the two of you in the parlor. Hester hasn't said anything, but chances are she's seen you two somewhere as well."

It was possible we had been indiscreet of late. "I see."

"Perhaps you should take more care in the future."

"Probably," I muttered, trying to banish the fire in my face.

Jonathan laughed again as he walked down the hall.

I stepped into my room, and Cethin raised an eyebrow. "So everyone knows I'm here?"

"Yes," I said, sitting next to him, "but we have maintained a modest front in line with societal and religious demands."

"Ridiculous," he grunted, dragging me onto his lap. Cethin pressed his lips against mine. "I'm incredibly grateful for you." He flopped on top of me, shoving my shirt off so his fingers could trace the thorny vines on my left arm. "Tomorrow we shall be wed in the human way as we already are in the fae way. There is no getting away from me."

"I never want to get away from you."

"And you never shall."

I rocked into him. "You're mine."

"Yes, Aidan. I will be yours even after the sun and moon cease to shine."

As my lips found his, my heart soared. Cethin and I would be together for the rest of our lives and even after. "Stay with me, my love."

"Forever, Aidan."

Cethin

I was always told that when I met my mate, my perfect match, I would know. The world would come into focus around them. There would be no question. No doubt. I scoffed at such romantic sensibilities. I had spent eons alive and no such person had called to me, no matter how much I searched.

The moment I opened my eyes, I knew the stories were true.

He hovered over me. His eyes were the fairest green I'd ever seen and his hair was as red as flame. His fingers held my face in such a gentle grasp while his melodious voice slid across my ears, the words without meaning.

At that moment, the universe aligned and my world centered on this one man. I had lived all of these years for him. He was the reason. My only reason. He was the sun and the moon by which I would live.

Acknowledgements

Writing this book was a unique experience for me, as it only took me five weeks to write the entire first draft. I was struck with an insane inspiration from a random writer's prompt: *You meet an injured man on the way to a graveyard*. It obviously changed from there, but it was so much fun! This, being the first spicy book I've released, caused me some stress, especially since my sister, Sage, felt the need to read said scenes out loud (do not recommend). But it was an interesting journey, and I hope you enjoyed this book!

I want to thank Sage (even though she embarrassed me many times throughout the drafting of this book) for reading Key of Iron & Fate even when she dislikes (more accurately hates) fae romance, Shonda, my ever-loyal beta reader, I could not do this without you and your encouragement, Etheric Designs for my gorgeous cover, and my editor Addie Hart, you made this book so much better.

Finally, a huge thank you to my readers, new and old. I appreciate every single one of you! I feel as if with each book, my support grows, and with it, my imposter syndrome shrinks, making me think I can do this indie author thing.

P.S. Yes, there will be more books with the rest of the single Byrne brothers. Stay tuned.

About the author

Katherine A. Darling, or Kat (he/they), is a transmasc author who adores writing queer characters. He's usually found, book in hand, cuddling a cat. He loves all things fantasy, sci-fi, and geek-related. If he's not writing, he's crocheting, gaming, or chilling with his horde of cats.

www.ingramcontent.com/pod-product-compliance
Lightning Source LLC
LaVergne TN
LVHW091020080826
845145LV00002B/301

* 9 7 8 1 9 6 1 9 7 2 0 3 2 *